HOUSE OF MURDER

ALAN E. LOSURE

HOUSE OF MURDER

Yorkshire Publishing
TULSA

ISBN: 978-1-960810-77-9
House of Murder

Copyright © 2024 by Alan E. Losure
All rights reserved.

No part of this publication may be reproduced, distributed, or transmitted in any form or by any means, including photocopying, recording, or other electronic or mechanical methods, without the prior written permission of the publisher, except in the case of brief quotations embodied in critical reviews and certain other noncommercial uses permitted by copyright law.

For permission requests, write to the publisher at the address below.

Yorkshire Publishing
2488 E 81st St.
Ste 2000
Tulsa, OK 74137
www.YorkshirePublishing.com
918.394.2665

Published in the USA

House of Murder

MAIN CAST OF CHARACTERS:

Lawmen of Gas City, Indiana

Justin Blake	Marshal
Wilbert Vance	Daytime Deputy
Michael Davidson	Nighttime Deputy
Philip Curtis	Nighttime Deputy
Russell Henderson	New Nighttime Deputy

Scofield Oil Company

William "Slick Willie"	Owner of Scofield Oil Co.
Ruth Ann Scofield	Wife of William
Garrett Jones	Oldest Stepbrother
Wanda Jones	Wife of Garrett
Anthony Jones	Youngest Stepbrother
Ethyl Jones	Wife of Anthony
Loreta Jones	Unmarried Stepsister
Matthew "Irish" Ferguson	Hot-Tempered Oil Worker
David Brown	Hot-Tempered Oil Worker

Other Gas City Characters

Cindy Moon "Half-Moon"	Miami Indian Housekeeper
Matthew Brooks	Barber/Owner Brooks' Barbershop
Jordan Brooks	Barber/Brother
Alvin Jensen	Reporter, Gas City Journal
Eugene Maxwell	Medical Doctor
Davis Huffman	Mayor of Gas City
Lowell Benson	Attorney for Scofield Oil
The Ragman	Street Beggar

-PRELUDE-
DEATH STALKS THE LAND

The Ragman

N obody knew his real name, or for that matter, where he came from, but the man quickly earned the nickname *The Ragman*. He just appeared one day, and lived, as people say, down by the river, separate from the occasional Hobo communities that frequented Gas City. They would say *The Ragman* had the art of begging for coins down to a tee, with his always-present donation tin can hung around his neck, ready to read aloud a few pages of scripture or shout, "Woe to those who deprive the poor!" He also knew the locations of all the local churches. Every Sunday, he would pick a new church and be found standing outside the main entry door begging for a few coins as the congregation came and went. *The Ragman* had no interest in any Christian charity offers of work, a bath, clean clothing, or a proper home. It seemed only coins mattered; coins to purchase homemade rot gut whiskey brewed illegally and peddled in dark alleys. People made a habit of pretending not to notice him walking around town, begging as he traveled. Any attempt to enter a saloon to help himself to the free lunch counter resulted in the bartender abruptly pitching him out on his backside. Most secretly wished he would go elsewhere. In a way, their wish would soon come true, but not in the way many expected.

Nighttime Deputy Michael Davidson was tired as he glanced at the office wall clock. He still had nearly an hour before Marshal Justin Blake and Deputy Wilbert Vance came in to relieve him. His shift had been quiet, and the hours had felt endless. *But why should I complain when things are peaceful and quiet,* he told himself. The image of bacon and eggs frying in a cast iron skillet replaced his thoughts. *You know, I can almost smell that bacon.* That was when an old man burst into his office.

"Deputy, come quick. There's a body floatin' down under the wooden bridge. My freight wagon is just outside and I'll be glad ta haul you down there if you like." The deputy's peaceful and quiet shift had just ended.

"Give me a second to write the marshal a quick note where to find me, Charlie," he told the farmer. Finishing, he grabbed his hat, and the pair stepped outside and climbed aboard the wagon. Just as quickly, the wagon rushed down the near-empty brick streets westward toward the Mississinewa River.

"I was on my way ta pick up some fence posts at the lumberyard when I noticed it. I saw it down the hill along the bank," the old farmer said as the wagon made its way down the near-empty morning street. Approaching the wooden bridge, the wagon halted and both men carefully made their way down the grassy embankment. "There it is!" Both men could see the body had become snagged in a tall thicket of brush and weeds with the legs submerged underwater and moving with the river's current like stalks of wheat in the wind. "Please stay back, Charlie," he said as he approached the body. It was lying face down, with the back of the head crushed in. This was no accidental drowning. He also recognized the man's odd clothing as the one folks called *The Ragman*. "Do you know where Doctor Maxwell's home is?" he asked the old farmer and received an affirming nod in response. "Good. I need to ask you to go to him and explain the situation and bring him here." Charlie said he would be happy to and departed. *It looks like the bacon and eggs would have to wait a while.* Until then, Deputy Davidson kept the curious bystanders from entering what he knew was an active crime scene.

* * * * * * * * * * * * *

Finding the office empty and after reading the hastily prepared note, Marshal Justin Blake and Deputy Wilbert Vance made their way down to the river. "Has Doctor Maxwell been contacted yet?" Justin asked. Maxwell was also the local coroner. Michael explained his instructions to the farmer to do so. "Has anything been touched or moved?"

"No, I wanted to stay back and wait for your arrival," Michael said. Justin thanked him and released him to go home. Justin began scouting the area, looking for footprints or evidence of another person. There were no footprints, but the crushed weeds indicated that the body had been rolled down the hill from above. The Ragman's single belonging lay half-submerged in the mud. Picking up the old rusted can, the marshal felt fifteen cents fall into his hand.

He searched the body for identification but came up empty. Returning to the top of the hill, Justin saw the ground was cross-hatched by so many muddy footprints it was impossible to discern one set from the next. He then returned to join Wilbert.

Wilbert began searching the grassy areas on both sides of the body. He found what he hoped to locate about fifty feet away on the south riverbank. "Here's the murder weapon," he announced, pulling the bloody weapon from between two logs. It was a common piece of two-by-four wood, approximately four feet long. One end contained fragments of blood and hair. Carefully, the murder weapon was retrieved as evidence.

At last, Doctor Maxwell's wagon came to a rumbling stop near the embankment, his leather bag of instruments clinking as he made his way down to the body. Making a quick examination, he determined the victim probably died instantly and did not suffer. "Help me load him in the wagon, deputy. I should have a medical report for you within a day or so." The doctor then departed for home.

"Wilbert, let's split up and interview the Hobo encampment along both sides of the river. Maybe someone saw or heard the victim arguing or fighting with somebody."

* * * * * * * * * * * * * * *

Justin was the first to return to the office and began making a fresh pot of coffee. Soon after, Wilbert entered, and the men compared notes. Unfortunately, they had learned little. The Hobos knew of *The Ragman* but gave him a wide berth as he didn't fit into their way of life. Nobody had seen or heard anything. Both lawmen were frustrated with the lack of useful information.

* * * * * * * * * * * * * * *

The doctor's medical report offered little information other than that the estimated time of death was between ten p.m. and midnight. Within days, *The Ragman* was buried at taxpayers' expense in a pauper's grave in the town's cemetery. There were no mourners. Despite their best efforts to find his killer, nothing further developed. An article in the Gas City Journal asked the public for any information that might assist the marshal's office in solving the murder. There were no responses.

CHAPTER 1
SEPTEMBER 6, 1901

Marshal Justin Blake   Deputy Wilbert Vance

"Justin, President McKinley has been shot!" an excited Wilbert Vance shouted as he entered the marshal's office. "I noticed a large crowd assembled outside of the Western Union and heard the news from them," he said standing halfway in the doorway breathing heavily. "Let's go inside to hear the latest developments."

It took Justin a split-second to comprehend the severity of what was said, and his first instinct was to follow his friend to the telegraph office, but instead, he hesitated. "No, let's go over to the newspaper office. They have a teleprinter machine and it's bound to be less crowded there." Justin stood, walked over to the coat rack to obtain his hat, and then glanced at the wall clock to check the time. *Good,* he thought. *I still have another hour before the interview.* Both men walked briskly across the street toward the front door of the Gas City Journal. A man on the street corner was already shouting the news to every passerby. Shocked citizens gathered in the streets as rumors began circulating throughout town. Justin and Wilbert entered the Gas City Journal and walked into the newsroom where reporter Alvin Jensen and a few others congregated around the teleprinter.

"You've heard, I take it?" the reporter asked. Both lawmen nodded.

"What's the latest? Was he hurt very badly? Did they catch the guy who did it?" Wilbert asked in quick succession showing shock and horror on his face.

The reporter shook his head, "We don't know much at this early stage. It happened at the Pan-American Exposition, you know, that big fair they're holding in Buffalo, New York? They say the president was shot twice, and the Secret Service has the shooter in custody. We've not heard anything more on his condition. I pray the president will live, or we'll be stuck with that goofy cowboy, Theodore Roosevelt! Now, gentlemen, if you'll excuse me, I have an urgent story to write for an important extra edition."

Justin nodded for Wilbert to follow him back to their office. Entering, Wilbert said, "One never knows what the day will bring, does it?" He walked over to the stove and poured himself a cup of coffee, then motioned to his friend, who declined the offer.

"I want you to remain in the office to help me interview this new man for the deputy position."

Wilbert smiled; pleased Justin valued his opinion. "What is the guy's name again?"

"Russell Henderson," Justin said. "Age twenty-eight, a past drifter, delivery man, and oil worker in Van Buren, unmarried, and looking, so he says, for a change in life. Other than that, I know little else."

* * * * * * * * * * * * * * *

Russell Henderson

* * * * * * * * * * * * * * *

"So, Mr. Henderson, why do you want the job of a nighttime deputy marshal?" Justin asked, evaluating his applicant's physical and verbal response.

"It's a respected position of authority in helping to keep our community safe." The man began, his hands folded in his lap. "I've always had the utmost respect for lawmen … that is, except for those thugs masquerading as lawmen over in Van Buren. Besides, I tend to be a night owl anyway, so the hours won't be an issue."

Justin frowned. "I take it you've had run-ins with the Van Buren police officers?"

"No sir, not me personally, but some of my oil worker mates had their skulls bashed in by their so-called lawmen. One man was beaten so badly he may never fully recover. I just stayed away from them and minded my own business."

Justin had heard stories about the so-called 'lawmen' before and decided to change the subject. "That was the best course of action on your part. In this job, you will be exposed to all kinds of men and, yes, a few rough women, too. Keeping calm and not taking any insults personally makes one a better lawman. As you know, alcohol can change a mild-mannered fellow into a raving troublemaker. An officer also must learn to count upon his partner to watch his back as well as the other way around, but remember, trust is a two-way street. You have to earn it, understand?"

"Yes, I do, Marshal. Please give me a chance to prove my worth. I won't let you, or any of my fellow officers, down." Justin paused and glanced over to get Wilbert's opinion. A slight smile and a wink provided the answer he was looking for.

"All right, Mr. Henderson, let's begin a thirty-day trial period and see how it works out. I'll be placing you under the supervision of Officer Michael Davidson. He is a very trusted and experienced man. Just do as he says. Two weeks later, you'll work with Officer Philip Curtis. Then, we'll see how things are from there. Your work shift is from seven in the evening until seven the next morning. We have a uniform contract with Evans Haberdashery and Fine Men's Clothing here in town. Go down there tomorrow, and they will fit you with three uniforms. By the way, you won't be issued a weapon until you become an official member of the department and receive proper firearm training. Can you start tomorrow evening?"

"I can start tonight, Marshal. I won't need a uniform to begin my training." His eagerness struck both officers as a good sign.

"Then you might want to get a bite to eat before your shift starts. I assume you have someplace to stay?"

"Yes, sir. I'm at the Mississinewa Hotel now, but I expect to start looking for a boarding house where they serve their boarders good food. I'm not much of a cook," he joked.

Justin and Wilbert stood, shook Deputy-in-Training Russell Henderson's hand, and welcomed him to the Gas City Police Department. Later, he was introduced to his fellow nighttime deputies and began his first shift.

CHAPTER 2
BROOKS' BARBERSHOP

B rooks' Barbershop was nestled inside the first-floor shops of the grand Mississinewa Hotel facing Main Street. If anyone wanted the latest news or gossip, the barbershop was the place to get it. All problems were easily solved by simply listening to each customer who, when sitting in the barber chair, felt enabled to educate the world on various topics. The news of the shooting was well-known by now, from reading the newspaper, but it was the 'why' and 'who' that captivated the citizens of Gas City.

On the morning of September 7th, 1901, the following article appeared in the latest edition of the Gas City Journal:

On September 6, President William McKinley was shot during the Pan-American Exposition in Buffalo, New York. The assailant was identified as Leon Czolgosz, an assumed foreigner and anarchist. The president was shot twice in the stomach at close range, with a .32 Iver Johnson revolver wrapped in a white handkerchief to avoid detection. Czolgosz was immediately apprehended by nearby citizens and security. President McKinley was rushed to the fair's medical center for treatment, but only nurses and interns were on duty.

The Exposition hosted a public reception for the president at the Temple of Music.

In line to greet the president was a twelve-year-old. She asked for his always-present good luck Red Carnation. The president smiled and handed the flower to her. Next in line was a tall man who appeared quite nervous. His demeanor caught the attention of a Secret Service Agents, but after shaking the president's hand, he casually walked away. Czolgosz was next in line. The president noticed the white handkerchief wrapped around the man's right hand and instinctively reached for his left. As soon as their hands touched, two shots were fired by the assailant.

By late afternoon, barbershop owner Matthew Brooks was getting tired of discussing the assassination, but through the years he had grown used to repetitive topics. However, his brother and fellow barber Jordan engaged in each conversation with his own pet theory: The shooting was of foreign involvement.

"Mark my words," he repeated over and over to customers. "That man is an anarchist from one of those European countries that wants to bring down our government. You saw his picture in the paper today. Just put a rope around his scrawny neck, and he'll sing like a Canary and give up all the names we need. Then, leave it up to our military to finish the job right and proper!"

One customer remarked, "I'll bet ya a beer he ain't no stinkin' foreigner but a Democrat!"

An old man said the shooting brought back memories of the Lincoln assassination.

"Don't forget James Garfield was killed back in '81," another offered.

"There ain't enough money in the world to make me run for president! What about you, Mat?"

"Oh, I don't know," Matthew replied. "Presidents have great power to pardon. So, if I do decide to run for the job, I guess my first official act would be to pardon Jordan here for masquerading as a real barber. I guess it's easy for some people to simply send off for a diploma from a Sears catalog." There were a few light chuckles.

"Yes, brother dear. I used the same catalog that you did." Matthew only shook his head.

Finally, another customer began. "I hear we got us a new night-time deputy."

CHAPTER 3
AN UNEXPECTED MEETING

Mrs. Ruth Ann Stanton

"I look forward to coming here every other Saturday morning, Irene," the widow Stanton said as she sat in the beautician's salon styling chair. "I don't get out as much these days, but when I do, conversing with you and the other ladies here remains the highlight of my day."

The beautician and owner of Irene's House of Beauty Salon smiled. "You're always welcome, Mrs. Stanton. I love your naturally curling hair, and it's a pleasure to serve you, but you really should try to get out and about more often. Sitting at home in that big mansion all day isn't good for you, dear."

"I know, and I agree, but society's antiquated Victorian rules require a widow to remain at home draped in black mourning clothing with the drapes all pulled shut. Irene, that lifestyle gets old quite fast, and I long to be out and about among people again and wearing something bright and pretty as before," she said.

Irene shook her head in sadness. "How long has your late husband been gone now?"

"George passed away last October. You know, he was fifteen years older than me and worked as an official with the Pennsylvania Railroad. Sometimes, I wonder why he took the time to court and marry me, as it seems now, he was already married to the railroad. Still, he did build us what I feel is the most luxurious home in Gas City and left me financially well off, as you can imagine."

"Think you'll ever remarry? Listen to me giving anyone marriage advice! I have avoided marriage my entire life, but perhaps love will find its way back into your heart someday."

"I don't know, Irene. I really can't say I loved my late husband, but I liked and respected him. Maybe that's all anyone my age can hope for."

"Nonsense, please don't cut yourself short. You're a lovely, cultured woman," the beautician said as she finished styling her hair. An appointment in two weeks was made, and Mrs. Stanton paid, along with the usual tip. Stepping outside into the mid-morning air, Ruth Ann Stanton thought she might casually walk by a dress shop and glance through the window. *I just cannot let anyone see me doing that.*

She was about a block from the salon when two hard-looking men stepped into her path.

"Hey there, missy," one of the men snarled through missing front teeth. "Why don't ya come with us and have ah few drinks from our bottle!" As he spoke, his partner grasped her arm and started pulling her toward their presumed lair.

"Yeah, we can show ya a good time too!" the other one with foul breath whispered.

Ruth Ann struggled. "Unhand me at once," she demanded and started to scream. That was when, out of nowhere, another man appeared.

"Unhand her," he shouted and socked the ruffian who had been holding her arm in the stomach, then shoved the other thug away. "I'll fight you both here and now," he told them. Both men looked at one another and decided otherwise, then ran off down an alley and disappeared.

The heroic man approached the trembling lady. "Are you all right, ma'am? Did those two brutes hurt you?"

Tears swelled in her eyes as she responded, "Oh, sir, I don't know how I can ever repay you for your kindness. It appears a lady isn't safe to walk our streets these days."

He removed his hat and introduced himself. "My name is William Scofield. Please allow me to see you safely to your carriage."

"I'm walking home today, Mr. Scofield. I greatly appreciate your kind offer. I'm Mrs. Ruth Ann Stanton." As the couple walked toward her three-story home, Scofield spoke a great deal and admitted to having seen her late husband a time or two from a distance.

Arriving outside her home, she said, "I'm delighted to have made your acquaintance, Mr. Scofield. Thank you again for your kindness."

Scofield removed his hat once again. "I hope we'll meet again soon." He bid her good day and watched from the sidewalk until she was safely inside. Scofield turned and laughed to himself. His plan had gone well. The entire episode had been a setup. He hired the men from Jonesboro to frighten the wealthy widow, enabling him to make a favorable impression and become her hero. *My plan's working out just fine. Soon, I hope to have complete control of her finances and then, I can form the company I have always dreamed of … the Scofield Oil Company.*

The following Monday evening, William Scofield decked out in his best suit, appeared at the Stanton doorstep with roses and a box of candy. The unfriendly housekeeper, who eyed him cautiously, ushered him inside the drawing room. His plan was now in motion.

* * * * * * * * * * * * * * *

Eight days after being shot, President William McKinley died of his wounds on September 14, 1901. He was fifty-eight years of age. His vice-president, Theodore Roosevelt, was sworn in as the twenty-sixth President of the United States. The following day, businesses closed for the day out of respect for the late president.

CHAPTER 4

William "Slick Willie" Scofield

Known for his ability to sell a legless man a fine pair of leather boots, William Scofield certainly earned his nickname. Born and raised in near poverty in Cleveland, Ohio, he was surrounded by loss from a young age. When he was just a child, his older brother, Able, drowned in a steamer accident on Lake Erie. At the age of eight, William's father died. Now in severe financial distress, his mother answered a Lonely Hearts advertisement. After some back and forth, two railroad tickets were mailed to her and William, and they picked up what was left of their lives and moved to Marion, Indiana. The pair married the day they arrived. William never got along with his stepfather and disliked his new stepbrothers and sister. By the age of sixteen, he had moved out and quit school to work as a laborer in the booming gas and oil business in Grant County. He sought wealth and power as he worked, prioritizing his career over a relationship. However, as time passed, he soon realized the wealth he desired would not come from working as a laborer and turned instead to selling. It didn't matter what he peddled, as the young man discovered he had the gift of gab and could convince anyone to part with their hard-earned money. While his new work provided an adequate living, William still wanted more and dreamed of owning his own oil company.

Due to a shortage of worker housing, oilmen often shared spare bedrooms in people's homes or rented spaces in barns and attics. William took advantage of the need for public housing. He opened a realtor's office in Gas City, quickly finding financial success by selling overpriced houses to families desperate for a permanent homestead. With the money earned from his realtor business, he acquired a group of cheap, low-quality cemetery plots and shamefully approached and sold them to grieving families for their dearly departed. One can easily see how the nickname 'Slick Willie' originated.

After hearing of William's financial success, his stepbrothers Bartlett and Anthony moved their wives to Gas City in search of new opportunities. William welcomed them, placing them in run-down, high-rent properties he owned and managed. Strangely, in doing so, he felt control over them. Last winter, stepsister Loreta chose to move from Marion into one of his rentals in Gas City. She remained unmarried and was determined to make good on her own.

* * * * * * * * * * * * *

William continued to become a constant visitor to the Stanton home, now more determined than ever to win the rich widow over. Soon, they were seen out together in public, and her grieving period abruptly came to an end. Ruth Ann's friends tried their best to warn her about William's reputation and that he was not to be trusted, and was only after control of her money. It had no effect. She was convinced she had finally found love and companionship. The events would soon prove otherwise.

* * * * * * * * * * * * * * *

Justin was pleased with the reports he was receiving on Russell Henderson. The new deputy had a relaxed demeanor that helped defuse saloon confrontations, and he wasn't quick to pull his nightstick; instead, he chose to reason with out-of-control drunks. However, one time, an individual sitting at a different table slowly stood, eyeing the back of Michael Davidson's head as he grabbed hold of a bottle. Russell saw what was about to happen and pulled his nightstick, striking the assailant's hand. The man was cuffed and taken to jail for attempted assault upon a police officer.

* * * * * * * * * * * * * * *

The topic at Brooks' Barbershop was the recent story published in the Marion Chronicle about an impending barber strike in their city. Journeymen barbers who worked for boss barbers demanded a minimum weekly paycheck of ten dollars. That amount was considered unacceptable to many of the larger barber-owner shops. Boss barbers had until midnight to sign the union agreement to avert a local strike.

"Say there, Jordan," a waiting customer asked. "Are you gonna go on strike against that cheapskate brother of yours?" Matthew

Brooks tried not to let the crack against his character show as he continued to shave the back of his customer's neck. Everyone waited for Jordan's reply, but his brother answered first.

"He's overpaid now," he jokingly said.

Jordan nodded toward his brother, saying, "But he insists on paying me in Confederate money!" A few soft chuckles rippled through the room.

"Jordan, ya better keep an eye on that brother of yours," said the old man, leaning into the conversation. "I read in the paper about some barber down in Vincennes who got paid a nighttime visit by about sixty Whitecaps." The other customers leaned in to hear the story.

The old man continued. "It seems the guy deserted his wife and family, mortgaged his place of business, and then took up with lewd women." The mention of Whitecaps brought silence and painful memories of the terrible events in Gas City only a few years ago. "The hooded Whitecappers stripped off his nightshirt, tied him up, and proceeded to give him fifty lashes with a cowhide, then told him to leave the community and never return under penalty of death. We sure don't need that kind of murderin' vigilante justice around here again."

To change the topic, another old man asked how many planned to attend the spirit demonstration over the weekend at Lovett's Opera House. "I read that Doctor Charles C. Foster will conduct a séance, pass on spirit messages, make tables rise in the air, and flowers appear out of nowhere."

The men smirked. The old man quickly added, "It ain't for me, mind you; it's the missus that believes in all that stuff."

Matthew saw an opportunity to add to the strange topic. "I remember seeing a so-called professor who swore he could cure all ailments through hypnotism. The funny thing was that the man walked with a noticeable limp."

* * * * * * * * * * * * * * *

Late that night, a house fire broke out on South 'C' Street. Deputies Curtis and Henderson managed to kick the door open and rescue a mother and two small children from the smoke and flames. Both deputies were publicly recognized for their bravery at the next city council meeting. Justin was thrilled for his fellow officers. Soon, Henderson's thirty-day trial period ended. He passed his marksmanship training with ease and was issued a weapon. He was now a permanent full-time deputy marshal.

CHAPTER 5
THEY RECALL HIM

This was the headline of the two-cent Marion Chronicle, also read by many residents in Gas City. Reportedly, the presidential assassin, Leon Czolgosz, spent some time in Marion before traveling east with the intent to murder the president. Postmaster Bradford and his clerk, Miss Prickett, said he called at their counter for several letters addressed to a Frederick Neiman. Recent photos published nationwide in newspapers confirmed it was indeed Czolgosz.

"He was of medium height, dark hair, dark complexion, and spoke with a drogue thought to be a foreigner," Bradford informed the Chronicle. The Grant County Sheriff's Department has confirmed contacting the U.S. Secret Service agency in Indianapolis with those details.

Another story published a few days later read:

Secret Service Detective Thomas Hall Secures Information

While Here, Czolgosz Went by the Name of Frederick Neiman and Associated with a Crowd of Discontents

From good authority, we have learned that the Secret Service has evidence that allegedly proves Leon Czolgosz, the murderer of President McKinley, was in the Indiana gas belt before leaving for Buffalo, New York. While here in Marion, he received mail by the name of Frederick Neiman and was seen in the company of known discontents, not necessarily avowed anarchists, as earlier thought.

Secret Service Agent Hall was an artful dodger who never volunteered information to newspapermen. When pressed on what he has learned up to this point, Hall replied, "We only got four counterfeit silver dollars during the state fair, which is the least number we have had reported before." It can only be assumed that is why they call their organization the Secret Service.

CHAPTER 6
SAY IT AIN'T SO

On Monday morning, Marshal Justin Blake sat in his office discussing a proposal for a new city ordinance with Mayor Huffman when Deputy Wilbert Vance and two other men entered. Wilbert's body language displayed deep tension that Justin picked up on, while the other two, Reverend Stokes and Funeral Director Ward, appeared uneasy and nervous. Wilbert pulled up chairs for the men and said, "Justin, you need to hear what they just told me."

The mayor stood, telling Justin he would speak with him later. Wilbert shook his head. "I thinkperhaps you should hear this too, sir." Huffman glanced at Justin, then sat back down. There was a brief silence before the reverend spoke first.

"Justin, you and I have been friends for many years, and I hate to be the one to bring troubling news, but … like I explained to Wilbert, I thought your new deputy was only joking with me. But unfortunately, he wasn't."

"Maybe you should start at the beginning, Reverend."

Looking deep into the mayor's concerned face, Stokes began. "Saturday afternoon, I was inside the church preparing for my Sunday service when your new deputy entered my office. After I welcomed him, he got right to the point. He said he required a twenty percent take of each Sunday's collection. I smiled at what I took as a jest, but he continued. Saying, quote, 'I have heard stories that this beautiful church of yours burned to the ground once before. If you want to keep it standing, you better have my money ready when I come by after lunch on Monday … or else.'"

Justin sat back in his chair, feeling like the wind had been knocked out of him. Mayor Huffman's mouth opened in surprise but remained silent. "It makes me sick to my stomach to feel like a trusted member of your department would stoop to extortion from the House of God."

Ward began clenching his fists as he spoke next. "He also threatened to burn my place to the ground and demanded a twenty percent cut of what I take in after every funeral. Marshal, I can't stay in business if I must make payouts to a crook. I debated coming straight to you then but decided to speak with Reverand Stokes about it after Sunday's service. I had no idea he'd also been approached. One can only wonder how many other store owners are being frisked down by that man."

Justin and Wilbert exchanged glances. "You say Deputy Henderson is to arrive at your office today after lunch to obtain his money, Reverend?" Justin asked, receiving a nod of affirmation in response. "Then, Wilbert and I will hide nearby to witness the transaction. I suggest you have some money inside a coin bag and wait until he demands it before handing it over. Do your best to act the part so he won't suspect it's a trap. I ask each of you to return to your home now and say nothing of this to anyone. We will arrive at the church around eleven o'clock and hide in the coatroom to wait. Thank you for bringing this to my attention." The men murmured their goodbyes before leaving the office.

"I'll also be going so you two can start planning," the mayor said. "I never would have thought that of Henderson. He seemed like a dedicated police officer. Please keep me informed as to what transpires. Goodbye."

* * * * * * * * * * * * * *

At eleven o'clock sharp, Justin and Wilbert entered the church through the back door and stepped into the large coatroom near the office. "Yes, this will do nicely," Justin said, looking around at the spacious closet. "I'm going inside to speak with the reverend. Make sure you can hear both of us. If not, we need to find another location to hide."

Leaving Wilbert, Justin found the reverend at his desk reading from his bible.

"We're here," Justin announced. "Do you have the money bag ready?"

"Yes, I do, but I wish it hadn't come to this." Justin silently agreed.

"Can you hear us, Wilbert?" he asked.

"Yes, but the reverend needs to speak up a bit."

"All right, Reverend, this is what I need you to say …"

Justin laid out the rest of the plan, Reverend Stokes nodding his understanding. He returned to his reading as Justin retreated to the coatroom as the two lawmen waited for Russell Henderson's arrival. Both men felt a queasy churn in their stomachs, dreading what would soon transpire.

* * * * * * * * * * * * * *

Ten minutes after one o'clock, a figure was heard entering the church's front door and walking toward the back. Russell Henderson entered the office and approached the reverend. "Do you have my money?"

"This isn't right," Reverand Stokes said, making his voice sound more confident than he felt as he recited what the Marshal had instructed. "The Sunday offering belongs to the church and was freely given. You, sir, have no right to steal from God's Altar."

The deputy laughed. "God can have his ten percent, but my expenses require more. Don't lecture me, old man. Remember, churches do burn in the dead of night. Pay up or go to bed each night, wondering if tonight will be the night it happens!"

Slowly, the reverend reached into a drawer and extracted the bag of coins. Just as the extortionist took hold of it, both lawmen burst from the closet, their guns drawn.. "Russell Henderson, you are under arrest for attempted extortion." Henderson showed no emotion as Wilbert cuffed him and marched him the short distance to the jail. Instead of working his night shift with Michael Davidson, Russell Henderson would now be spending the night behind bars. His ex-coworker was shocked to learn of his arrest and tried to ask the prisoner questions after the day crew left. He was met with silence. Word of the arrest spread quickly, and reporter Alvin Jensen begged to interview the prisoner. Initially, Davidson refused the request but agreed when Henderson asked to speak with him.

"A man has got to make money any way he can. What's a few dollars to those who have plenty!" he offered. "I just didn't expect to get caught so fast. In the past, I have milked suckers for months at a time as an oil roughneck. It now seems my mistake was not cutting the Marshal into the scheme. It worked well in Van Buren."

How many businesses have you presented your ultimatum to in Gas City?" The reporter asked.

"Just those two. I had more planned, but that squealing preacher put the word on me!"

Jensen thanked him for the interview and knew he had a long night of work ahead of him. Despite this, he was thrilled to have secured a news scoop for tomorrow's edition of the Gas City Journal.

The next morning, with the written charges in hand, Wilbert escorted his prisoner to the Marion jail. The story was soon in every Grant County newspaper. It wasn't every day that a lawman got arrested and put behind bars. The story brought shame to all the honest, hardworking lawmen in Grant County.

CHAPTER 7
THE WIDOW BECOMES MRS. RUTH ANN SCOFIELD

The Three-Story Scofield Mansion with a live-in maid and cook

Their marriage ceremony was a private affair, performed by the justice of the piece and attended by only two of Ruth Ann's friends. Neither woman spoke to the new husband, which didn't bother Slick Willie one bit. Within days of their ceremony, he took the marriage license to the bank to have his name added as an equal partner on all her accounts. That evening, he explained to her his desire to start exploring for oil and the huge profits they would receive from it. At first, she objected, but he slapped her across the face and growled, "I am the keeper of the coins in this household now, so keep your trap shut, and we'll get along just fine." The look on his face appeared more like a mad dog than the man who had sweetly courted her those past months. With a cold feeling settling in her stomach, she realized her friends had been right all along. *I have been played for a sucker! I see now why people refer to him as Slick Willie. Oh, my God, what have I done?*

* * * * * * * * * * * * * * * *

Cook, Mrs. Sylvia Tyler

Housekeeper, Cindy Moon aka Half-Moon

Both women have served in her mistress's employment since she and her first husband built their fine home. The two women resided on the third floor of the home, and while they had their own bedrooms with access to separate balconies, they had to share the bathroom. Both women hated each other and only spoke to the other when required. Here are their stories:

Mrs. Sylvia Tyler lived in the town long before it changed its name from Harrisburg to Gas City. A widow and mother of three strapping sons, she had become a hired cook out of necessity long before Ruth Ann and her late husband employed her. She immediately disliked William Scofield and suspected the feeling was mutual. She also witnessed her employer getting slapped and felt instant rage and hatred. *That terrible man is out to bankrupt poor Ruth Ann. He must be stopped at all costs.*

Cindy Moon, aka Half-Moon, was born to a Miami Indian mother in the large Osash Village east of Peru. Her father was an unknown white man. Growing up, she never felt accepted by either race. By age twelve, she decided to call herself Cindy Moon and lived and worked in the white community as a housekeeper. Either through her rough outward attitude or because of her visible Indian features, she didn't last long anywhere. She bounced from job to job within Grant County, eventually settling in Gas City. She also despised the new man of the house. Drawing upon her people's beliefs in good and bad spirits, she called upon Kachina, the bad spirit, to put a deadly curse on William Scofield. Mrs. Tyler overheard her nightly chanting before bedtime, which filled her with fear for her own life and an intense loathing for the Indian woman.

* * * * * * * * * * * * *

At one o'clock in the afternoon on October 29th, presidential assassin Leon Czolgosz was executed by electric chair in Auburn,

New York. The prisoner expressed no regrets. His last words were, "I am sorry I did not get to see my father."

Reports that Czolgosz had been in Marion before the shooting proved to be false, indicating either misidentification or, perhaps, wishful thinking.

* * * * * * * * * * * * * *

William Scofield sipped his morning coffee as he read the newspaper report about the untimely death of the owner of Giles Drilling Service, a subcontractor who supplied oil and gas exploration equipment. This was the opportunity he had been hoping for so he made plans to approach his wife's Gas City Attorney, Lowell Benson. *If that man works for me, he can prevent Ruth Ann from trying to stop me legally.*

* * * * * * * * * * * * * *

Attorney, Lowell Benson

"Mr. Bensen, I wish to hire your services, and if we are successful, you shall be my legal representative for the Scofield Oil Company," Scofield said.

The lawyer had already begun evaluating the man and was not overly impressed with his demeanor and flashy suit. "Exactly how am I to help you, sir?"

"I want you to reach out to the widow of the Giles Drilling Service and offer to purchase her late husband's drilling equipment on my behalf. Before making an offer, I need to inventory everything. I aim to make a generous offer, roughly fifty cents on the dollar. Keep that figure just between us. Encourage her to accept it, ensuring she can walk away clean and start her new life with financial security. What steps are involved, and how soon could I have possession?"

The lawyer smiled. "I'll be happy to represent your interests. I have also heard that Mr. Gile didn't have a business partner, so all company assets will become part of his estate as laid out in his will, of which I can only assume names his wife, Lois Gile, as the sole beneficiary. That is, providing he had a will in the first place, but it is standard practice for all businessmen to have one. Then, an advertisement must run in all Grant County newspapers informing those who may be owed money for services not rendered to contact the representing attorney and present their claim within thirty days. After any debts have been paid, the estate can be closed, and if an agreement is reached, you may make the purchase. I assume you have the capital to make such a purchase?"

Scofield made a sour face but nodded. "More time wasted, but you can still represent me with my offer and ask that I be allowed to inventory all of the drilling equipment."

The attorney agreed. "I will call her or her representing attorney to see if she is receptive. No doubt, she'll want to consult with her attorney before deciding. Then, he and I will begin the financial discussion." Reaching into his desk, Attorney Benson extracted a new client form and handed it over. "Please fill this out and leave it with my secretary. I'll be in touch with you soon. Good afternoon, Mr. Scofield." The prospective oilman, his heart pounding in anticipation, stepped into the adjoining office, sat at a small table, and filled in the needed contact information.

Days passed by without hearing from Attorney Bensen. *I hope the widow jumps at my offer and all the equipment is here in Grant County. If so, it must be stored away somewhere. Maybe I can rent or purchase that building too?* Finally, Bensen called with good news. The widow was open to his proposition and gave him a name to contact to schedule an inspection of the materials at the warehouse in Marion. Things were indeed looking up.

CHAPTER 8
TRAGEDY STRIKES

It was a pleasant Sunday morning when Ruth Ann Scofield began dressing for church. Ever since the slapping incident, she had moved into another bedroom, wanting nothing to do with her new husband. Perhaps, she thought, maybe time will heal her hurt and frustration. She remembered bitterly that she had begged him for her pastor, Reverend Stokes, to perform their wedding ceremony, but William adamantly opposed it.

Today was the day of the week she enjoyed the most: escaping from her self-imprisonment and being out and about with other people. Sunday was also the day their live-in cook and maid had the day off. After sleeping in for a change, both women left the home for the day quite early and returned late after dark. Ruth Ann could not blame them one bit for staying away. Where they went, or who they saw was unimportant to her. At least they knew enough to manage a longer escape than she was free to do. The thought of speaking to her kindly pastor about her unhappy marital situation had crossed her mind several times but was ultimately rejected. *No sense in other people knowing of the hell I have unleashed upon myself.* After dressing, she proceeded downstairs to the kitchen and, as her morning ritual, consumed an apple from the seasonal bowl of fruit placed there by the cook. After washing up, she stepped out the back door toward the stable. Soon, Ruth Ann Scofield's carriage was on its way to the Friends Church and a brief salvation.

* * * * * * * * * * * * * * *

It was a welcome relief to enter her church and mix again with those she loved and respected. Taking a seat on the wooden bench next to a friend, Ruth Ann attempted to get caught up with the latest church news. Soon, services started as the organist began playing a popular hymn. Before the music had ended, Ruth Ann began to cough. *I must have swallowed my saliva wrong*, she thought. As she coughed, she noticed a strange metallic taste, and soon, she felt as if she couldn't breathe in fully.

I must be coming down with the flu. I better leave as I think I may vomit. She struggled to get to her feet, swaying back and forth before fainting into her friend's lap. Confusion among the congregation spread quickly, bringing Reverend Stoke's message to an abrupt pause. "Someone has fainted," he announced. "Is there a doctor or nurse present?" There were none.

"Take her outside in the fresh air," someone yelled, and two men came forward and gently removed her from the seating.

Once outside, two women came forward and attempted to revive her by patting her hand and speaking softly. It had no effect. An older man who had served as a stretcher bearer during the Civil War became alarmed at her difficulty in breathing. "Help me get her into my carriage," he instructed. "I'll take her to Doctor Maxwell's home."

The carriage raced through the streets, and soon the old man pounded on the front door. "Doc, come quick. I don't know if she is breathing or not."

Maxwell realized the seriousness of the situation, and together, they carried her inside and into his treatment room. The old man watched helplessly as the doctor did everything in his power to save the woman. Finally, he suspected the worst and listened once again to her heart with a stethoscope. Without saying a word, he draped a sheet over the body. "Do you know her name?" he asked.

The old man shook off the anxiety he was feeling. "Yes, she is … ah … was Mrs. Ruth Ann Stanton until recently marrying that man everyone calls Slick-Willie. Ruth Ann was a fine woman.

"Someone needs to call her husband and inform him of the terrible news. I'll make contact with the marshal's office to do so unless you want to do the honors," the Doctor said. The old man declined and left to return to pick up his stranded wife at church. Maxwell picked up the candlestick telephone kept on his desk and placed the call. "Hello Deputy. This is Doctor Maxwell. I'm afraid I have an unpleasant task to ask of you …"

Deputy Davidson wrote down the information but dreaded the task before him. *There isn't any easy way to inform someone their loved one has died.* The old Stanton Mansion was well known to him, three stories in height, but the new husband by the name of Scofield was a stranger. After arriving, he knocked on the elegant front door. There was no response. *Perhaps he has already been contacted. I'll* come back later, just to make sure. By the end of his day, he was still been unable to contact the husband, and the large home remained dark. With the shift change, his coworker, Philip Curtis, was now responsible for notifying the new widower of his loss. As evening fell, Curtis approached the house once more and was met by the housekeeper, who took the news with no emotion, which struck Curtis as quite odd.

* * * * * * * * * * * * *

Monday morning brought a light rain to the town as Justin stared out his office window. He knew he desperately needed to hire a replacement nighttime deputy to prevent Wilbert Vance from being bounced around from working days to nights as a fill-in. His advertisement in the Gas City Journal had yet to produce a qualified applicant. His desk telephone rang, breaking his concentration.

"Marshal Blake, this is Doctor Maxwell. I was hoping to catch you as I have something very important to show you here in my examination room."

"Sure thing, Doc. I'll come right over." Blake hung up the receiver and put on his coat and hat before heading out in the rain to the doctor's residence. After arriving, Blake hung his wet garments on the nearby coat rack inside the doorway.

The doctor greeted him at the door, saying, "Sorry to get you out on such a bad day, Marshal, but you need to see this." Justin followed him into the exam room. There, on a table, lay a covered body. "I'm sure your deputy informed you of the death of Mrs. Scofield."

Justin said he was aware of it. The Doc continued. "When I began my initial examination of the body, I presumed the woman died from a heart attack since she appeared very healthy. Then, I noticed her lips were turning blue, a possible side effect of poisoning. During the autopsy, I examined the contents of her stomach and found she had consumed a single apple laced with Mercury Chloride. I took a blood sample, and it showed positive for Mercury Chloride to confirm it was in her system."

Justin's face showed surprise. "What are the chances of this being an accident or even a suicide?"

"I would think the level of concentration in the apple would rule out an accident, but I'm a physician, not a police officer. But if it was a suicide, why would the lady then go into a packed church to die in front of her congregation? Here is the medical report; it's all in here." Justin took the file and slipped it into his vest pocket.

"Am I free to turn the body over to the family now?" Justin nodded and thanked the doctor for contacting him. After donning his coat and hat, Justin stood on the doctor's front porch watching the rain fall and thought of the old proverb, 'Into every life, a little rain must fall.' Now, he had a second murder investigation to conduct. He had finally concluded that *The Ragman* was probably killed in a robbery attempt gone wrong and that the assailant hopped on a train out of town to parts unknown. At least, that theory made sense.

CHAPTER 9
QUESTIONING SUSPECTS

Justin arrived outside the Scofield Mansion and knocked. An elderly woman he assumed to be the housekeeper answered. "I am Marshal Blake. I must speak with Mr. Scofield on official police business."

The woman's face showed no emotion as she replied, "I'm sorry, Marshal, but Mr. Scofield isn't here."

"Where can I find him, ma'am? It is most urgent that I speak with him."

"Come in, sir, out of the rain," the elderly woman offered, taking his coat and hat. "As to where he is, we haven't any idea. He left here sometime Friday and hasn't returned. I'm afraid Mr. Scofield doesn't inform us of his whereabouts."

"You mentioned 'we.' Who else is here that I can speak with?"

"A Miss Moon, the housekeeper. I am Mrs. Sylvia Tyler, the Scofield's cook. Please have a seat in the library while I look for her." Justin had heard stories about the elegant beauty of the home's interior but was still taken aback by its fine craftsmanship. Within a minute, both women appeared. Rather than sitting next to each other on the nearby couch, they chose to sit separately away from each other on hard chairs. Justin noticed this and assumed they were not close friends.

"Miss Moon, my name is Marshal Blake, and I need to ask you a few questions concerning the murder of your mistress, Mrs. Scofield." Neither woman reacted in the slightest at this information. Justin became suspicious of them at this point but continued. "I can't help but notice that neither of you showed any surprise when I said she was murdered. Why is that?"

Both sat in silence until one glanced at the other. "Very well, sir, I shall go first," Mrs. Tyler said. "I have worked for Mrs. Stanton … I mean Scofield, for many years. Though a widow, she seemed to handle her grief well enough, and her life in the house was uneventful. You see, Miss Moon and I live on the third floor. My working conditions were fine until that dreadful day he came here."

Justin asked, "By he you are implying William Scofield?" Both women nodded.

"Marshal, any fool could see he was trying to win her over for her money and social position. I even overheard a couple of her friends warning her of his intentions and saying that he is known around town by the name of 'Slick Willie.' Unfortunately, the poor dear, desperate for happiness, fell for his scheme and married him. Rest assured; If she was murdered, he is responsible."

"What about you, Miss Moon? What can you tell me?"

"He has an evil spirit residing within him. Money and power are all he craves. I witnessed him slapping her when she objected to his careless use of her money. He never loved our employer and only used her to get his hands on her income. Death and destruction await all those associated with him. I know, as the spirits have shown me, what will soon occur. That is all I have to say."

"So, tell me about the apples?"

Both women appeared confused by the question. Mrs. Tyler then asks, "If you're referring to the Red Delicious apples we try to maintain on hand for her, they are in a bowl on a small table in the kitchen. What's so special about apples?"

"Show me," Justin stated, and the two women led him into the kitchen.

"Over there. Like I said, they ..." The bowl of fruit sat empty. "I don't understand. I filled it with at least eight or nine Red Delicious apples I bought at the fruit market on Saturday," the cook stated. "Maybe he took them on his trip, though I can't recall ever seeing him eat one before." Justin walked out the unlocked kitchen door and into the backyard, both women watching curiously. He approached the metal barrel used to burn trash and looked inside. There was no sign of apples. He then walked through the backyard searching. Nothing was found. Justin's search for answers continued as he reentered and looked through the pantry. It didn't take long to discover what he was hoping to find. Sitting behind a bottle of bleach was a half-empty bottle marked Mercury Chloride.

"What do you use this for?" Justin asked. Both women said they knew nothing about it. Justin pocketed the bottle as evidence. "The minute your employer returns home, call me, day or night. Both of you need to remain in town until I tell you otherwise, understand?"

The women nodded.

Justin left the Scofield Mansion and visited the Pennsylvania Railroad Depot. Unfortunately, nothing was learned of Mr. Scofield's travel. Arriving at the Union Traction Company depot, he asked about William Scofield buying a ticket to leave town. "Yes, Marshal," the streetcar agent remembered. "I sold him a roundtrip ticket on the trolley to Marion last Friday afternoon. Why do you ask?"

"I need to speak with him, that's all. When is the next Marion streetcar due in?" After hearing in about an hour, Justin left to visit the town drugstores searching for those that might sell Mercury Chloride. Most carried the bottle on their shelves but kept no record of its prior purchases. No one could recall selling a bottle to any of the occupants of the Scofield Mansion anytime lately. Feeling he had struck out, Justin returned to the streetcar depot to await the next Marion streetcar's arrival. *If he hasn't returned by evening, I will contact the Marion Police to take him into custody,* he thought.

That didn't prove necessary, though, as William Scofield returned to Gas City carrying a small suitcase. "Are you Mr. Scofield?" Justin asked. "I am Marshal Blake, and I need to have a private word with you." Justin had already spoken with the ticket agent about using one of their empty offices, so the men headed inside.

Setting down his suitcase, Scofield asked, "What's this all about, Marshal?"

"I'm afraid I have some bad news for you, sir. Your wife collapsed in church yesterday and later passed away." He purposely refrained from saying she was murdered so he could judge the man's reaction but was surprised that he stood there without any display of emotion.

Finally, Scofield asked, "Did she have a heart attack or something?"

Justin ignored his question. "It appears you don't seem all that upset about this news. That seems quite strange to me, sir. What have you been up to since leaving here Friday afternoon?"

Being questioned by the marshal about his whereabouts began to upset the man as he fidgeted with his hat. "Not that it's any of your business, but I'm starting my own oil drilling company. I was permitted to conduct an inventory of some equipment I'm in the market to purchase. I also met with an individual who owns oil leases on Gas City and Van Buren properties and spent many hours haggling over a selling price with that hardhead. I stayed at the Spencer Hotel for three nights, completed my business, and am only now returning home. You can check with the hotel if you don't believe me. Now, if you'll excuse me, it appears I need to make some funeral arrangements, so if you don't have any more prying questions …"

"One final one, sir. Do you enjoy eating Red Delicious apples?"

Justin expected to see some reaction on the man's face, but only annoyance showed. "I dislike their taste, but the wife enjoys them. What a stupid thing to ask a grieving husband! I don't appreciate your attitude, Marshal, not one stinkin' bit. I intend to speak with Mayor Huffman about your lack of compassion and professionalism. Good day to you, sir!"

Grieving husband my eye, Justin thought. *We need to watch this guy very closely.*

* * * * * * * * * * * * * * *

Though he suspected his wife would have wanted her funeral to be conducted at her church, William Scofield rejected the idea outright. Instead, he held a brief ceremony at one of his cheap cemetery plots. Only a moderate amount mourners attended, including the cook and housekeeper, as he seemed to be in a great hurry to have her buried and be done with it.

He told himself that nothing would stand in the way of fame and fortune now.

Arriving back at the mansion, now in his name, he instructed Mrs. Tyler to fix him a grand supper of steak, potatoes, corn on the cob, and rolls. There would be no mourning period within the Scofield Mansion. While he waited, he sat in the library, sipping a glass of sherry. Both the housekeeper and cook later recalled seeing him sitting in that oversized stuffed chair, smiling as if all his problems had been solved.

* * * * * * * * * * * * * * *

After verifying with the hotel, Justin discovered that William Scofield had stayed three nights at the Spencer Hotel in Marion and that no additional tickets from the Union Traction Company had been purchased. *I guess that rules out traveling back and forth to commit the murder. But he could have hired someone else to do it. The shop owner did confirm the cook purchased red apples on Saturday. That puts those two strange women higher up on my list of suspects.*

* * * * * * * * * * * * * * *

Alvin Jensen, the reporter for the Gas City Journal, had heard rumors about Mrs. Scofield's suspicious death but knew nothing of the details. He tried to interview the household staff, but the housekeeper and the cook refused to talk to him. Out of respect, no attempt had been made to speak with William Scofield who was seen not wearing the traditional black armband on his left arm, as was customary for a grieving spouse.

Marshal Justin Blake felt frustrated he didn't have enough proof to arrest any of his three suspects. His frustrations would only increase due to the dire predictions of the Indian housekeeper that death and destruction involving William Scofield would soon come to pass.

CHAPTER 10
THE TELEPHONE CALL

On Thursday morning, just as Mr. Scofield finished reading his morning newspaper, the phone in the hallway rang, cutting through the silence of the large house. "I have good news for you, Mr. Scofield," said Attorney Lowell Bensen as a way of greeting. "Your counteroffer was accepted by the widow Giles. She is anxious to complete the legal transfer as quickly as possible. As agreed upon, full payment shall be by a certified check from the First National Bank. Would one o'clock tomorrow afternoon work for you?" Mr. Scofield said it would. "Fine. I'll have everything ready for your signatures. Goodbye." William Scofield now felt on top of the world. *It's all coming together just as I've planned! Now I'll need to go into Marion and arrange for wagon loads of my new drilling equipment to be brought into Gas City and stored in that rented warehouse next to the lumber yard. But there is one problem I need to overcome first before I go.*

That evening, he appeared outside the small house rented by his stepsister Loreta and knocked. A startled look appeared on the woman's face as she answered the door. "You're about the last person on Earth I ever expected to pay me a visit, my dear, evasive brother." Without being offered the chance to enter, William stepped inside.

"I heard that rich widow you married died under mysterious circumstances," she said with a questioning voice. William didn't reply. "So why are you here?"

He then explained that the Scofield Oil Company would be formed tomorrow and offered her a job to handle the office bookkeeping and payroll. "The warehouse I rented sits beside the lumber yard and has a small side office. Your title would be Office Manager. Interested?" He then quoted her salary, which was slightly higher than her present employment. But the offer intrigued her, and she saw a better future in a family-owned company.

"I will agree to your offer, but only under one condition. You need to hire Garrett and Anthony, too." As he pondered the idea, she continued. "Garrett is smart, and you'll need someone to handle the operational supervision of your oil rigs, reviewing oil lease contracts, ordering supplies, and such to help you."

William knew she was right, and having Garrett assisting him would be useful. "You can't be everywhere all at once," she continued. "You'll need eyes on the ground at your oil rigs."

"I don't need Anthony, though. He's just a punk kid and doesn't know crap about anything."

She shook her head. "It's all of us or nothing." He knew he had to relent, though the idea of the kid working as an untrained oil roughneck did strike him as funny. "All right, I'll do it," he relented. "You tell them to be in my office at eight o'clock sharp on Monday morning. Tell Garrett he will work as my number two man in the company and the kid will start as a roughneck. I plan on having all our purchased equipment delivered here on Saturday. I'll see you and the boys then, sister dear." He then left. *The idea of being around those half-wit siblings again wasn't appealing, but I'll be able to dictate my terms and make their lives a living hell if I so desire. Now, the only things I'm missing are a qualified drill supervisor, an experienced oil roughneck crew, and the best places I know to find unemployed men in the town's saloons.*

William, no stranger to saloons himself, visited most of the drinking holes in search of the one key man who could make his dream of being a rich oil tycoon a reality: that elusive, hard-to-find, experienced drill supervisor. Without his skilled help, there would be little hope of striking oil.

-MEET THE FAMILY-

Miss Loreta Jones

Loreta Jones had no love for her stepbrother and stepmother, who forced their way into her life that awful day years ago. She could not understand how her father could replace her deceased loving mother so quickly with another woman. That woman's son, William, now the oldest of the children, attempted to exert himself as the new top dog in the food chain. He was a bully, strong and determined to have his way against Loreta and her brothers at every opportunity. She was thrilled when he finally moved out of their home, never to return. Now, their paths crossed again, and he has control of their lives and future financial livelihoods.

I hope this isn't a mistake, she told herself as she left to speak *with* her brothers about his offer of employment.

Wanda and Garrett Jones

Garrett Jones was the oldest of the two Jones boys. He had sought to protect his younger brother from the abuse suffered at the hands of the new boy in their family and always came up short on the losing end. William seemed to enjoy breaking what few toys his younger brother Anthony possessed as a child. Now grown men, Garrett still had no love for William, and he wondered if accepting the position of second in command of the new Scofield Oil Company was wise. This was a career field he knew nothing about. *Knowing William, he'll probably fire me within the week and enjoy every minute!* "What should I do, sis? You know as well as I do how he is," Garrett asked.

"I think we should accept, or we might kick ourselves one day for not becoming a part of the new family-owned company," his sister replied. Garrett turned to his wife, who smiled and nodded in agreement.

"All right, consider me in." Loreta left to visit their other brother.

Wanda Helbling was a young woman working as a seamstress when she met Garrett Jones. He entered the tailor shop, needing repairs for his only suit jacket. She was immediately taken by his appearance and encouraged by the lack of a wedding ring. Six months later, she had solved that problem by becoming his wife.

Throughout their marriage, she had never heard her husband mention his stepbrother until he offered them a rent house in Gas City. She was discouraged by how small and rundown the home was, but Garrett encouraged her to make the best of it. However, despite living in the same town, she and Garrett were never invited to William's magnificent home. Knowing her husband had nothing good to say about his stepbrother made her suspect the worst of the man. Still, the job opportunity was good, and she hoped they could move up socially within the community.

Ethyl and Anthony Jones

Anthony Jones was the youngest of the Jones siblings. As a child, Anthony lived in fear of William Scofield. Years later and recently married, he hoped to provide a better life for Ethyl and, one day, his children. He wasn't sure exactly what the position of roughneck entailed, but it didn't frighten him. He had a strong work ethic and was willing to start at the bottom of the rung and work himself upward to prove his worth. *Maybe William has changed*, he kept telling himself. *Maybe.*

Ethyl Dobbs was a recent graduate of the class of 1899 at Marion High School. She met Anthony through a mutual friend who knew him from the feed store where he worked. He appeared to be a nice young man, a bit shy but honest and sincere. After only a few dates,

Anthony asked her to marry him. She was taken aback by his quick proposal and insisted upon a few days to mull it over. Eventually, she agreed. Though financially poor, the young couple made the best of their situation until fate seemed to step in when Anthony received an offer to work in the family's oil company.

CHAPTER 11
FALLING INTO PLACE

On Saturday afternoon, three wagonloads of oil drilling equipment were seen crossing the wooden covered bridge into Gas City. William Scofield drove one, while the other two were handled by two of his newly hired employees. Each wagon also had a return driver sitting on the bench. The wagons made the short distance to the awaiting warehouse, where everything was unloaded onto the ground. With a wave of their hands, the other men hustled their wagons back over the bridge towards Marion. Though tired from the prior loading and hauling, Scofield was determined to have all his drilling equipment safely stored away. By late afternoon, it was finally finished. "I want to thank you, men," he said, handing each a dollar coin. "Go have yourselves a few drinks on me. Irish, I'll see you Monday morning." Now feeling exhaustion setting in, William made his way home to take a long nap.

The nightly chanting continued.

Matthew (Irish) Ferguson
Derrick Drilling Manager

Known by the nickname 'Irish' due to his Irish accent, he had quickly worked his way up from one of the roughneck men due to his love of drink, hot temper, and fast-moving fists. Irish had worked for many Indiana gas and oil drilling companies but hadn't lasted long anywhere. He and a few of his other colleagues became well-known within the industry as knowledgeable but unreliable. They were suspected in the rash of fires and on-sight accidents that occurred during his watch, though nothing was ever proven. Irish had sized up William Scofield as a greenhorn wannabee in the industry and someone he could control.

He has left the hiring of my new crew all up to me, and I know just the type I want on my team, he thought as he drank shot after shot of whiskey, courtesy of the silver dollar. The other hired man sitting next to him had the same mindset but would not be attending the Monday morning meeting.

David Brown, Roughneck

David Brown had grown up fighting. Born with a dark birthmark above his right eye, he soon earned the hateful nickname 'Brown Spot.' At the age of sixteen, David nearly beat a man to death after he was jokingly called 'Spot.' It took three bystanders to pull him off the injured man. That day, David left town and never returned. Day after day, he continued to feel rage at those who slighted him or brought reference to it. Being a roughneck proved a very satisfactory job, allowing a simple fistfight to put rude men in their place. After working with Irish on several oil derricks, he had grown to trust him.

* * * * * * * * * * * * * * * *

Monday morning's meeting went well. William announced that their first oil derrick would be located three miles south of Gas City on leased property he had acquired. Garrett Jones and Irish worked together to estimate the amount of lumber required to construct the oil rig. As second in command, Garrett, referred to as Mr. Jones by Irish, was put in charge of purchasing materials and transporting equipment and supplies. Irish announced he had acquired an adequate work crew to assemble and operate the new oil derrick. An over-optimistic William named their first derrick Bonanza #1. Construction would begin within a few days. All hoped it would live up to its name. Loreta Jones had not responded to the enthusiasm of the moment. Instead, she occupied herself with figuring out how an office manager begins the process of forming the bookwork for a new company. "Mr. Irish, I'll need a full list of our employee names for payroll purposes as soon as possible," she instructed, and everyone noticed the man's smile at being addressed as Mr. Irish.

* * * * * * * * * * * * * * * *

That afternoon on November 4th, an event occurred that would impact both Gas City and Jonesboro well into the next year.

* * * * * * * * * * * * * * * *

Alan E. Losure

Extra!
Covered Bridge Fire

Special Edition of the Gas City Journal

The Jonesboro-Gas City bridge was destroyed by fire this afternoon. The bridge caught fire shortly after 1:30 p.m., and in less than an hour, it was a mass of ruins. The fire first started in the dwelling house of Herbert Daily, which stood south of the bridge. Despite the bucket brigade's attempt to extinguish the flames, their efforts were powerless against the growing fire. A stiff, northerly wind carried the sparks over to the covered bridge as the roof caught fire in several places at one time, and within a few moments, the old landmark was wiped out of existence.

Some of those who had started to fight the fire at the dwelling now left and made efforts to save the bridge, but their work was to no avail; the wooden structure burned like tinder. The men who were fighting the fire drew back from the hot, scorching flames and sought safety with the crowd that had gathered on the riverbank. It was a grand spectacle as the timbers gave way, and the trolley rails fell into the water with parts of the burning structure. An hour after the fire had started, nothing but charred ends of the structure close to the foundation of the bridge were left to mark the spot. The bridge burned down to the water's edge.

* * * * * * * * * * * * * * *

Justin stood among the crowd of people, surveying the bridge's ruins. It had been a lifeline for the community, used for foot and wagon traffic, and the Union Traction Company streetcar service, but with it now gone, traffic into Jonesboro would have to rely solely upon the Tenth Street Bridge. Justin was about to leave when a familiar voice called out.

"It looks bad, doesn't it, Marshal?" Asked his friend Brad Lockridge, the owner of a gasoline/kerosene repair service station located on the corner of the street leading to the cemetery. Brad had worked under Justin as a nighttime deputy before resigning to join the army during the late Spanish-American War. Upon returning to Gas City, he and a silent partner opened the first service and repair station in Grant County.

"Hello, Brad. Yes, the loss of the bridge will certainly hurt our downtown businesses. I wonder if we'll need to rig up a temporary rope bridge across the river for foot traffic."

Brad's lips twisted in skepticism. "With winter fast approaching, heavy snow and ice would probably bring it down in no time." The two men stood in silence for a moment, looking out across the debris of the burned bridge, before he continued, "I saw your advertisement in the paper for another deputy. Have any luck finding one?"

"No," Justin said with a dejected sigh. "After that last guy, I've been very particular in reviewing potential candidates. So far, though …"

"A lot of my automotive repair work from Marion will be curtailed now with the demise of the bridge, so I was wondering if I could fill in for anyone who comes down sick or takes a vacation," he offered. "I don't want you to feel compelled to say yes; just think about it. I fully understand if you would rather wait for the right man to come along."

As Justin pondered over the situation, a glimmer of hope began to form. *Maybe that bridge burning is a gift in disguise*, he thought. "I don't have to think about it. The answer is yes. Let me speak with the mayor about a salary offer for your part-time employment, and I'll get back to you. We would be happy to have you rejoin our office."

Brad grinned. "You know, my old deputy uniforms still hang in my bedroom closet at my parent's house. I'll drop by and see if they still fit." Justin shook Brad's hand and welcomed him back.

* * * * * * * * * * * * * * *

William smiled at his good fortune. He had been able to get his equipment across the bridge days before it burned. *The luck of the Irish is with me. Nothing can stop me now!*

* * * * * * * * * * * * * * *

Inside the Scofield Mansion, a deeply depressed Mrs. Tyler contemplated quitting her job, but at her age, her options were limited. Mr. Scofield didn't bother to inform her if and when he would be home for a meal, which made meal planning nearly impossible. On the occasion she was able to ask him if he would be home for dinner, he ignored her or said he didn't know. Then Cindy Moon, aka Half-Moon, began her ritual chanting every night. *She is a stupid crazy Injun, always chanting at night and driving me crazy, reciting her mumbo-jumbo. I don't know how much more of this I can take! She refuses to eat anything I've cooked, preferring her secret strange Injun' concoction, most likely made up of missing neighborhood cats and dogs.*

* * * * * * * * * * * * * * *

Just as the first snowfall began to cover the Hoosier landscape, the Bonanza #1 Oil Derrick was finished, and the steam engine began pounding piping into the ground.

William's attorney had advised him that forming a will would be wise since he was now a businessman. Attorney Bensen thought it prudent to prepare for the eventual reality that anything could happen, and it was best to be prepared for the worst. After giving himself a few days to think about it, William sat in his library one evening and wrote his final requests for the distribution of his company. He called both women in to witness his signature, then sign their names and date. Both women were highly suspicious of what they asked to sign, but William ignored their questions. Once completed, he sealed the paper inside an envelope addressed as the 'Will of William Scofield.' He would hand it over to Attorney Bensen to file away in his office safe the next day.

Day after day, the derrick's steam engine continued to pound metal piping further and further into the ground in its search for oil and vast riches. Also on site was a portable work shack on wheels with a wood stove for warmth. This gave the men a place to get out of the elements and eat whatever food they brought that morning during breaks. Wall hooks provided for a change of personal clothing to be hung up as well. A pot of hot coffee could generally be found to help warm their insides from the cold November weather.

Alan E. Losure

CHAPTER 12
FIRST TIME'S A CHARM

Scofield's First Oil Gusher
Bonanza #1

Why is crude oil important?

In 1852, it was discovered that crude oil—originally used as a tooth medicine—could produce kerosene, which could burn longer and cleaner than whale oil. Oil prices soon soared as crews, making as much as twenty-one cents an hour for a ten-hour workday, used steam power to pound metal piping into the ground. Oil was then collected in wooden barrels and transported to railroad cars to be taken to oil refineries. Through necessity, tanker cars were eventually built to hold the oil and eliminate the transportation of leaking wooden oil barrels altogether. Ninety percent of all U.S. refineries were owned by one company: Standard Oil. They also owned twenty-five percent of all oil-producing wells. Who was the president of Standard Oil? Mr. John D. Rockefeller.

Standing a safe distance from the derrick, William and Garrett watched in awe as Bonanza #1 continued to burst forth valuable crude oil. At its base, the crew of roughnecks, under the supervision of derrick manager Irish Fergusen, continued their valiant efforts to affix a shut-off valve to the casing to stop the flow of oil. "Garrett, I need you to take the train to Fairmount today and bring back the Standard Oil representative," William instructed. "Tell him we will not sell our well but seek a contract for our oil's collection, transportation, and refinement. Don't discuss any figures; only remind him that their tanker cars run right through Gas City anyway on the Pennsylvania Railroad tracks." Garrett nodded and mounted his horse for the short trip to the railroad depot. *Here's my chance to prove to William that I'm capable of the position of authority he's placed me in.*

It would be another evening before the oil-soaked roughneck's tireless efforts succeeded in shutting off the flow.

* * * * * * * * * * * * *

Once the crew had finished their work, they entered their shack for the evening, took off their oil-soaked clothing, washed up, changed clothing, and dropped them in the empty laundry barrel outside.

"You there, punk kid," David Brown shouted at Anthony Jones. "The new guy has ta wash everyone else's clothing in dat barrel with Fels Naptha Soap, then string up da close line. Get busy, or I'll come over there and knock your front teeth out!" A few of the men chuckled Most of them had also undergone the bully's threats in the past as the new guy on the crew. This had not been the first time David accosted Anthony. Just yesterday, the man people referred to as Brown Spot had grabbed Anthony by the throat and slammed him into the wall. "How ya like dat," David joked. "Dem brothers of yours, all dressed up in their fancy suits and stayin' clean while sending ya down to do derrick work fer a lousy twenty-one cents an hour. Dey must hate your stinkin' guts, and I don't blame them none. I hate da very sight of ya myself. You is about as worthless as they come. I think I'll be ah callin' ya Baby Jones from now on."

Irish Fergusen laughed and joined in on the confrontation. "And the next time I hear you calling me Irish, I'll look the other way while Davey Boy here pounds you into the ground. Only my friends and folks I respect call me Irish. You, worthless excuse for a roughneck, will address me as Mr. Ferguson. You hear me, Baby Jones?"

"Yes, Mr. Ferguson."

"Now, do what you were told and start cleaning our clothing," Irish said.

As he worked for several hours hauling fresh water, cleaning, dumping the dirty water, refilling the wash drum, and more washing, Anthony Jones questioned his decision to work for the family business. *Garrett's love for me must have changed to put me through this physical and mental torture,* he told himself. *I hate Spot's and Irish's guts, but they are right about one thing. My brothers have no respect for me, which may soon prove to be a two-way street.*

It was nearly midnight when Anthony finally finished, and his body felt leaden with exhaustion. "Where have you been?" Ethyl cried as he stumbled through the front door of their rental home. "I was so worried that something happened to you."

"It's bad enough that William and Garrett treat me like a stranger off the street and work me like a slave, but Irish and a man named Brown are making my life a living hell," he replied. "I don't know how much more of this I can take. They now refer to me as Baby Jones."

* * * * * * * * * * * * * *

Within days, the Standard Oil Company and Scofield Oil contract was drawn up. William and Garrett reviewed the agreement and found everything in order. They brought it to William's attorney, Lowell Bensen, for his review. Once approved, the contract was signed by both parties and notarized. William's dream of owning a successful oil company had become a reality. Both brothers then began discussing the next leased property and the upcoming construction of another derrick.

* * * * * * * * * * * * * *

That evening, William decided it was time to celebrate his good fortune. He was seen in the company of a young woman while out celebrating on the town. Money, it seems, can make one forget the sweet wife recently buried in a pauper's grave. People took notice of this and instantly felt contempt for the man. Soon, William announced to everyone in his family that he intended to bring another woman to Saturday night's theater performance at Lovett's Opera House. Sylvia

Tyler and Cindy Moon felt utter contempt for their employer's bad behavior. The cursed chanting by the Indian housekeeper continued that evening, stronger than ever.

* * * * * * * * * * * * * * *

Construction began on a replacement wagon bridge across the Mississinewa River one square north of where the old bridge used to stand. There would be no streetcar tracks on the new bridge. It was said that the county commissioners had agreed to let the Union Traction Company use the new bridge for $100 a year. Still, the company wanted to be the only one allowed to use the bridge and to stop all other railways and lines from crossing it. They also insisted that the city make a landfill on Main Street from the bottom of the hill to the new bridge. These demands were rejected. It was assumed the Union Traction Company will forge the river sometime in the spring at another location.

CHAPTER 13
A NIGHT AT THE OPERA HOUSE

Third-Floor Lovett's Opera House, Bank
Building, and Ward's Funeral Home

Once word spread that the wealthy William Scofield was in the market for female companionship, he had no difficulties finding beautiful young women. The thought of landing the rich oil tycoon as a future husband caused ladies to lower their standards and give him a second look. He was more than happy to take every advantage he could. Finding a trophy wife was not on his immediate horizon, but he did want to be seen out and about in the envious public eye. Tonight's eye candy was a young woman named Rachael. He hadn't bothered to remember her last name as there'd be another new face next week. Together, William and Rachael walked through the crowd up the center stairs to the third floor and took a seat near the aisle to await the start of the play. Tonight's showing was a comedy called, "The Governor's Son." It was about a well-to-do young man who finds himself attracted to a poor housekeeper's daughter. William instantly pictured himself as the dashing young man, but the very thought of finding love in the arms of a housekeeper's daughter was appalling to him. *No, I'm going to play the field to pick my future queen,* he thought. After the second act began, he heard a commotion of voices coming from behind them. Then suddenly, someone yelled, "Fire! Fire!" The play didn't stop immediately, but two players stepped out of character and began to point toward the northwest corner of the room, where heavy smoke was accumulating. Panic erupted as the audience leaped from their seats, causing the center aisle to become blocked. People tend to be creatures of habit, and the patrons began to force their way toward the doorway leading to the downward steps they earlier entered, rather than take the exit side door fire escape. Screaming voices and cries of panic drowned out the leading actor, attempting to direct the audience toward the east side exit. Terrified people began to trip over someone who had fallen in the aisle, desperate to get out of the theater, now filling with smoke.

Theater staff directed everyone outside while the manager grabbed a pump water extinguisher from the lobby and rushed into the theater. What he found amidst the waning smoke was a trash container in the back corner full of smoldering oily rags. Anger swept through him as he realized this entire episode had been some foolish prank, probably by a couple of juvenile delinquents. After emptying the contents of the extinguisher onto the rags, he directed one of his staff to assist him in carrying the smoldering container down the front steps and out onto the street's sidewalk. He then returned upstairs and propped open the east door with the empty fire extinguisher. With the exit door now open, the smoke began to clear. That was when he noticed the body of a trampled man lying in the center aisle.

"Sir, sir, are you all right? Should I call for a doctor?" the manager asked as he arrived but paused in horror. Buried deep in the man's back was an ice pick. The final curtain call of William Scofield's days of playing an important bigshot around town had ended.

* * * * * * * * * * * * * * * *

The crowd had dwindled to a few curious pedestrians by the time Deputy Philip Curtis was located and informed emergency at the theater. The volunteer firemen soon determined that no fire had occurred and were in the process of returning to the fire station. Assistant Fire Chief Briles remained on the scene waiting to speak with the theater manager to complete his report, having been informed of a fatality by one of his firemen. Doctor Maxwell arrived and made his way up the flight of steps to the third floor. To better assist, the manager brought up the gas lighting to provide better visibility. Curtis was then informed of the oil-soaked smokey rags incident that caused the patron stampede to occur. Approaching the body, Curtis asked who it was.

"William Scofield, the oilman." "This is the last thing we need," the distraught manager said as he shook his head in disbelief. "Once word of this spreads in the theater industry, it will be hard to book future quality entertainment here."

"Was he alone tonight? Did anyone see who killed him?" Curtis asked.

"I was his date tonight, sir," said a soft voice from behind, a trembling woman emerging from the shadows. "All I can tell you is that when the smoke started filling the theater, everyone seemed to jump up at once and head for the aisle. I lost sight of William then but I was only concerned about exiting and not burning to death. When I reached the ground floor, I noticed he wasn't there, but I assumed he was probably helping others to escape. Most of us stood away from the entrance to allow the firemen in, but later, I heard one of them say there was a dead man upstairs."

"What's your name, miss? And how well were you acquainted with the deceased?"

"Rachael Raymie, sir, and this was our first date. May I leave now, sir? I'm not feeling very well."

Curtis nodded and wrote down the woman's name in his pocket notebook. He then turned to the doctor who was waiting to speak with him.

"Judging from the angle of entry, Deputy, I would guess the ice pick penetrated the heart and that death was almost instantaneous. I'll know more after I make a closer examination."

"Fine, Doc. Thanks." Curtis returned outside and began questioning the few patrons who remained. Nobody saw how the fire started nor who murdered the man. He then left to go to the marshal's house and brief him on the situation.

After hearing all the acquired information, Justin said he suspected the smoke was only a diversion so the assailant could attack Scofield amid the smoke and confusion. Curtis said he agreed with that idea and was on his way to the Scofield Mansion to speak with the man's staff.

It was a short walk to the mansion. Arriving, he was met at the door by Mrs. Tyler and informed her of Scofield's murder. Curtis thought he detected a slight smile on the old woman's face. "Do you know if the deceased has any family close by?"

"Sir, I believe he has a brother … or brothers … but I have never seen them or heard him mention where they live. That is all I can tell you." She then wished him goodnight and began to close the door.

"Wait a second. Is Miss Moon at home, and if so, have you both been here all evening?"

"I have been here, sir, but I don't know the whereabouts of that stinking Injun." She then closed the door. *What a strange household*, Curtis thought as he made his way back to the office.

* * * * * * * * * * * *

The following morning, a man and woman entered the Marshal's office. "Marshal Blake? My name is Garrett Jones, and this is my sister Loreta. We are the stepbrother and sister of William Scofield. We were hoping you might tell us more about his murder and where you stand in the investigation." Justin offered both a seat. "I'm afraid not much is known at this point. Did your brother have any recent run-ins with anyone he might have mentioned?" Unfortunately, neither did. "Were you both on friendly terms with your brother?"

Justin noticed a slight pause before Garrett answered. "I take it you didn't know him, sir. Our stepbrother was a difficult man to be around, someone who sought control over others. Money and power were all he ever spoke about. He hired each of us and our younger brother to work in his oil business. I served as his number two man,

Loreta as his bookkeeper and office manager, while our younger brother Anthony had to work as a roughneck."

Justin asked for their addresses as well as Anthony's. "We'll do all we can to find your brother's killer. Please contact this office day or night if anything should come to you regarding a possible motive or of any individual we should investigate."

"On behalf of my sister, I want to thank you for your time and efforts, Marshal. Please keep us informed." As they rose to leave, Garrett turned to Loreta and said, "I think we should pay a visit to our company's attorney, Lowell Bensen, to see if we still have a job."

* * * * * * * * * * * * * *

Once the Jones' arrived at the attorney's office, Garrett introduced his sister and explained the reason for their unannounced visit. After hearing the news, Attorney Bensen said, "Your stepbrother does have a will on file here, so that will alleviate some of the more challenging probate difficulties. Tell you what, give me some time to review his final instructions, and I'll contact you soon."

"Our priority must be the continuation of Scofield Oil. As you are aware, we have a signed contract with Standard Oil," Garrett said.

"Just continue as before until we get things settled out," Gensen replied. Garrett and Loreta left to find Anthony and discuss what they had learned.

* * * * * * * * * * * * * *

Two days later, the body of William Scofield was laid to rest in a pauper grave next to his late wife Ruth Ann. Very few people attended the funeral.

* * * * * * * * * * * * * *

Three days later, a letter arrived at the company office addressed to Miss Loreta Jones. It read:

Dear Miss Jones

You are hereby notified that you have been named the executor of the estate of the late William Scofield. You are directed to make contact by letter with the following individuals, also named as beneficiaries. Inform each person to meet in the library of the Scofield Mansion, on Monday, November 19th at nine o'clock. Wives are welcome to attend. The mentioned beneficiaries are:

Yourself
Mr. Garrett Jones
Mr. Anthony Jones
Mrs. Sylvia Tyler
Miss Cindy Moon

                          Lowell Bensen
                          Attorney at law

CHAPTER 14
THE MEETING

It was a strange feeling for members of the Jones family and their attorney to now be sitting inside the library of the Scofield Mansion, a house none of them had ever been invited into before. Sylvia Tyler and Cindy Moon silently sat behind the group, curious as to how and why their names were added to their ex-employer's will. Attorney Bensen sat behind Scofield's impressive wooden desk and called for everyone's attention.

"Now that everyone's here, let's get down to business, shall we?" Bensen began. "As you already know, Miss Loreta was named executor of Mr. Scofield's will, mostly due to her experience in money matters. She will be responsible for settling debts, collecting monthly payments on his rental properties, and any other estate liabilities, which I assume will be next to nil as Mr. Scofield hasn't been in business very long and paid cash for everything. Also in our favor is the fact that Indiana has not yet passed a bill to collect income tax from her citizens like a few other states already have. I also wouldn't be at all surprised if the federal government won't go that way sometime in the future. Anyway, this should all work out in your favor as listed but in the meantime, you are free to continue the operations of Scofield Oil as before. Before I proceed to the stipulations of his will, do any of you have any questions?" There were none. The attorney removed the will from its opened envelope and began to read aloud.

I, William Scofield, a resident of Grant County, Indiana, being of sound mind and body and being at least eighteen years of age, do hereby make, publish, and declare this to be my Last Will and Testament.

1. *If I am married at the time of my death, I hereby bequeath my home and all financial holdings to her. Should I be a widower with stepchildren, no said financial holdings shall be passed onto her children, but instead be distributed as outlined below.*
2. *If I remain single, the following individuals shall become heirs to my estate, providing the following stipulations as outlined in paragraph (3) are strictly adhered to.*
   Garrett Jones
   Anthony Jones
   Loreta Jones
   Sylvia Tyler
   Cindy Moon
3. *All parties mentioned, as well as their wives, are required to move into my residence one week from the reading of this will and remain there until the final Probate has been completed. There are ample bedrooms within my home for your comfort. I task Mrs. Tyler and Miss Moon with the responsibility of carrying for my family and maintaining a log-in book signing, swearing that each heir continues to sleep there nightly in good faith. I can see the possibility that Garrett might require overnight travel to expand our business, but this is not to be abused by him, or more than three nights per month. Should this mandatory requirement fail to be met by anyone, that individual will forfeit all rights and privileges under the terms of this will, with his/her share going to the others. Any attempt by an*

individual or individuals to challenge the legality of this document will cause their forfeiture of all rights to future money.
4. During the Probate period, Loreta will be tasked with paying the cook and housekeeper a dollar per day in monthly salaries while they perform their official functions to service our new guests.
5. I know that each of you hated me, and I have felt the same for you. I wish I were there to see the looks on your faces right now, knowing that to come into my money, you must become one big happy family living inside this huge tomb of a house. Perhaps you will kill each other off, and whoever is left can take the final prize!

William Scofield
November 12, 1901

Sylvia Tyler
Witness

Cindy Moon
Witness

The terms of the will caught everyone by surprise. Neither wife was anxious to move into the house and share it with the others. After a bit of griping, everyone finally accepted the fact and sought out individual bedrooms to make their claim upon.

* * * * * * * * * * * * * * *

Within the required time, everyone settled in for what they knew would not be a happy experience. It didn't take long for the wives to start arguing among themselves and develop issues with the cook and that rude Indian housekeeper, who finally was forced to stop her annoying chanting. The nightly logging of everyone's presence continued without issues.

* * * * * * * * * * * * * *

Garrett, Anthony, and Loreta were grateful to be able to find an escape through work. The first royalty check from the Standard Oil Company soon arrived, just in time to meet payroll needs. A new derrick was under construction as the roughnecks fought the cold, bitter elements of snow and wind. At least the portable worker's shack was on-site, and the coffee pot on the hot stove helped warm the workers.

The physical and emotional abuse suffered by Anthony continued. If anything, Irish and David Brown were more determined than ever to break the spirit of the young man and send him packing. Anthony was resolved not to speak of his terrible predicament to his brother, whom he now avoided altogether. An icy chill hung in the air inside the Scofield Mansion.

CHAPTER 15
THE FIGHT

A man can only take so much before being compelled to finally act in his own self-defense. That's what happened toward the end of the workday at the new Derrick site. All day long, David Brown had kept after Anthony with his Baby Jones this, and Baby Jones that, taunting until finally, the young man had had enough and struct Jones squarely in the jaw. The hateful roughneck had been taken by surprise by the attack and was knocked down. Jumping to his feet, Brown shouted, "Let's finish this here and now, punk!"

"Whatever you say, Brown Spot!" Anthony replied as both men began to struggle while their fellow workers cheered. The loud disruption caught the attention of Garrett, who had been on site checking on supplies. Seeing his brother's involvement, Garrett's first reaction was to rush in and break up the fight, but he quickly decided not to become involved. *If I did, Anthony would feel shame and embarrassment in front of those men. He must learn to fight his own battles.*

Both fighters slipped and fell on the snow as they struggled to finish each other off. Irish happened to glance across the property and saw Garrett Jones watching. "Hey, hey, you guys, break it up. The boss is watching! You can finish this off later under better time and conditions." He then separated both men. "I got an idea. Since everyone here, except Baby Jones, enjoys having a few brews every Saturday night with his pals at Clancy's Bar, why not postpone your brawl for a couple more days and finish it in their storage room? In the past, Clancy preferred that over having his tables and chairs smashed to pieces. Then, we can all celebrate Davy's one-punch victory over the baby with a few beers!"

Brown seemed not to hear what Irish had said as he seemed determined to end it now. "Nobody calls me that name and keeps their front teeth!" he shouted as other men began restraining his arms.

The men would soon remember the fire in Anthony's eyes as he replied, "I'm gonna lay you out flat, dead as a doornail, all ready for the vultures to pick your dirty bones clean." Irish then ordered all the men back to work as he smiled and approached Mr. Jones.

"Just a friendly little disagreement, Mr. Jones. Nothing to be concerned about. I handled it."

* * * * * * * * * * * * * * *

That evening at the supper table, Garrett sensing the tension in the air, asked his brother about the quarrel. Anthony lost his temper and slammed his fist down hard on the dining room table. Everything that had been bottled up inside Anthony suddenly came out in a loud voice recanting all the verbal and physical punishment he had to endure as a lonely roughneck. Garrett was shocked. "Do you want me to fire them?"

"No! That would be the worst thing you could do. I need to fight Brown Spot fairly or I'll never earn the crew's respect. So please, stay out of it. I'm not afraid of him." Anthony began to calm down.

He then turned to his wife Ethyl and asked, "Honey, would you still love me if I lost my front teeth?"

* * * * * * * * * * * * * *

The following two workdays were tough. Anthony could feel the tension among the roughnecks who were giving him the silent routine, no doubt via orders by Irish. The odds maker hadn't taken long to offer eight to one against Baby Jones coming out on top. By Saturday morning, both fighters had agreed to appear at nine o'clock that evening. No weapons were allowed by either man. Irish had already gotten the bartender's approval the night before, and a crowd of curious men were expected to witness the fight and make their bet after the fighters arrived. As a precaution, crates of whiskey were moved away to give the fighters extra room to brawl. This type of free entertainment was bound to draw a larger-than-usual crowd into the saloon. All day long, Anthony Jones and David Brown remained apart but flipped each other off when they saw one another. By six o'clock, work ended, and each man began to wander off to await tonight's fight. "Baby Jones ain't got da guts ta even show up," Brown bragged to his co-workers.

* * * * * * * * * * * * * *

Anthony chose not to go home but walked along the frozen riverbank for over an hour, trying to clear his head before entering the local dinner to eat, relax, and waste some time. To him, the hands of the wall clock seemed to move slower than usual. Finally, at eight-thirty, Anthony left and began the walk towards Clancy's Bar with his hands buried in his coat pockets. He had somehow misplaced his leather gloves from his work jacket, and today's cold wind numbed his fingers.

I hope I can put up a decent defense, he told himself.

Entering the saloon, Anthony was called to the back storage room, where he removed his coat and hat to await the arrival of his opponent. A few men had already arrived with drinks, and more soon entered. Anthony avoided the small talk, concentrating instead on his task at hand.

Nine o'clock arrived, but there was no sign of David Brown. The crowd became restless, and a few returned to the saloon to await the man's arrival. By nine-thirty, it seemed that there would be no fight.

"Where is your thug, Mr. Irish, sir?" Anthony asked in a sarcastic voice. The supervisor could only shake his head in disgust. While none of his co-workers could bring himself to say it out loud, each thought the word *coward*.

Soon, Anthony got tired of waiting and left for home, thinking *at least I had the guts to show up. How is he going to explain this Monday morning?* Anthony slept soundly that night, but soon, his real-life nightmare would soon begin.

On Monday morning, the roughneck crew discovered the body of David Brown at the back of the drill site. His rear skull had been crushed inward.

CHAPTER 16
THE MURDER SCENE

Justin Blake was reading through the night logbook while Wilbert Vance made a fresh pot of coffee when a man they didn't know entered. "Are you the marshal?' he asked.

"Yes, how can I help you."

"You need to come with me to the Scofield Oil Derrick outside of town. I'm the supervisor there, and one of my roughnecks has been murdered. We have the man who done him in. He's the owner's younger brother, Anthony Scofield. I have my wagon outside ready to take you." *Here we go again,* Justin thought in disgust as he and Wilbert began donning their heavy coats and hats.

"We'll need to make a short stop to bring our coroner, Doctor Maxwell, with us, Justin explained." The men boarded the wagon and drove the short distance to the doctor's home. Arriving, Justin jumped down and disappeared inside. Shortly after, both men exited the house and climbed up on the seat while Wilbert seated himself in the back. *I wouldn't want to be in Justin's boots right now,* Wilbert thought. Justin decided to wait until their arrival before asking any questions of the supervisor. Technically, any crime committed outside of the city limits fell within the jurisdiction of the Grant County Sheriff's Office. However, the time it would take to send one of their deputies would result in the loss of fresh evidence. Justin's department had a good working relationship with the sheriff's office, and all evidence collected would be preserved and presented to them.

The derrick soon appeared in the distance, a towering object that seemed out of place with the level farm ground. After arriving, the group approached the noisy worksite and walked toward the assembled workers. "Can someone shut off that noisy steam machine?" Justin asked. Irish did so. "Thanks. Now we can hear each other without having to shout." There, before him, lay the body of a man half buried in the snow with fresh boot tracks covering the area. Doctor Maxwell did a quick examination and pointed out the severe damage to the rear of the skull. Each worker then began describing the bad feelings between the deceased and Anthony Jones.

"They were to have a fistfight Saturday night to resolve the matter, but Davy here didn't show up. That's because Baby Jones had already done him in!" The rest of the crew agreed. "We got the murderer inside the shed all tied up like a Christmas present for ya," one of the workers said.

"Have any of you messed with the body or moved anything?" Justin asked. The men all said no. "Wilbert, while I'm inside questing the suspect, I want you to scour the area." The deputy nodded and began to search. Justin and Irish entered the shed. Before him sat the trembling young man all tied up. "Take that rope off of him at once," Justin directed. With reluctance, the supervisor complied. "Mr. Jones, I don't know if we've met before, but I am Marshal Blake. What can you tell me about this murder?"

"Marshal, I swear on a stack of Bibles, I had nothing to do with it! Yes, we had our troubles and were to settle things Saturday night, but he didn't show up. Irish was there and will testify to that fact."

"Ask him what he did after leaving work then. He must have doubled back and killed poor Davy!" the supervisor stated.

"Sir, I must ask you to remain quiet." Irish nodded his consent to comply.

"Marshal, I can tell you. After work, I was greatly troubled about the upcoming fistfight with Brown Spot, as I hadn't been in a fight since the third grade. I walked down to the river and prayed to God he wouldn't hurt me. Then, I went into the diner, ate, and stayed until it was time to go down to Clancy's Bar for the fight. I waited and waited, but he didn't show up. Secretly, I was thrilled as he bragged that he would knock out my front teeth. Greatly relieved to still be in one piece, I went home to bed. That's all I know. I had nothing to do with any murder!"

"Do you have any witnesses that will corroborate with seeing you down by the river?" The young man replied he did not know.

At that point, the door opened, and Wilbert entered. He was carrying a two-by-four piece of lumber and a pair of gloves. The end of the board had a frozen red substance staining it, as did the gloves. Wilbert peeled back the glove to display the owner's name: A. Jones. "I found these down the way half-buried in what appears to be a splattering of blood."

Wilbert held the gloves up to the suspect's face. "Are these yours, sir? They have your name written on them."

The suspect's mouth hung open in surprise. "Where did you find them? I noticed they were missing from my work coat Saturday morning when I came in, and I had to work outside all day in bare hands. These men will attest to that!"

"That proves nothing, you stinkin' little runt!" Irish hatefully sneered said. Justin gave him a dirty look that shut him up. Justin then motioned for Wilbert to follow him outside to speak in private.

"So, what do you think? He had the motive to kill; there are no witnesses he saw to prove he was elsewhere, and we have work gloves he has identified as his with blood on them: that and the murder weapon you discovered close to the bloody gloves. I feel we have enough evidence to bring him in for additional questioning. Maybe he will admit to the truth once we get him away from these men." Wilbert said he agreed. "I'll help the doc load up the body in the supervisor's wagon and have him take us back into town. You stay here and get written statements from those men. I'll obtain the supervisor's statement at the office, and then send him back to pick you up. All right?"

While Justin returned to the shed to inform the supervisor of what was to happen, Wilbert began speaking with the other roughnecks and writing down their statements. "Anthony Jones, you will have to come with us to the marshal's office for additional questing," Justin said, cuffing him and leading him to the wagon. As they passed the gathered roughnecks, they glared and taunted him. If the hatred in their eyes could kill, Anthony Jones would be a walking dead man.

"I swear to you, Marshal, I didn't do it! I am innocent!" the young man pleaded as he was taken away. "I want to speak with my brother, Garrett."

Justin said it would be arranged as soon as possible as the wagon returned to the doctor's home office.

* * * * * * * * * * * * * *

Garrett, you gotta get me out of this!" Anthony pleaded from inside the jail cell. "I'm being held on suspicion, but it sounds like they are just waiting for a sheriff's deputy to come and take me to the Marion jail. I swear, I know nothing about this murder!"

"I called Attorney Bensen before coming here. He said he doesn't practice criminal law and can't help us but that the court will appoint a defense lawyer should it come to an actual trial. Hopefully, they'll let you go, but if not, try to remain calm, little brother, and know the family believes in your innocence."

* * * * * * * * * * * * * * *

After hearing the severity of the possible charges against Anthony, the family ate their supper in near-silence. Finally, Garrett spoke, "I asked Mr. Bensen about using company funds to hire an attorney, but he advised against it. He said local criminal attorneys take turns acting as the court-appointed lawyer anyway, so Anthony should be in good hands, and it won't drain our resources. We all heard him say how much he hated Mr. Brown, and apparently, they have witnesses that he made some serious threats to do away with him. Also, some of his personal property was stained in blood." All eyes fell upon Ethyl Jones, who ate her soup in silence.

* * * * * * * * * * * * * * *

The following day, a sheriff's deputy appeared in the marshal's office. While Anthony could only hear bits and pieces of what was being discussed, he knew the evidence discovered at the crime scene pointed to him as the killer. Almost all the witness statements contained his threat to the victim, the roughnecks quoting him saying, "I'm gonna lay you out flat, dead as a doornail, all ready for the vultures to pick your dirty bones clean." Finally, his jail cell was opened, and the sheriff's deputy entered, cuffed him, and placed him under arrest. With the murder weapon and bloody gloves taken as evidence, Anthony and the deputy were whisked away by the Marion trolly car. That night would be the first of many nights that he found himself behind bars.

* * * * * * * * * * * * * * *

Due to the loss of two workers and the approaching Christmas and New Year's Eve, Garrett and Loreta decided to halt drilling operations. Irish's attempt to hire the needed replacements so far had been unsuccessful, as word on the street was that Bonanza # 2 was an unlucky workplace, wrought with danger.

* * * * * * * * * * * * * * *

Despite the family's attempt at optimism for Anthony's full acquittal, Ethyl could not be coaxed out of her depression. Garrett's wife, Wanda, privately advised her husband that she feared for the emotional well-being of her sister-in-law. The next morning, Ethyl did not appear at breakfast. When Wanda asked Cindy Moon if she had seen her, the housekeeper replied, "Yes. She left the house with her suitcase very early this morning." Anthony's wife was never seen again.

* * * * * * * * * * * * * * *

The search for oil at Bonanza # 2 started again the first week of the new year. Eight days later, oil was struck, though not as many gallons per minute as the prior well. The Standard Oil Company was happy to transport the new oil to their refinery. Garrett had been successful in purchasing additional oil leases. With Loreta's permission, each member of their now expanding workforce received a small bonus for bringing in a successful well and, hopefully, keeping them happy on the job. The profits continued to flow into the company's bank account as construction began for Bonanza # 3.

* * * * * * * * * * * * * * *

Despite their best efforts, the murder of Mr. and Mrs. William Scofield remained open in the Gas City Marshal's Office, though Justin now assumed the younger brother was most likely the killer, with money as the prime motive. Justin officially requested to view the contents of William Scofield's will, hoping to find a motive. Attorney Benson initially refused the request, citing privacy issues, until Garrett and Loreta gave verbal permission.

CHAPTER 17
SPRINGTIME, 1902

Miss Loreta Jones had a big responsibility in the Scofield Oil Company, managing the books, receipts, expenses, and payroll. Luckily, she has always been good at math, and along with the helpful aid of a Burroughs Adding Machine, Loreta kept their books balanced. One can easily understand the difficulty of concentrating in a noisy office with people coming and going, with the shrill ring of the telephone echoing around the office. That's why she made it a point to arrive early every Thursday morning before the office opened for business. Today would be no exception as Loreta hurried down the sidewalk just as the sun began to rise. Typically, by mid-morning, she would excuse herself and walk over to the local diner for a quick breakfast. So far, her one-day schedule has been working quite satisfactorily.

The Scofield Oil Company's office was located on the south side of Main Street next to the grain store. After unlocking the entrance door, Loreta walked to the back wall and turned on the gas lighting. The room became fully illuminated. She then removed her coat and hung it up on the coat rack. Pausing to contemplate her busy morning schedule for a few seconds, she turned and walked toward her desk to sit down. That's when the front window suddenly shattered inward, spraying glass fragments all over the floor.

Brad Lockridge, the part-time deputy, was finishing his morning patrol when the sound of a rifle shot penetrated the quiet morning air. From his experience in the late Spanish-American War, he knew the sound of rifle fire, instantly registering it to be of a smaller caliber and that it had come from a block ahead. He started running, looking along both sides of the street for any activity. One office was well-lit ahead, and he instinctively approached it. Arriving, he could see the damage to the glass window and knew he was in the right location. Rushing inside, he saw a woman holding the receiver to a desk candlestick telephone. "Sir," she shouted. "I was trying to get ahold of someone in your office. I don't know what happened, but I'm scared half to death. That window just exploded all over the place!"

"Are you all right, Ma'am? Did you see who took a shot at you?" She replied she was unhurt and sat as her hands began trembling. "Shot? Someone shot at me? Oh, my God, why?" She began sobbing. Brad ran outside and across the street to the wooded park, searching for the shooter. *Whoever did it is gone*, he told himself.

"You're Miss Jones, aren't you?" he asked, stepping back into the office. "I suggest you return home and rest up a bit. You've been through quite an ordeal this morning. I'll be happy to escort you there safe and sound." She thanked him, and they walked the short distance to Scofield Mansion.

Once home, Loreta stumbled into the dining room looking distraught. She tried to remain calm as she faced her family, but the words came tumbling out as she cried, "Somebody took a shot at me in the office!" She then ran upstairs to her room, and her sister-in-law, Wanda, followed her. A shocked Garrett stood up, tossed his unused napkin down in anger, and marched out of the house, demanding to know what the heck was going on. In the kitchen, Mrs. Tyler heard the loud commotion and wished they all would march out of the house and stay gone. The housekeeper, Cindy Moon, began chanting to herself as she went about her cleaning duties.

* * * * * * * * * * * * * * *

Entering the company's office, Garrett found the marshal and a deputy prying something out of the back wall with a pocketknife. "Looks to be .22 caliber," Wilbert Vance offered. Justin concurred.

An angry Garrett began demanding answers. "What are you two doing to protect my family? Ruth Ann was poisoned, William was murdered, our employee David Brown was beaten to death, and instead of finding the real killer, you arrest my innocent brother, Anthony. Even his wife, Ethyl, couldn't take any more of this and walked out. Now you'll probably tell me he broke out of jail overnight just to shoot his sister and then returned to his cell to await his trial tomorrow morning! I thought we had real lawmen in this city, not escapees from Barnum and Bailey's Circus! Marshal, you must know that young man is innocent, but you had to pin those crimes on someone, and he was an easy choice."

The words stung both lawmen. "Mr. Jones, right now, all our efforts are on investigating who took a shot at your sister. Has she expressed any trouble with anyone that you are aware of?" Justin asked. Garrett only shook his head and stormed out. He walked the streets for over an hour, trying to regain control of his emotions, before going home to check on his sister. After lunch, Garrett and Loreta returned to the office. There would be no delays in meeting payroll on Friday while they attended their brother's murder trial in Marion.

* * * * * * * * * * * * * * *

The murder trial of Anthony Jones lasted two and a half days. He was happy to see his brother and sister in the courtroom but saddened when he didn't see Ethyl. The defense's claim that Anthony took a walk after the bitter confrontation with Brown didn't sit well with the jury, and no witnesses could confirm his statement. In the end, the jury found him guilty of first-degree murder in the death of David Brown. Superior Court Judge Albert Flynn sentenced him to twenty-five years to life at the Indiana State Prison in Michigan City.

* * * * * * * * * * * * * * * *

The Union Traction Company began constructing a replacement bridge across the Mississinewa River. It would be built to rest on the old abutments of the old covered bridge and used exclusively as a railway bridge by the company.

CHAPTER 18
QUESTIONS ASKED

Matthew "Irish" Ferguson was an angry man. His efforts to control Garrett Jones had failed. Irish suggested several times that he should be included in business meetings with Loreta, but he was always rebuffed. *I'm being treated more like a glorified roughneck myself who directs other roughnecks. If it weren't for me, Bonanza wells four and five would not have produced a drop of black gold. But I did enjoy the look on Garrett's face when three proved to be a financial bust!* Irish had dropped hints among the crew that they should be paid higher wages. When Garrett began offering small bonuses to the workers for their efforts, it upset his plans to stage a worker's mutiny. Still, there was time to create on-site chaos, as Bonanza #6 was now built and fully operational. Plans were also underway for Bonanza #7.

* * * * * * * * * * * * * *

While waiting for their evening meal, Garrett and Wanda continued their continuing argument within the confines of their bedroom. "Please try to see things from my perspective," Wanda told her husband. "I simply cannot stand another night in this depressing mausoleum of a house. I can feel the walls closing in on me, can't you? Let's move out and give everything to your sister. She will keep you working in your current job anyway!"

Garrett shook his head. "I don't want to work for her or anyone else when I can hire someone to run the company for me. Don't you understand, dear? This is our golden opportunity to become wealthy and set for life."

"I'll tell you that this awful house has driven off poor Ethyl, put Anthony in prison for a murder he didn't commit, and as driven Loreta crazy as she hasn't been the same since that shooting incident weeks ago. Can't you see that William's will was intended to destroy the very family he secretly hated?"

Garrett said nothing as he considered his options. "I'll tell you what. Tomorrow, Loreta and I will try to meet with the attorney and ask how much longer all this legal mumbo-jumbo is going to take. I remember him saying it may not take a full year, so an update of information would greatly benefit everyone. Please trust me and give it time to work out. Now, let's go downstairs and eat."

* * * * * * * * * * * * * *

The following morning, Garrett asked his sister to call to their attorney and see when they could meet with him to discuss the status of Probate. An appointment was made for two o'clock that afternoon.

* * * * * * * * * * * * * *

A man is only a number inside this god-forsaken place, Anthony thought, eyeing the black 08859 stitched into his jumpsuit. His three new roommates had given him the nickname 'Little Darlin',' an implied meaning he certainly wanted no part of. He received a letter from an attorney in Marion the day before informing him that

Ethyl was initiating divorce proceedings. The news struck Anthony hard, but he was beginning to accept his fate and that she needed to get on with her life.

Anthony stood, grasping the cell bars as he thought about her and how she didn't care about attending his trial. His thoughts broke when he heard a rough voice from behind saying, "Ya can't do nuttin' about it, 'Little Darlin',' so ya might as well curl up next ta me and keep me warm!" The men laughed at his discomfort.

At that moment, Anthony Jones wished he were dead.

* * * * * * * * * * * * *

"Everything is moving along just as I expected," Attorney Bensen informed Garrett and Loreta. "I hope to have everything wrapped up by the end of next month."

"We're all counting the days until we can move out of that retched old house and sell it the first chance we get," Loreta said, and Garrett nodded his agreement.

"You should make a pretty penny for it. Oh, and once we're done, will the name Scofield Oil continue to be used for your company, or will we change it? If so, I can easily handle the necessary paperwork."

"We've talked about changing it but haven't settled on another name yet," Garrett replied.

Glancing at the wall clock, Attorney Bensen said another appointment was coming in and promised to keep them informed. Satisfied, brother and sister returned to their office.

* * * * * * * * * * * * *

That night, around two in the morning, the sound of fire bells startled the residents of the Scofield Mansion awake. Most of the occupants simply turned over and tried to go back to sleep until the ringing of the upstairs hallway telephone got everyone's attention. Wanda finally answered it and was informed by the night watchman that Bonanza # 6 Oil Derrick was on fire. Garrett dressed, saddled a horse, and proceeded to the location. Upon his arrival, only a charred pile of rubble now occupied where the wooden framework of the derrick had once stood. Once the site had cooled down for inspection, Garrett saw that the pumping equipment had been damaged but the shutoff valve holding back the flow of oil had luckily done its job and held the flow of oil back.

Knowing that the ground had been covered in spilled oil, Garrett concluded that an unknown spark had started the blaze. By noon, work crews had removed the rubble and began making necessary repairs to put the machinery back into operation. "It could have been much worse," Garrett told his sister.

Dear reader … have you solved the mystery yet?

< > < > < > < > < > < > < > < >

Think back to the murder that took place at Lovett's Opera House. Someone lit a barrel of oily rags atthe back corner wall while, during the panic that ensued, William "Slick Willie" Scofield was fatally stabbed with an ice pick. Wouldn't you say it would've taken more than one person to pull this off? I have compiled groups of *possible* suspects for your consideration. Please review and make your pick to see if you are right! So many to choose from. Good Luck!

Anthony & Wanda	Benson & Irish
Anthony & Ethyl	Benson & Loreta
Anthony & Loreta	Benson & Wanda

Anthony & Irish
Anthony & Benson
Cindy Moon & Anyone
Ethyl & Wanda
Ethyl & Loreta
Ethyl & Irish
Ethyl & Benson
Irish & Wanda
Irish & Loreta
Wanda & Loreta

David Brown & Anyone
Henderson & Anyone
Mrs. Tyler & Anyone
Garrett & Wanda
Garrett & Ethyl
Garrett & Loreta
Garrett & Antony
Garrett & Irish
Garrett & Benson
The Evil Spirits

CHAPTER 19
BRAINSTORMING SESSIONS

Just before lunch, Justin and Wilbert sat in their office trying once again brainstorming the murders of The Ragman, Ruth Ann Scofield, her husband William, oilfield roughneck David Brown, and finally, the murder attempt against Loreta Jones. It seemed that the answer was right in front of them but just out of reach. "Mayor Huffman is demanding answers … answers we just don't have at the moment," Justin said with disgust in his voice. It must be someone associated with the Scofield Oil Company. But we've interviewed everyone in that family and all their workers without learning a thing. Someone must know something."

"My head hurts just thinking about all this. I think I'll go get me a bite to eat. Want to come along?" Justin declined the offer. The lawmen found themselves back where they started, with … no proof to arrest anybody and fearful that the murderer was not finished.

* * * * * * * * * * * *

Barbers Matthew Brooks and his brother, Jordan, each had customers in their respective chairs when another man entered the shop. It was Gas City Mayor, Davis Huffman.

"Good to see you, Mr. Mayor," Matthew said. "We'll be with you shortly."

"No rush, Matt." He then picked up a two-year-old magazine, glanced through it quickly, and returned it to the pile. "You fellows really ought to get newer reading material in here. This one came over on the Mayflower," he joked. His comment had been heard many times before and was ignored.

"We were told the city is spreading gravel out on the roads and installing curb siding," Jordon offered.

"Yes, we're extending Main Street a mile east and west and First Street one-half mile north and south. It should make for quite an improvement in traveling, especially in the rain," Huffman boasted.

"It's always good ta see our tax dollars put ta useful work and not linin' some dang dirty politician's pocket!" the grumpy old man in Jordan's barber chair stated. Everyone smiled at the unintended humor of the statement. After hearing no objections from anyone, the old man continued. "Also, don't be ah buyin' any of them dang ol' horseless carriages with our money. Dems worthless pieces of expensive, noisy junk are all bound fer da scrapyard. Give me ah good, old, reliable horse any day!"

CHAPTER 20
THE BEGINNING OF THE END

When the Hoosier gas and oil rush began, many homeowners started renting out spare bedrooms to make a few easy bucks. The Poindexter family was no different, except Mrs. Poindexter refused to allow some filthy oilman into her home on East South B Street, next to the High School. Determined to cash in on this money train, Herman Poindexter began to eyeball his seldom-used rear tool shed. After adding a much larger addition and a heating stove, it was furnished with the living necessities. Since only a few of the modest townhomes were equipped with running water or indoor restrooms, the renter would have to share the family's backyard privy. The improved shed was rented out and, through the years, provided some much-needed extra income for the older couple. One day, a new oilman appeared on the scene as their renter. His name was Matthew Ferguson.

The call of nature can affect people at different times of the day or night. Herman Poindexter awoke to answer that occasional call during the early morning hours. Being an old Civil War Veteran of the 17th Indiana Regiment, he had learned long ago to flow through life as it comes. Tonight was one of those odd nights. *I hope I can go back to sleep*, he reasoned. Leaving through the home's back door, dressed in his nightgown and slippers, Herman entered the wooden privy. Moments later a single gunshot echoed through the night. *My God! That sounded like it came from my backyard*, he *thought.*

Exiting the privy, his eyes focused on his rental shed. The door was open, the interior illuminated by a single oil lamp. He then heard glass shattering, and instantly, a flame appeared. Just as Herman was about to run forward to investigate, a figure stepped out of the burning shed. "Hey there," the owner yelled. "What happened?" The reply of a bullet whizzed by his head and embedded into the wooden walls of the privy behind him. Instinct told him to duck as he watched the figure running north onto Fourth Street and disappear into the darkness.

Herman ran over to the shed calling out, "Is anyone in there?"

He thought he heard a weak moan calling for help through the smoke. Bending down nearly to the floor where the smoke was thinner, Herman could see what appeared to be a man's head and shoulders. Grabbing hold underneath the victim's armpits, Herman dragged the injured man out into the yard to safety, far enough away from the heat and smoke. Two blocks away, the bell at the fire station sounded. Looking back at the shed, Herman knew it would be a total loss.

His terrified wife appeared at his side, drawing his attention away from the burning shed. "I called the operator to report the fire."

"Call for a doctor. Mr. Ferguson has been shot. Then, bring me some clean towels to help stop his bleeding. Hurry!" He turned back to the man as his wife ran off, examining his body for the source of the bleeding. "Mr. Ferguson, Mr. Ferguson! It's me, Herman Poindexter. Hang in there, my friend. Help is on its way!" The injured man's chest wound brought back forty-year-old memories of comrades injured and dying in battle, but Herman pressed on and was eventually successful in slowing the flow of blood. The fire department arrived and began extinguishing the flames. Soon, the shed was just a smoldering pile of rubble when Doctor Maxwell arrived.

"Help me get him into my wagon and back to my office," Maxwell ordered. Two of the firemen assisted and accompanied the doctor the short distance. As the wagon pulled away, Mr. and Mrs. Poindexter huddled together, shocked at what had just transpired on their property.

* * * * * * * * * * * * * * *

Before Temporary Deputy Brad Lockridge heard the report of the shed fire and attempted murder, he found himself in the northern part of town answering the call of a reported assault and battery with a deadly weapon. Earlier, a terrified wife said her husband had returned home from a late-night drinking binge and was beating their sixteen-year-old son, threatening to shoot her if she intervened. The husband's name was Mark Temple. Just as Brad arrived at the address, he could hear people shouting inside and suspected he might have his hands full. *A drunk with a gun is a dangerous combination,* he told himself. *I think I'll enter without displaying my pistol and try to reason with him in a less threatening manner.* Not bothering to knock, the deputy slowly opened the door and found the family in a back bedroom. As he entered, the loud sound of fire bells ringing in the distance caught his attention. *That's great! Two emergencies at the same time. Well, that one can wait.* Then an idea came to him. *It's worth a chance.* The bedroom door was open when the deputy appeared. The drunk man stood in the middle of the room, one arm wrapped tight around a young man's throat while he leveled a pistol at the terrified wife trembling in the corner. "Mr. Temple," Brad began, his voice low and stern. "We need your assistance. Can you hear those fire bells ringing? I'm here to collect every abled man I can find to assist in an emergency. The fire is raging out of control and may burn down the entire south side. Your neighbors said you are a good man that can be counted upon. Time is of the essence, and you can handle your family issues later. Come on, let's go!"

Brad held his breath, waiting to see how the man would react. Slowly, Mr. Temple released his son, who ran towards his mother's arms. "Yes," Temple said with an intoxicated slur. "I can be counted upon."

"Good, that's good. Now, put down the weapon. It won't do you any good against a fire." Brad held his hands up placatingly, and with reluctance, Mr. Temple set it on the dresser. "Let's go, young man." The men walked out of the room and onto the street. This dangerous situation was disarmed by quick thinking. In the distance, flames from the burning shed could easily be seen as the men picked up their pace, running toward it. Brad hoped the exertion from running and the cool early-morning air might start clearing Temple's head.

After arriving on Main Street, the men were still two blocks away from the fire, but they could see there were enough men to tame the blaze, and their aid was no longer needed. "It looks like all the men we assembled have brought the fire under control, so you won't be needed after all. I want to thank you, Mr. Temple, for your assistance. I have a pot of coffee on the stove in the marshal's office. Why don't you go inside and enjoy a cup while I finish investigating the cause of the fire? I won't be too long, and maybe I'll bring a few other men back with me. I know they'll want to see you, sir, and thank you for your eagerness to serve our community. Who knows, maybe all of your names will appear in the next edition of the Journal!" Brad would have seen the man's smiling face if it had been daylight hours. It worked as Temple gave a half-hearted wave and staggered toward the jail. With the cell door standing open, Brad hoped he'd find the man sound asleep on the cot upon his return. *I'll make a quick check of this fire situation, then get right back in the office.*

His wish for a quick return *was* dashed as he interviewed Mr. and Mrs. Pondexter and learned of the shooting. Ferguson's name and association with Scofield Oil had been discussed at great lengths within the police department. He considered waking up Justin and briefing him on the situation but decided to hold off. Knowing that the gunshot victim was probably undergoing surgery, he informed the homeowners that the marshal would be back later that day to interview them.

Brad left for the office and was a block away when a thought hit him. *Oh my God, what if Temple returned home and was at this moment assaulting his family? I would be responsible!* Brad quickened his pace, but his fears were soon put to rest. Inside, a snoring Mark Temple lay sleeping away inside the open cell. Relieved, Brad locked the cell door, and proceeded to pour a cup of coffee to start writing out his log report. Once he got settled at his desk, he called Mrs. Temple to assure her that her husband was in police custody and that her husband being asked to help fight the fire had been a ruse. "I'll be in sometime after lunch to press charges against him. This is not the first time we have endured his drunkenness, but I swear it will be the last," she said. Brad was pleased with her statement. *Boy, what a night!*

* * * * * * * * * * * * * * *

Justin and Wilbert listened as Brad relayed everything that had happened that night. Both lawmen recognized Ferguson's name. "So, another associate of the Scofield Oil Company comes into play," Justin said as he reached for the telephone and called the doctor's office to check on the patient's condition. *I pray he is alive and can tell us who shot him*, Justin thought.

Wilbert motioned for Brad to step outside. "That was some ruse you pulled on that drunk. How did you even come up with it?"

Brad appreciated the compliment. "It came to me when I heard the fire bells and saw the flames. It probably wouldn't have worked if he hadn't been so intoxicated."

"Well, it did, and you may have saved that family's life. We'll watch for her and draw up the complaint. He probably won't see the insides of a bottle again for quite a spell."

"You know, I was thinking afterward about my military fighting in Cuba. We used medical corpsmen inside a wagon stocked with basic first-aid supplies. That way, trained corpsmen quickly treated the injured and then transported them to a field hospital for care. Rather than have one of our doctors called to the scene of, say, a shooting and then transporting the man to his office, we would save time and lives if we had our version of corpsmen housed in the fire station ready to respond."

Wilbert nodded. "You're right, but we both know that our stingy city council would never authorize the added expense. Maybe one day, though. Go home and get some sleep if you can. You've certainly earned your pay today."

Wilbert returned indoors just as the marshal hung up the telephone. "Maxwell's nurse said that the patient survived surgery but remains unconscious. I hope he comes to long enough to tell us who's behind all this. I have little doubt that someone wanted to eliminate him from talking, just like they did with David Brown. Now, all we can do is wait and hope. Let's go interview Mr. and Mrs. Poindexter. Maybe they have seen visitors come and go from Ferguson's shanty."

* * * * * * * * * * * * * *

On his way home, Brad couldn't shake the idea of a corpsman's vehicle. Being a mechanic and owner of an automobile service station, he envisioned not a horse-drawn wagon but an automobile with the rear seat removed. Then, by extending the frame, an enclosed wagon could be mounted upon it. At the rear would be a doorway for loading the patients, not by the standard pole and cloth stretcher, but a metal one with small wheels. *It's a grand idea. Maybe one day I will build it.*

* * * * * * * * * * * * * * * *

Just before noon, a dejected Justin Blake entered Brooks' Barbershop for a haircut. Matthew couldn't help but notice his friend's sad demeanor. "What's wrong, Justin? Did Wilbert run off and join the circus or something?"

"Worse than that, Matt. I just got a call from Doctor Maxwell. His patient never regained consciousness and passed away. Now our investigation is back to square one."

Soon, word of the death of the man known as Irish spread all over town. Reporter Alvin Jensen begged for an interview, but Justin turned him away.

The morning edition of the Gas City Journal informed its readers that perhaps it was time for the city council to ask for Justin Blake's resignation and to bring in someone more qualified to solve this murder spree gripping the town.

CHAPTER 21
THE PHONE CALL

The following late afternoon, Justin and Wilbert were completing their paperwork when the telephone rang. Justin picked it up on the second ring. "Marshal's Office, Blake speaking."

"Marshal, our mystery patient's fever has broken, and I think he wants to speak with you," Doctor Maxwell said. Justin was thrilled. This was the news he had been waiting, hoping, and praying to hear.

"That's wonderful news, Doc, but are you sure his head is clear enough to provide an official interview statement?"

The doctor laughed. "It must be as he can't seem to stop flirting with Nurse Pieper." Justin knew that Valorie Pieper was very attractive, so he couldn't blame Matthew Ferguson one bit.

"That proves he is coherent. Give us a little time to round up a stenographer; then we'll be right over. Thank you again for assisting in our little ruse." He hung up. "Wilbert, we're in luck. He's talkative now. Let me write a quick note for Michael to remain here in the office if we're not back. If this goes the way I'm hoping, we can use all the help we can get. Grab your hat, and let's go see the mayor about borrowing his stenographer for the evening."

* * * * * * * * * * * * * *

Mayor Huffman listened intently as Justin explained why he had purposely spread the false rumor that Furguson had died. The killer was bound to be worried about being seen and heard after taking a shot at Mr. Poindexter. "We're now hoping that Ferguson will open up and start informing, once I charge him with being an accessory to murder."

"So, I gather, if you want to spread a rumor quickly, tell it in a barbershop." The mayor chuckled as Justin and Wilbert nodded. The mayor called the stenographer, Miss Lee, into his office and shut the door. "Miss Lee, you are to accompany the marshal here to the office of Doctor Maxwell and take down a confession. I don't have to remind you to keep everything you see and hear confidential. If the marshal is successful, type it up quickly. Any questions?"

"No sir, I'll get my notepad and pencils and meet you gentlemen outside."

The mayor offered some fatherly advice. "I pray that your effort will bear fruit as I don't have to remind you that there has been some discouraging talk among the council members. Best of luck and please keep me informed." Once outside, the group made their way to the home of Doctor Maxwell.

* * * * * * * * * * * * * *

Entering the doctor's home, they proceeded into the treatment room. Looking up at his three new visitors, a chipper Matthew "Irish" Ferguson lying in bed smiled and said, "You're bringing me another pretty lady to flirt with!" Miss Lee understood his statement well enough that she felt her cheeks momentarily blush. The doctor seated her at a small desk, ready to begin her work.

"Mr. Fergson, you look well. We're happy you have survived your terrible ordeal, and I hope you will tell us what happened. You are in a difficult position, so I must warn you that you're being charged as an accessory to murder. It may be all over for you, but why allow your accomplice to escape justice scot-free? Who shot you and why?"

"I've already come to that conclusion and am ready for what's to come. I'll talk, Marshal, if you remove these handcuffs from my ankle. They're digging into my skin." As a precaution, this had been done earlier to secure him to the bedpost.

"Sorry, we can't do it, but I'll move them over to your other ankle," Justin said, pulling a set of keys from his belt to adjust the cuffs. Irish thanked him for his kindness Nurse Pieper entered the room with some salve to administer to his roughened skin.

As she applied the lotion, Irish thanked her and asked, "Marshal, do you know why God gave men two arms?"

Justin wasn't there to exchange jokes, but to keep their conversation friendly, he shook his head.

"It's so we can grab hold of two beautiful women at the same time! Let's see if my arms still work!" Irish then laughed at his stupid joke.

The nurse ignored his statement. "I liked him better when he was unconscious, Marshal." She bid the men good day and left the room.

"Let's get back to business, Irish. Who shot you and why?"

The injured man seemed to cherish being the center of attention. "All right, Marshal. I'll tell you everything you want to know. The person who shot me ... the one who poisoned Mrs. Scofield ... the one who insisted upon the killing of David Brown ... the person who shot at Miss. Jones ... and the one who shot me ... and attempted to burn me to a cinder is … my old proxy mother … Mrs. Sylvia Tyler."

CHAPTER 22
THE CONFESSION

The name surprised Wilbert, who asked, "Are you sure about that?" A quick nod answered his question.

"Perhaps I should start at the beginning, then you can ask your questions afterward. Is that all right? Good. My story begins when I was only five years old. You see, my mother died, and my father quickly found a replacement woman who moved in, but they never married. I hated my father for this and never got close to the woman you now call Mrs. Tyler. Her name then was Miss Edwards, or at least that's the name she gave us. She lived with us until I was almost thirteen. Father came down with cancer that kept him bedridden and in great pain. One morning before school, I entered their bedroom to find her holding a pillow over his face. He was struggling to breathe, but she pushed down even harder. I tried to pull the pillow away, but it was too late. She had killed him. She then turned to me and said, 'I did him a favor. You wouldn't let a dog suffer. No, you'd put it down. That's all I did, but you better forget what you saw today, or some night, a pillow may be coming for you!' So, killing meant nothing to her. Nobody suspected the truth. My father was buried and forgotten. Soon after, I packed a bag and snuck out in the middle of the night, never to return.

"Many years passed, and I became an oil and gas roughneck. I felt I was pretty good at my job, but I have a habit of saying too much and getting work crews all stirred up. As a result, I lost a lot of jobs. It was a total shock when I bumped into her here in town. Neither of us had suspected the other lived close by. She suggested I start calling her Sylvia and that we go someplace to have a cup of coffee and let bygones be bygones. I agreed to her idea. She then smiled and asked if I would like to one day become the manager and half-owner of an oil company. I naturally said yes, and she began by telling me her name now was Mrs. Tyler, and she was employed at the Scofield Mansion as their cook. She then told me of her plans. I didn't know about the apple poisoning. Strangely, Sylvia said she liked the woman, but her presence stood in her way, and she hoped the Indian would be blamed.

"It seemed that her employer, Mr. Scofield, had requested Sylvia and their housekeeper, some dumb Indian woman by the name of Cindy Moon, to sign as witnesses to his new will. The Indian went first, which gave Sylvia time to glance over the wording and see her name listed as a beneficiary to his estate. This was a golden opportunity Sylvia had only dreamed about. She said her new employer wanted to start an oil drilling business and suggested that I 'accidentally' bump into him, probably in a saloon, and be receptive to his ideas. That worked like a charm, and I was hired and told to find other oilmen to make up a crew. Again, it all happened just as she had planned.

"Then came time for us to do away with that weasel, William Scofield. His family members often discuss private things among themselves without realizing their hired help can hear everything. The morning of his murder, Sylvia overheard him on the telephone making a date with some floozy to attend the theater. She had a system to signal me using a pocket mirror if she needed me during work hours, so before lunch, she flashed me. I told the crew I was sick and going home and met her in a safe location. She then explained her plan and my role in it. I was to carry two boxes full of rags and newspaper up the stairs to the third floor of the theater an hour before showtime. In one of the boxes was also a Mason screw-top jar filled with oil. I was to place the jar inside a trash can in the corner, pack the rags around it, and then spread the newspaper on top like normal trash to hide the jar.

"I was surprised that not a soul paid any attention to my presence. I left and waited until the appointed time. Once the play started, I was to stand close to the barrel, wait until the second act started, pour the oil all over the contents, and then light it. During the confusion and smoke, I exited with the crowd. Sylvia was dressed as a man and sat several rows behind Scofield with an ice pick ready in her coat pocket. After stabbing him, she casually entered an alley and dumped suit jacket and tie, returned to the mansion, entered through the kitchen door so as not to be seen, and returned to her third-floor room to dress. Again, everything worked just like she said it would. By now, I had total faith in her ability to make us rich.

"I guess I left out the part about David Brown. I knew him from the past to be somewhat of a hothead and suggested to her that with a cash incentive, Brown could make Anthony Jone's life unbearable on the job. He agreed and was more than happy to receive a bonus for picking on 'Baby Jones.' He did a fine job, too, and I'm surprised the kid took it as long as he did. When I told her it was all coming to a head, Sylvia instructed me to suggest a public fight somewhere. Then she told me the bad news. If I wanted to remain a part of her plans, I had to kill Brown before the fight and leave evidence that Baby Jones did it. That worked, too, and off to jail he went for a crime I committed. I hated to kill him, but after all, money speaks louder than friendship.

"We would meet at my shack about once a week in the middle of the night and plan the next move. I owned an old Stevens .22

rifle that Sylvia borrowed. That was the gun that fired through the window and narrowly missed Miss Loreta. She's cute, so in a way, I was happy the bullet missed, but in the end, she has to go also. By the way, Sylvia owns a Smith and Wesson Ladysmith Seven-Shot Revolver. If you go after her, remember, she isn't at all afraid to shoot you. Last week, we were trying to devise a way to kill off Barrett and Wanda Jones simultaneously, but the idea wasn't working out.

"Which brings us to my shooting. I thought we would be discussing another plan to rid ourselves of the husband and wife, but instead, Sylvia informed me that my usefulness had expired and from now on, she would act alone. I guess I should have expected betrayal, but she caught me off guard. Marshal, she laughed as she pulled the trigger. After I had fallen from the pain, she smashed the lit oil lamp against the wall and tried to burn me alive. I was barely aware of someone pulling me to safety. I think it was my landlord, or did I dream that part?"

Justin answered, "No, he was outside at the time and was shot at by someone he couldn't identify. Well, Mr. Ferguson, I appreciate your full cooperation. Unfortunately for you, your admission of killing Mr. Brown will result in a full charge of murder. You haven't mentioned the murder of the beggar called *The Ragman*. Who killed him and why?" The prisoner seemed confused about the name and said he'd never heard anything about any *ragman*. Justin conceded that his original idea that perhaps another tramp had killed him and left town was most likely correct. "I understand I did wrong, Marshal, but at least I won't be hanging alone! I hope you take her alive," Irish said.

Unfortunately, the whole truth would never be known to anyone. The street beggar known as *The Ragman* was, in fact, Sylvia Tyler's older brother. Years ago, he had contracted a disease called Neurosyphilis from a prostitute. The highly infectious disease spread into his brain and would one day be known as Dementia. During brief periods, he remembered who he was and demanded money from his sister in exchange for maintaining his silence about being her brother. After three payments, Sylvia decided enough was enough and laid in wait one dark evening to rid herself of her pest once and for all. It had all been so easy, and she felt no remorse, only relief.

CHAPTER 23
THE SEARCH FOR MRS. TYLER

A confident Justin Blake and Wilbert Vance returned to their office to find Deputy Michael Davidson waiting, as the note instructed. "Mike," Justin said. "Great news. The prisoner provided a full confession, admitting his involvement, and named the primary suspect, Mrs. Sylvia Tyler. She's armed and dangerous, so before we pay her a friendly visit, check your firearm and make yourself ready to use it. I hope we can capture her alive, but if necessary, shoot to wing her if possible."

Michael shook his head and grinned. "I was leaning toward the brother being the criminal organizer, not that old woman! It would be like shooting my grandmother!"

"Except this grandmother would not hesitate to shoot you right between the eyes. I want you guys to be on constant guard," Justin stated. A quick inspection of their weapons showed that everyone was ready. "Come on. Let's end this nightmare tonight once and for all." The group left for the Scofield Mansion.

Justin halted about a half-block away to give final instructions. He looked at the time on his pocket watch and said, "It's after seven o'clock. The family may be having their evening meal or are finished. We'll have to play things as we find them. The important thing is to determine if she is inside the home and then get everyone else outside safely before we attempt to place her under arrest. Since we won't know her whereabouts, I'll take the front door and Wilbert the back. Mike, you remain at the side, ready to respond in either direction as needed. We'll signal you, so watch both locations closely. If I discover she isn't home, we'll meet back up and come up with another plan. Any questions? Good. I'll take the lead." Once everyone was in position, Justin prepared to knock.

The Jones family was seated in the dining room eating their evening meal. It had been served, not by the cook as usual, but by the housekeeper, Miss Moon, who had informed the family that Mrs. Tyler had gone to bed with a headache. Wanda was deep in a conversation with Loreta. "… and there in Fletcher's Grocery Store window was a sign that read the price of a dozen eggs had gone up to twenty-two cents!"

"That's outrageous! There ought to be …" A loud knock at the front door interrupted Wanda. The family remained seated as a second series of knocks began. "What's taking her so long for her to answer?"

Finally, Miss Moon appeared and opened the door.

In a strong voice, Justin said he needed to speak with Mrs. Tyler immediately on official police business. "She's upstairs on the third floor in bed with a bad headache," the housekeeper said. "Perhaps you could come back later?" Justin ignored the statement and pushed the door open. He saw the startled family sitting at their dining room table, wondering what was happening.

Garrett jumped up angrily and threw down his napkin. "What's the meaning of this, officer? I demand to know what gives you the right …" Justin told him to shut up and listen carefully. Garrett turned red with anger and clenched his fists.

"I don't have time to explain, sir, but we need all of you to vacate this house immediately! He then stepped back outside and motioned for Michael to wait outside. Justin entered the dining room and began to shout, "Everybody, outside now!" While all of this was going on, Miss Moon casually walked up the stairs to the third level. The women sitting at the table froze in place in confusion.

"Nobody comes into our house and issues orders, young man!" Garrett angrily said. "I'll have your badge for this!" He then turned to the ladies and reluctantly motioned for them to comply.

Upstairs, Miss Moon entered Mrs. Tyler's private bedroom. Turning to the figure lying on the small cot, she said, "Your day has arrived. They are here for you."

The old woman stood up and replied that she had been expecting them. "How did you know the police were after me?"

The Indian woman replied, "The spirits informed me what was to come. They have all the answers."

Mrs. Tyler walked over to her dresser, removed her revolver, and pointed it at her visitor. "Did your spirits tell you I was going to kill you?"

In a calm voice, she answered. "Yes, I know exactly what will become of me … and of you."

"Then join your spirits!" The gunshot echoed through the house, startling the women, who ran to Garrett outside.

"Tell me what's happening? Did one of your officers shoot our cook?" Garrett demanded of Michael Davidson, who ignored the question and tactfully told the group to go out on the sidewalk and stay out of the way.

The body of Cindy Moon's body tumbled over the third-floor banister and crashed down the stairs.

"You'll never take me alive!" came a loud shout from up above. With their weapons already drawn, Justin and Michael advanced up the stairs in search of their hidden adversary. Retreating to the safety of her bedroom, Sylvia Tyler glanced about, searching for a way to escape. Of course, there was the outside balcony where she could have a final shootout with her opponents. *No, they might wound me, and I'd have to face trial and hang. I know! Why not go out in a blaze of glory and take them with me?*

On her dresser sat an oil lamp and matches. She removed the chimney and lit a match to the burner to ignite the flame. Then, taking hold of the lamp, she advanced toward the doorway and peaked downstairs. The shadows of two men advancing upward danced on the wall. With excitement in her voice, she yelled, "Here ya go, boys! Enjoy a hotfoot!" She dropped the oil lamp down the second-floor stairs. Upon impact, it spewed burning oil everywhere. Justin and Michael instinctively jumped back to avoid injury. Upstairs, a voice, clearly from a mad woman laughed and shouted for joy. Seeing there was no way the officers could combat the spreading fire, they were forced to retreat outside. Michel appeared and was told to run next door and call the operator to report the fire.

The three Jones members all began demanding answers. "Why did you set our house on fire!" Garrett shouted. The mad laughter from the third floor could still be heard by all, but soon, the entire structure was ablaze. There would be no more laughter heard that night.

CHAPTER 24
–EPILOGUE–

Word spread that the terrible murder spree that had plagued the town had finally ended. The following day, townspeople made their excuses to visit the scene where the beautiful three-story Scofield Mansion had stood. Now, all that remained was a heap of smoldering rubble. Gas City Journal Reporter Alvin Jenson obtained an eyewitness account of the terrible event from Mrs. Wanda Jones. "We simply had no idea a murderer was living under our roof!" she was quoted as saying. Readers found her story fascinating. Many of today's customers inside Brooks' Barbershop boasted they had suspected the old lady all along. Justin Blake felt as if a giant weight had been removed from his back, and the pressure from the city council ceased abruptly.

* * * * * * * * * * * * * * *

As soon as Barrett and Loreta heard that Anthony was innocent and it had been Matthew Ferguson who killed David Brown, they consulted with Attorney Lowell Benson. "Now that the man confessed, how soon can we get Anthony released?" they asked.

"I'm afraid it may take some time. First, the accused must stand trial and be found guilty of the murder. If that happens, I will file with the court to dismiss the indictment. Once the judge sets aside the original verdict, we will seek a full pardon from the governor. Then, and only then, will your brother be set free. A full pardon would completely relieve him of the conviction and any consequences, such as **denying** voting rights and the ability to serve on a jury. Please inform your brother that this process may, unfortunately, take a year or more. Until then, he **must** keep his nose clean and wait."

Sadness reflected on the faces of the brother and sister. "That brings us to another point, Mr. Bensen," Loreta said. "We have talked and would like you to hold off on closing William's estate until our brother has been freed. We feel that the false imprisonment should not cause his violation of the terms of the will and that, in the end, the three of us are to share equally."

The old lawyer smiled. "That is very commendable of both of you. As soon as I hear something, I'll be in touch."

* * * * * * * * * * * * * * *

Matthew Ferguson's trial took place in the fall. The defendant waved his rights to a jury trial and pleaded guilty to the murder of David Brown. He was sentenced to life imprisonment without parole at the Indiana State Prison in Michigan City. While confined, the man known as Irish would have ample time to reflect upon his foolish actions for many years to come.

* * * * * * * * * * * * * * *

In June of 1903, Indiana Governor Winfield T. Durbin signed a full pardon for Anthony Jones. Twenty-four hours passed before the southbound Pennsylvania Railroad train stopped at the Gas City depot. Garrett, Wanda, and Loreta waited for Anthony's arrival, anxious to see and try to help their younger brother adjust to the life of a free man again. They were shocked by his appearance, as Anthony appeared to have aged ten years during his time spent in prison. Tears flowed freely at the happy reunion. "Come," a smiling Barrett said. "Wanda has prepared a welcome home dinner at our house where you'll be staying. It's so good to have you back, Anthony." The four entered the carriage and proceeded to their home on East North D Street. As the carriage passed by the old Scofield lot, only tall grass and weeds remained. It was a sad and depressing sight.

Everyone had much to say in an attempt to bring Anthony up to date on the success of their family business. He said very little in return. Though everyone was dying to hear about his terrible ordeal, nobody could bring the subject up. Finally, Anthony did ask one question. "Have any of you heard from Ethyl? Our divorce is final, you know, but I have always wondered how she is." This was a question all had dreaded being asked as they exchanged glances. Once his brother's release was guaranteed, Garrett hired a private detective to locate her whereabouts. A few days later, he received a short, written report. Garrett dreaded informing his brother of the contents.

"I thought that perhaps you might ask this question, so I hired a man to track her down. She lives in Kokomo and is working as … a woman of the night. I'm so sorry to have to tell you that." There was no change in Anthony's facial expression one way or another as he took in the information. It was clear that his time in prison had diminished his outgoing personality. Where a young and exuberant young man once existed, now a hard and suspicious man sat before them.

"Tomorrow, I'll contact Attorney Benson and inform him of your return," Garrett continued, changing the subject. "Everything will be split evenly three ways, like we told you. The rental properties can either be sold, or we can split the income between us. William had a couple of unused cemetery lots that Loreta and I thought we could donate to the city. Several people have been interested in the old homestead lot on Main Street since it's prime real estate. We do have a couple of options for you to consider, though. Standard Oil has expressed an interest in purchasing our twelve active oil wells and the unused property oil leases. The price they offered would take your breath away. Or we can change the name to the Jones Oil Company and continue on, but with three equal partners. Two of us could buy out the third partner, or even one could buy out the other two. Have you given it any thought, Anthony?"

"Yes, I want the money," Anthony said decidedly. "I'll be leaving for Nevada once everything is settled. You have to understand, being cooped up in a cell, day in and day out, makes one desire wide-open spaces. I spent a lot of time researching the prison library atlases and found a little spot in the middle of nowhere. A regular desert oasis. There, I'll purchase as many acres as possible and build myself a home. I want to sit out on the front porch in the evenings and enjoy the open sky and the nighttime stars. Maybe, one day, I can even start trusting women again, get me a good wife, have kids, and pass the large spread onto a new generation of Jones. By leaving here, I'm leaving all my troubles behind at the boundary of the state, and I'll be free to start a new life where nobody knows the hell I was put through."

"What's the name of this place in Nevada?" Wanda asked.

"It's a tiny Spanish-sounding community they call Las Vegas."

Alan E. Losure

But Wait! What Happened to The Disgraced Deputy, Russell Henderson? Find Out in The Following Chapter

CAST OF CHARACTERS

Russell Henderson	Disgraced Ex-Deputy
Leo Montgomery	Marshal of Van Buren
Ben Emery	Nighttime Deputy
Scott Emery	Nighttime Deputy
Jim Moore	Owner of We Haul Everything Freighting Co.
Able Doby	Freight Hauler
Chet	Saloon Owner
Aunt Millie Carswell	Owner of Boarding House
Paul Eastman	Councilman, Owner of Hardware Store
Brian Eastman	Adult Son, Hardware Store
Dr. Thomas Wells	President of the Town Council
Roger Paxton	Councilman, Town Druggist
Johnny Day	Freight Company Stableman

CHAPTER 25
A REMINDER OF HOW IT ALL HAPPENED

Ten minutes after one o'clock, a figure entered the church's front door and walked toward the back. Russell Henderson entered the office and approached the reverend. "Do you have my money?"

"This isn't right," Reverand Stokes said, making his voice sound more confident than he felt as he recited what the Marshal had instructed. "The Sunday offering belongs to the church and was freely given. You, sir, have no right to steal from God's Altar."

The deputy laughed. "God can have his ten percent, but my expenses require more. Don't lecture me, old man. Remember, churches do burn in the dead of night. Pay up or go to bed each night, wondering if tonight will be the night it happens!"

Slowly, the reverend reached into a drawer and extracted the bag of coins. Just as the extortionist took hold of it, both lawmen burst from the closet, their guns drawn. "Russell Henderson, you are under arrest for attempted extortion."

* * * * * * * * * * * * * * *

Russell Henderson, the disgraced ex-deputy marshal, was a free man. After spending thirty-three days incarcerated inside the Grant County Jail, Henderson was brought before a courthouse judge and was sentenced to time already served. Henderson became quite the celebrity in the Grant County newspapers during his stay. After all, it isn't every day that a deputy sheriff turns criminal, and a few of his old pals in Van Buren might consider his actions a badge of honor. Henderson had only lived in that small town for a better part of three months, but he could see the right kind of man could make easy money.

He reached into his front pocket and pulled out a couple of dollars in change. *Not much to make a new start*, he told himself. Henderson began walking towards the streetcar traction depot and approached the ticket window. "One ticket to Van Buren."

* * * * * * * * * * * * * * *

When the first post office was established in 1872, the town took its name in honor of Martin Van Buren, the eighth president of the United States. Before that, it had many unofficial names: Stringtown, Roods Crossing, and Rood's Town, presumably to honor George H. Rood, an early settler and founder of the first sawmill. Van Buren remained an unimportant little backwater town until 1880, when the Toledo, Delphos, and Burlington Railroad were built. It was initially constructed with narrow gauge three-foot rails, and by 1887, the company had decided it was too time-consuming to change to the standard gage 4-foot, 8 ½ inch rails. Then, an exciting and impossible-sounding idea was put forth: accomplish the entire two hundred and eight miles between Toledo, Ohio, and Frankfort, Indiana, in one day! The organization of such a bold venture took a great deal of planning. Still, on June 26, 1887, all available farmers, their sons, and numerous volunteers worked feverishly in forty gangs of fifty men up and down the entire route. The one-day miracle happened, and by four o'clock that afternoon, the first trains, with all new equipment, rolled out of their terminals.

In 1890, the gas boom began in Van Buren despite the little interest in oil. That would soon change. Since the town was about halfway between Delphos and Frankfort, the railroad erected a coaling tower to service their engines, placing Van Buren on the map. With oil and gas workers arriving daily from the east, its population jumped to nearly fifteen thousand people.

Around 1894, heavy oil production caught the attention of the Standard Oil Company, who built a pipeline in the oil field. Soon after, the Buckeye Pipeline Company constructed a pumping station two miles northeast of the town. A glass factory appeared briefly, producing bottles.

Let no one think that life in Van Buren was all work and no play. Rather, on the contrary with the opening of the brand-new second-floor brick and stone Riley and Duckwall Opera House. It was located on the corner of Main and First Street. Housing five hundred patrons, it was packed for its for the production play, "Under Two Flags," on opening night. Riley and Duckwall were two local business partners in the general merchandise business for many years and built the first floor for their expanding business.

Don't let it be said that the town didn't have its share of decent folks who followed God's Ten Commandments. Van Buren most certainly did, but as in life, it seems only bad individuals tend to be remembered. As a result, some prospective families choose to live elsewhere upon hearing unfavorable stories.

East Main Street Looking West

CHAPTER 26
THE ARRIVAL

VAN BUREN, INDIANA

It seemed strange for Russell Henderson to return to Van Buren as he stepped off the traction trolly car. His stomach told him it was time to find somewhere to eat as he picked up his lone bag and walked toward a nearby diner. *I wonder if she still works there?* He thought to himself as he pictured the diner's waitress and daughter of the protective owner. *I can't blame him one bit. She's cute, and this town is full of hard men; most, I'm afraid, possess dishonorable inten-*

tions. Approaching the advertising display sign outside the diner, it read: "Today's Special: Beef Stew for Twenty Cents." As nice as it sounded to his hungry stomach, Henderson decided it best to order a beer and eat at the free salted meat counter in the nearby saloon. *Once I land a job, it'll surely be a tasty beef stew meal.*

Chet's Saloon was known as a dark and rundown drinking establishment that catered to the working man's desires for drink, gambling, and perhaps a place to settle a personal score. The combination of alcohol, knives, or hidden pistols, mixed with hardened men, had resulted in the town doctor's medical skills being employed on many late-night hours to save the injured and dying. The owner of the establishment was a mountain of a man known only as Chet. Whatever his full name was, or where he came from, went unanswered. Perhaps, some speculated, he killed a man and fled to greener pastures. Either way, he found a safe environment in Van Buren, a place known to be the roughest, least desirable town to live in Grant County. It's safe to say that most crimes committed there go unpunished. Oil and natural gas workers were the bread and butter of the town. They worked hard, drank hard, and a few enjoyed the company of a few late-night wayward women who were happy to help a working man part with his money. Most townspeople tried to overlook what they only heard vulgar whispers about.

Chet's Saloon was located a half-block east of the town's new opera house that was soon to open. Upon entering the saloon, Russell Henderson saw Chet laying out salted meats, thinly cut slices of bread, and pickles bar's free lunch counter. Two eager old men watched and waited from the sideline, all ready to make their move, provided they possessed at least a nickel for a beer. If not, any attempt at a free handout would result in an unfortunate incident of pain and suffering at the hands of the owner. Both men knew the rules and patiently waited with their nickels in hand.

Russell walked up to the bar and laid his nickel down. Hearing the familiar sound, Chet began pouring the beer for his new customer. Flies had already started to light upon portions of the salted food. Picking up a relatively clean-looking plate, Russell piled on food. Chet brought the beer to him, setting it down with a dull thud.

From a back table, Russel heard a low voice say, "He's a brave man to eat that." Glancing up to see what Chet's reaction might be, Russell saw the owner either hadn't heard the comment or chose to ignore it this early in the day. Russell glanced toward the table and recognized one of the men he had worked with briefly before leaving Van Buren for Gas City.

"Brave, probably not. Hungry, you bet! How are you, Doby?" Picking up his plate and drink, Russell walked over to the table and a chair slid out for him to sit. "You know, I never did learn your last name." Their newcomer then began to devour his food.

The man smiled. "Doby is my last name. The first is Able, but I prefer not to be called Able as it seems to cause some idiots to make stupid cracks about being 'able and willing.' Anyway, meet Mr. Jim Moore, the owner of 'We Haul Everything Freighting Company.' I work for him now." The men shook hands. "You probably read about my friend here, Mr. Moore. He certainly made exciting headlines in the Chronicle-Tribune recently. Imagine, as a deputy marshal trying to extort money from a preacher's church collection plate!"

"My first and last attempt along those lines, I assure you. Frankly, I stink as an extortionist but … I'm very good at hauling freight. I could certainly use a job, Mr. Moore, any job now that my criminal days are behind me," Russell said.

Doby and Moore looked at each other before Moore asked, "How come you're free? You didn't break jail or something, did you?"

Russell shook his head. "The judge said that since it was my first offense, and I hadn't possessed anyone's money, he sentenced me to time already served and let me go with a stern warning."

Moore nodded. "We are down a hauler now because of the incident here last evening." He then began to explain. "I don't know if you've had much dealings with our Marshal Montgomery or not while you lived here. Perhaps you know of the two evil brothers serving as his deputies." Russell said he had steered clear of those two many referred to as 'The Mongomery Men.'

Freight Hauler Able Doby   Freight Co. Owner Jim Moore

Looking side to side to make sure he wouldn't be overheard, Moore said, "This is the story I was told. My other freight hauler was in here last evening, apparently having a few drinks but not bothering anyone. And then, our illustrious nighttime deputies, brothers Ben Emery and older brother Scott entered and paused to looking over the crowd. Deciding upon their prey, both deputies advanced through the tables of men and approached the end of the bar where my hauler was standing, minding his own business. The witnesses stressed that every man in the saloon stopped what he was doing and watched, suspecting what was about to happen.

"Then, each brother separated and stood on opposite sides of the man. After exchanging a few words, both deputies pulled out their nightsticks and beat my hauler silly. Even when he hit the ground, the pair kept on beating and kicking him. Then, they walked out without a word, smiling at everyone who had witnessed the ordeal. I heard later that they'd fractured his jaw, broken his right arm, separated his left shoulder, broke two front teeth, and after the severe kicking in the lower area, he may never be able to have children if you catch my meaning." Both men nodded.

Russell asked, "What about witnesses? Won't anyone come forward and make a formal complaint?"

"A man tried once, saying he would appear at the next town board meeting, but that very night, his place of business mysteriously burned to the ground. Realizing the hopelessness of the situation, he and his family left town. From then on, people understood there would be no justice here."

"What about your newspaper? Why won't they expose the corruption in the marshal's office?"

"We only have a political publication paper. Perhaps in time …" Doby replied.

Mr. Moore pulled out his pocket watch. "I'll tell you what, Henderson. I'll hire you today if you give me your word that nothing I've said today will be repeated. I want to keep my business and go on living."

Russell readily agreed. Moore then turned to Doby. "Then he can take the place on our two o'clock, two-wagon haul. I better be going. Good luck, and make sure your criminal days are behind you."

After the boss left, Doby explained they hauled everything, from people's furniture to store supplies to and from the railroad and heavy dray wagon equipment. "Those will be our two loads today, out to the Ajax Gas and Oil Company west of town. I hear they are pumping four hundred barrels of oil per day!" Doby then asked if his friend had a place to live yet. Russell said no. "We have time; let's go to Aunt Millie's Boarding House. A lot of workers, including me, stay there. She has a vacancy, so she'll have space for you as long as a cot and a storage trunk for your clothing in the cool basement won't bother you. In the winter, it's warm and comfortable with the furnace, and cool in the summer. I prefer it over those upstairs rooms. Everyone calls her Aunt Millie. She is the sweetest old woman you will ever meet and extremely religious, so I don't suggest telling her about your attempt to extort money from a preacher."

Van Buren Nighttime Deputies Ben and Scott Emery

Alan E. Losure

CHAPTER 27
MEETING AUNT MILLIE

Miss Millie Carswell

"Russell Henderson, may I introduce to you the kindest lady you will ever know, Miss Millie Carswell. My friend Russell here is looking for a good place to board, and I told him there are no lodgings finer than here with you. Now that Mr. Brock has been seriously injured in that terrible beating and unable to work, I was hoping Russell might have that vacant basement bed," Doby said.

Russell, with hat and hand, smiled upon the face of the kindly old woman. "Yes, ma'am, I'll be working side by side with Doby here at 'We Haul Freighting,' and I promise I won't be a bother to you."

The old woman smiled. "Please, call me Aunt Millie. Everyone else has called me that for so many years that hearing my full name seems strange." She told him the rental cost, which seemed fair to Russell. "I do have a few house rules that I expect all my guests to follow, Mr. Henderson. The first and most important is there will be no cussing or taking of the Lord's name in vain in my home. I also feel that cleanliness is next to godliness, so each guest must remain as clean as possible before entering my home. I have a water pump out back if you need to wash up and a sink with running water and towels in the basement you'll have to share with the other guests. There is a convenient bathhouse down the street beside the barber shop that I hope each of my guests will utilize at least weekly. It's not my intention to point out a working man's odor, but I will if I must. I won't allow any women to be brought into your sleeping area, nor the consumption of intoxicating liquor to be consumed in my house. I provide breakfast every morning promptly at six for my guests, and I give thanks to the Lord before we begin. I insist upon everyone's participation, or at least their cooperation. All your other meals, as well as your laundry, are your responsibility. Do you find the conditions of my house rules acceptable, Mr. Henderson?"

He did and managed to make the weekly rental from the few coins that remained in his pocket. There would be no beef stew for him in the foreseeable future. "Let's go into the basement so you can drop off your bag. Then, we need to hurry if we're gonna get to work on time," Doby said.

* * * * * * * * * * * * * *

Russell knew of the large freight company building on the south end of town but hadn't any reason to enter it when he lived here months ago. Doby informed him that the freight company he and Russell had worked at before had gone out of business. Seeing how nice 'We Haul Freighting' was, he understood how that could happen. The structure had two large wooden swinging doors on both ends, kept open during nice weather, and a side door facing the street entrance. After entering, Doby said, "As you can see, we're a pretty large outfit. We even store other people's furniture and equipment until they're ready for delivery. That other side door over there connects to our stable, where a dozen or more horses are housed. One of Aunt Millie's boarders is our stableman, Johnny Day. He cares for the animals and maintains our different capacity hauling wagons in tip-top condition. On many mornings, Johnny skips breakfast or returns here before bad weather just to care for his babies. We tease Johnny that he considers them his children. He even cares for Aunt Millie's horse and volunteers to drive her carriage to and from church on Sundays and Wednesday evenings. Try to get to know him, Russell. He's about the nicest guy you'll ever work with, and this company couldn't get along without him. We affectionately call him, 'Johnny the Stableman.'"

As he spoke, both men watched Johnny bring their team and delivery wagon into the warehouse. Owner Jim Moore exited his office and approached Doby carrying a piece of paper. "Here's the list of items to pick up. You know the routine: just work with the railroad unloading supervisor to make sure we get everything listed here.

Also, good luck on your first day on the job with us, Mr. Henderson." Russell was surprised Mr. Moore remembered his name. The men then mounted their freight wagon and were soon gone.

As the noon lunch hour approached, the men stopped outside the fruit market and purchased some fruit to eat. Tonight's meal, which required the last of his coins, would be sliced meat and bread from the butcher shop. With payday still two days away, Russell wondered how he was going to make it until then, but the problem was solved by the generous loan of twenty-five cents from his friend Doby.

Johnny Day aka 'Johnny the Stableman'

CHAPTER 28
THE TOWN COUNCIL

Paul Eastman, Councilman   Dr. Thomas Wells, President   Roger Paxton, Councilman

"Gentlemen, please be seated. We need to talk about the beating of that poor man at Chet's Saloon before the marshal arrives," Council President Doctor Wells said. The three men sat inside the town hall where meetings were held. There would be no public meeting tonight, no treasurer present, and no minutes taken. Instead, Marshal Leo Montgomery had been summoned to explain the recent actions of his deputies. "I was there and treated the victim before having him transported to Marion Hospital. I've already explained the extent of his injuries to each of you. Still, for the life of me, I cannot understand why we continue to tolerate the appallingly low quality of lawmen who are supposed to protect, not terrorize, the public."

"I agree, and I don't understand why it must have a unanimous vote among the three of us to fire all of them," Councilman Eastman said.

In reply, Councilman Paxton said, "We've been over this subject many times. The unanimous rule was adopted years ago because two prior councilmen tried to run things their way. It's a good safeguard to have at our disposal. As for the action of the deputies, well, sometimes these oil and gas men get out of line and …" He was interrupted by doors banging open. Marshal Mongomery had arrived.

"You wanted to speak with me?" he said as he straddled a wooden chair. There was clear defiance both in his voice and in his body language.

Marshal Leo Montgomery

An awkward pause elapsed before the council president spoke. "Yes, Marshal. We need to ask you questions about last evening's severe beating of the man by both your deputies."

The marshal appeared quite smug. "Not much to tell. My men were making their normal rounds and entered Chet's Saloon. In the back, standing at the bar, was a man flipping off both his middle fingers at them. My men approached him to acquire about his rudeness, but they were cussed out and told their mothers were both whores. Ben and Scott maintained their professionalism, but when that idiot spit into the face of younger brother Ben, Scott came to the rescue, and both lawmen lightly worked the man over. Too bad his fall caused his main injuries. This needs to be a lesson learned by everyone: respect lawmen who put their lives on the line to protect the public."

Doctor Wells continued. "That story is a bunch of lies, and you know it. We have countless witnesses who say your men singled him out for a beating and that he hadn't done anything except stand, minding his own business, enjoying a drink."

The large marshal jumped to his feet. "Listen, old man. Nobody calls me a liar and gets away with it! The Emery brothers can produce witnesses to counter yours, who are the liars, not us. So, if you're finished with your absurd accusations, I need to …"

"Nobody said we were finished asking questions, Marshal," Councilman Eastman interjected. "I suggest you interview a few other witnesses yourself and then compare the stories." The look on the marshal's red face implied that it wasn't about to happen anytime soon. The councilman continued. "Can you update us on the progress you've made investigating those string of home and business break-ins occurring at night?" The marshal said he had nothing new to report. That statement didn't go over very well either with the three councilmen.

Doctor Wells spoke again. "It would seem that your office is incapable of providing the public trust, and I can't help but wonder …"

"Then, why don't you fire all of us? Oh … yeah! … that would take a unanimous vote from your council, and I understand that ain't about to happen anytime soon!" Both councilmen glanced at the saddened face of their member, Roger Paxton, who had remained quiet during the interview.

Councilman Eastman said, "Maybe we should vote to cut your pay to only five dollars a month!"

The marshal laughed. "You can cut it to five cents, for all I care! We're not going anywhere. Now, if there isn't anything else, I want to go home." Before anyone answered, the marshal stood up and left, slamming the door behind him.

Seeing that their talk with the marshal hadn't produced anything positive, the informal meeting adjourned. As they stepped outside, Doctor Wells turned to his friend, Councilman Paxton, and asked, "Does that man have something on you, Roger?" The question went unanswered.

* * * * * * * * * * * * * *

During the early morning hours, bandits forced open the back alley door of the Eastman Hardware Store and successfully made off with a variety of expensive items. The message sent to Councilman Eastman was quite clear. Don't rock the boat, or be prepared to pay the price.

Eastman Hardware Store, Visible Above the Wagon on the Right Side.

CHAPTER 29
BREAKFAST IS SERVED

Russell Henderson spent his first night comfortably at Aunt Millie's Boarding House. The following morning, after washing up in the basement sink and dressing for work, Russell joined his friend Doby at the breakfast table. Six other guests lived in the home, and all seemed to be day workers like himself. He smiled and nodded to each man as they waited for Aunt Millie to start serving their breakfast. Seeing her enter the room with a large plate of scrambled eggs and another of biscuits to sit on the table, Russell stood and pulled out a chair for her. She smiled at his gesture. "Thank you, kind sir." Everyone waited patiently until she finished her somewhat longer-than-normal prayer of thanks before the food was passed around. She then spoke up. "I would like to introduce our new guest, Mr. Russell Henderson, to you. Please introduce yourselves, gentlemen." Each reluctantly did, clearly more interested in their food than any howdy to the new guy. Russell could not blame them as he, too, was hungry. Coffee was served during the meal. There was little table talk as each man's work shift would begin shortly. One by one, they quietly departed.

"Here, let me help you carry those dishes into the kitchen, Aunt Millie," Russell said.

She smiled. "No, thank you, Mr. Henderson. I have a young girl who comes by later and takes care of the dishwashing for me." The men left for work. Today, he and Doby would haul a couple's household furniture over to their new Marion address, a full-day delivery job, and back.

* * * * * * * * * * * * * * *

"There. That should hold the door more securely," Paul Eastman said after installing a heavy-duty slide bolt to the door's interior. How's our missing inventory list coming along, son? I wonder what's delaying the marshal's arrival."

Son Brian Eastman had gone over everything missing from last night's break-in. "I counted seven .45 caliber revolvers, six boxes of various ammo, two .22 'thumb trigger' Winchester Rifles, and a few hand tools among the stolen items. I guess it could have been much worse. As for the marshal, I don't understand him either. I sent little Tad from next door to report the break-in over an hour ago. He said he told the marshal, who replied he would come when he was able." The owner felt he already knew the answer but had chosen to remain silent, at least for the moment.

Finally, after lunch, Marshal Mongomery entered the hardware store. "I hear you had a little trouble here last night," he said. Brian showed him the repaired damage to the door and then handed the marshal a list of the stolen items. "I'll check around and get back to you," he said as he walked out. The marshal's demeanor didn't strike Brian right. He had heard stories about him and decided to follow behind the lawman. After walking two blocks, Brian saw the marshal wad up the list and toss it down on the brick street. Shock at the marshal's actions swept over Brian as he began to realize the stories people were whispering might be true. After retrieving the paper, he returned to the hardware store and briefed his father on the marshal's actions. Paul Eastman always remained quiet about what was discussed during the private town council meetings but decided it was time to tell his son what had occurred the evening before. Anger flowed through Brian's body upon hearing the final pieces of the puzzle. *Something must be done, but what?* By late afternoon, he was beginning to form a plan.

Brian Eastman

CHAPTER 30
THE HUNTERS BECOME THE HUNTED

First Street Looking South

B rian Eastman felt it was now up to him to implement his plan. After speaking with his parents that evening, Mrs. Eastman, though concerned for her son's safety, agreed to fill in for him during peak hours at the hardware store. Brian chose to live in the tiny apartment above the store after his parents vacated it years ago after purchasing a home. At his age, he desired to be out on his own anyway. *Why hadn't I heard those robbers break in?* He kept asking himself. His plan seemed simple enough: get as much sleep as possible during the daytime and track the whereabouts and activities of the two nighttime deputies Monday through Saturday night. Due to the Nicholson law, the sale of alcohol was prohibited in Saloons on Sundays, and he expected the deputies would not be working. *Maybe I can catch them in the act of violating the law.* Brian knew that if his plan had any hope of success, he'd have to dedicate many, many hours and, most likely, multiple nights out on the hunt. The following morning, Brian remained wide awake, and as hard as he tried, he couldn't go back to sleep. *After I'm up all night until daybreak, I'm bound to be tired enough to sleep in the daytime.* At least, that was his hope. Tonight, the hunt for actual proof would begin.

* * * * * * * * * * * * * * *

Dressed in a long trench coat, dirty work boots, a long-haired wig he once wore at a Halloween party, and a worn hat, Brian waited until darkness before beginning his search. His first night out was anything but successful. He walked the entire town and did not even see the Emery brothers. *They must have a place where they hold up*, he told himself. *Tomorrow will be different. I'll sit on that wooden bench across from our store and wait for them to appear.* The following night, his plan began to work. The brothers were seen uptown. Brian remained on the opposite side of the road to ensure they would not take notice of him. Still, the night didn't produce any real results. The next night, he trailed them to a house rumored to contain prostitutes and waited behind a bush across the street. It was nearly two hours later before the brothers emerged. With the absence of a full moon, trailing them was quite challenging, and at times, he lost sight for a while before locating them again. Night after night, he waited impatiently on the bench for them to appear. A few locals, somewhat intoxicated, approached and tried to strike up a conversation with him. Brian, fearing recognition, said little and moved on. Once, the Emery brothers walked past him as he sat but paid him no attention. The next morning, he learned that two homes were burglarized of jewelry and money while the occupants were at church choir practice. Brian began to lose hope until the chance he'd been waiting for finally happened.

The Greer-Wilkinson Lumber and Coal Company, Van Buren, Indiana

That night, Brian sat on a bench waiting for the Emery brothers to appear when they suddenly walked past him again. This time, the younger brother, Ben, stopped, pulled out his nightstick, and pointed it at Brian. "You there! What are ya ah doin' just hangin' around here? Be gone, or I'll introduce ya to this!" He slapped the stick into his open palm. The message was clear. Both nighttime officers laughed as they wandered away. Brian suspected he should give in to the threat and left the bench, walking across the street. The stars in the sky were bright and twinkling. Brian wished there was an easier way to keep track of the brothers as he lost sight of them briefly before realizing they were walking west and away from downtown. Brian managed to keep them in view.

A few blocks away, the Emery brothers joined three other men outside the Greer-Wilkinson Lumber and Coal building. Brian hid across the street and tried to hear their conversation but could not make anything out. Then, the three new men, one of whom appeared to be holding a bucket, disappeared into the darkness around the back of the building. Brian heard glass breaking, and then the Emery brothers turned back toward town, walking briskly. Brian assumed a robbery was in progress until flames emerged from the back of the structure. By the time the fire was reported and the volunteer fire department arrived on the scene, the building was completely engulfed in flames. Shocked by what he had just witnessed, Brian returned home, took out paper and pen, and began documenting everything he witnessed that night while it remained fresh in his mind. As far as he was concerned, there was no further need to follow the nighttime deputies. He had all the proof he needed that the deputies were working hand-in-hand with local criminals.

The fire department concluded that the fire was started by arson, most likely by kerosene poured over the pile of coal inside the rear coal storage building. The destruction of the lumber and coal company was a great loss to the citizens of Van Buren, and the two owners pledged to rebuild again, bigger and better by spring.

By noon the next day, Brian returned to his job at the hardware store and informed his father of what he witnessed. "I wrote a complete report of everything I witnessed, signed it, and will mail it to the sheriff of Grant County, pledging to testify at the Emery Brother's trial." His father was proud of his son's efforts. "Then, all we have to do is wait to be contacted." The long letter was soon mailed. A week passed, and then another, but no response came. By the end of the third week, Brian gave up hope of being contacted. *The sheriff must think I'm some kind of nut-job.* The atrocities committed by the Mongomery Men continued unabated.

* * * * * * * * * * * * * * *

Wednesday morning, Jim Moore waved Doby and Russell into his office. "Doby, I have an extra task for you this morning while in Upland," the owner said. "Our eight-year-old nephew, Billy, has spent the week with us but needs to return home as school starts next week. I would appreciate it if you'd see him home safely. Johnny Day is hooking up the dray wagon for you as we speak. Take it to my house and pick him up. He'll show you where he lives in Upland. Then, proceed to Wicker's Storage and load up a dozen, sixteen, 4" excess drilling pipes I purchased. There'll be someone there to help you load it. I think you've been there before, right?" Doby nodded that he had. "Good. Now, Henderson, tomorrow morning, you'll deliver Doby's load to the Atlas Drilling Company site somewhere on the outskirts of Warren. It's just over the Grant County line in Huntington County. Ask someone there, and they'll direct you to the drilling operation. Make sure you bring back their payment check. Then, go to their railroad depot and see a man named Tooms. Somehow, my order of wagon axles was unloaded there by mistake, so bring them back. Any questions?"

"No, sir. What'll I do today?"

The owner reached into his desk drawer and removed a sheet of paper. "Here. I've been making a short list of things I'd like fixed on our building and some general housekeeping tasks before the weather turns cooler. See what you can accomplish today."

As the men returned to the warehouse, Doby saw that the heavy-duty dray wagon and team were ready and waiting. Johnny Day asked him to be gentle with the horse called Boxcar. "He's been a bit off his feed lately," he cautioned, much like a parent would when speaking of their child. Doby assured him he would do so, mounted the wagon, and proceeded toward the owner's home. After pulling up to the home, a woman he took for Mrs. Moore and a young boy stepped out and approached the wagon, suitcase in hand. Doby got down, removed his hat, introduced himself, and helped the young boy into the wagon. Doby then placed the small suitcase in the back, climbed aboard, and said, "Well, Billy, are you ready to go home now?"

"Yes, sir."

"Just call me Doby, young man." The pair hit it off quickly, and Doby was surprised that a boy of only eight could speak so much. By late afternoon, he had returned to the warehouse, where the wagon of piping was parked indoors for tomorrow's trip to the small town of Warren.

Little Billy, Doby, Walnut, and Camera-Friendly Horse Boxcar

CHAPTER 31
AN INVITATION TO CHURCH

That evening, Aunt Millie descended the stairs, all dressed for the evening prayer services at her church. Several of the lodgers were sitting inside the parlor talking politics. At times, the conversation became quite heated until she entered the room. Johnny Day smiled. "I have your carriage all hitched up and ready for you, Aunt Millie."

"You are so kind, Mr. Day. I greatly appreciate everything you do for me, but I do wish you might consider attending services with me. It will require more than kindness on your part to enter the Kingdom of Heaven."

"The minute I walked in, a tornado would smash your church to pieces, and an earthquake would destroy the town," he joked. "Thanks, Aunt Millie, but I'll pass. Anyway, I think we might have a storm coming in late tonight, so I better go check on my horses. I'll be sitting out front of the church afterward, waiting as usual when your services are over. Take your time, no rush."

"Then, I guess I'm ready whenever you are," she said. "Good night, gentlemen."

Once she left, one of the men returned to the prior subject. "If it were up to me, I'd fire that whole worthless bunch in Congress …"

* * * * * * * * * * * * * * *

It was well after dark when Johnny Day pulled up beside the side entrance door of the freight company warehouse. After exiting the carriage, he reached into the back and removed two items: an oil lantern and a small tote bag. Johnny lit the lantern and approached the side door. He fumbled a bit, trying to insert the correct key before successfully entering. Once inside, he approached the rear of the parked dray wagon. The lantern lit the area enough for him to see what he needed to accomplish. He removed a small cloth from the bag and inserted it into the bottom middle pipe of the load brought back the previous day. The stableman grabbed a nearby broom and used the handle, pushing the rag further into the pipe. After withdrawing the handle, he reached into the open bag, extracted small wrapped packages, and inserted them into the pipe. To secure everything in place, he shoved another rag into the pipe. After returning the broom, he scanned the small storage shelf until he found a can of blue paint the workers used for the front and back folding wooden doors. He pried open the lid with a screwdriver. Johnny removed a third rag, dipped the edge into the paint, and applied it to the rim of the pipe, just enough to make quick identification possible but not enough to attract unwanted attention. He then buried the paint rag deep into a nearby trash barrel. Now satisfied that everything was ready, Johnny left with the lantern and bag, relocked the door, extinguished the lantern, put the items in the carriage, and returned to the church to wait for Aunt Millie. What he didn't realize was that someone had followed him and watched everything he did through the side window.

CHAPTER 32
OFF TO THE TOWN OF WARREN

Russell Henderson rechecked his coin purse to ensure he had enough money for lunch. Johnny the Stableman had just finished harnessing two other horses to the dray wagon. "How is Boxcar doing today, Johnny?" he asked.

"Much better, I'm happy to say. Still, I prefer that he remains in his stall for a couple more days so I can monitor him. I gave you a pair of strong horses for your delivery today, Able and Cain."

Russell couldn't help but comment upon their odd names. "As long as Cain doesn't slay Able on the way, we'll be fine." The stableman only shook his head, now quite tired of the biblical jokes of the horse's names. *If you label two horses by those names, Johnny, you're bound to be teased*, Russell thought. *People here are right. He does treat those horses as his children.*

Jim Moore approached. "Henderson, just take the road north out of town for three miles, then turn right. Once you cross over the railroad tracks, the town is just after the wooden bridge. You won't have any trouble, and please, after you find the rig and deliver the piping, don't forget to bring back their payment check!" With a small wave, the owner returned to his desk. Russell mounted the wagon.

This should be a breeze. Speaking loud enough for others to hear, he said to the horses, "All right let's go, and please, no family squabbles until we return!" The dray wagon left the warehouse, went through town, and proceeded north. The ride was proving to be uneventful. Russell had thought of bringing a canteen of water as he knew it would be hot by midday. After the three-mile stretch, he could make out the wooden sign pointing east toward the town. It was bumpy crossing over the rough railroad tracks, but the dray wagon was solid, and its tied-down load remained securely in place. Soon, he reached the wooden bridge, the town visible on the other side. Looking down at the river, he could see two men and a small boy fishing along the bank. *I should try fishing again. I haven't tried it since I was a young boy with my father.* Memories of the past filled his thoughts. Exiting the short bridge, a loud shout of "Hold it right there!" was heard as a group of uniformed men appeared almost out of nowhere and circled the wagon.

* * * * * * * * * * * * * * * *

Main Street, Van Buren. Note: Barbershop Pole by Steam Bakery

Marshal Montgomery enjoyed having an audience as he went on and on, bragging about his crime-fighting abilities while seated comfortably in the barber chair. Across from him sat two waiting customers. Their expressions indicated they were not buying his boasts. One man finally asked, "Marshal, have you ever shot anybody with that pistol you're always carrying around?"

"To do so would be my last resort," he replied. "Of course, I wouldn't hesitate if need be, and I am a crack shot. But my first reaction would be to try to de-escalate any potentially serious situation before it ever reached that point." Even the barber's face made a slight smirk that the waiting men couldn't help but notice. Once finished with the haircut, Montgomery stood and paid the barber, offering up a five-cent tip.

At that point, two uniformed men entered the shop. "Leo Montgomery. We're from the Grant County Sheriff's Department. You are under arrest." One of the men reached over and removed Montgomery's pistol from its holster as the other began handcuffing their prisoner.

"What! You can't arrest me. I'm the marshal of this town! I'll have your badges for this!" The officers ignored his complaints and marched him out of the shop. Suddenly, the large marshal appeared quite small and weak in the eyes of the men in the barbershop. Within the hour, news of his arrest quickly spread all over town.

* * * * * * * * * * * * * * * *

While Montgomery's arrest was underway, three other officers appeared at the front door of the house where the nighttime deputies were sleeping off last night's shift. As the officers pounded hard upon the door, a very irate Scott Emery jerked the door open. "You better have a darn good reason for waking us up, or I'll knock some sense into you!" He was easily subdued and pushed back inside.

"Scott Emery. You are under arrest." The other two officers entered, pulling the angry younger brother from his bed. "We'll give you both two minutes to get dressed unless you want to ride the trolly car to the Marion jail in your long underwear." Reluctantly, both men dressed but offered several threats that Marshal Montgomery would soon see to their immediate release. "I wouldn't count on that," the deputy said as they were handcuffed, "as he'll be riding along with us very shortly."

* * * * * * * * * * * * *

Across town, four uniformed officers entered the We Haul Everything Freighting Company and entered the office of the owner, Jim Moore. "Sir, we're from the Grant County Sheriff's Department and need you to round up all of your employees in one group for questioning immediately. Out in the bay will do just fine."

Mr. Moore was shocked by the order. "Not everyone is here, I'm afraid. One of my drivers is out delivering a load of piping to a client in Warren."

Within a few minutes, everyone had assembled. "Which of you is Johnny Day?" the deputy in charge asked. The stableman didn't answer, but the looks everyone gave pointed to their man. "You are under arrest for transporting stolen jewelry using this company's resources. His wrists were cuffed. While searching their prisoner, they found a small caliber pistol tucked away inside his boot. It was confiscated.

Moore spoke up. "I think you're making a big mistake, Deputy. Johnny is one of our most trusted employees. He wouldn't do anything like that!" All the assembled men began agreeing.

"I'm sorry, sir, but we have all the proof we need. We'll be questioning each of you separately, starting with the owner. Your office will do. I suggest the rest of you sit down and wait your turn."

Moore began to protest. "You can't shut us down like this! We have a large furniture pickup and delivery to make." The deputy replied he would see that the deliverymen involved would be interviewed right after him. Realizing he had no choice but to comply, Moore reentered his office to be interviewed by the officers.

CHAPTER 33
-EPILOGUE-

That same day Gas City Marshal Justin Blake finished an all-to-rare lunchtime break at home with his wife Virginia and small son Kenny. As she removed their used dishes from the table, Justin picked up his son and announced, "I think it's armpit time!" Kenny laughed and compressed his arms tightly against his small frame to try to avert the tickling he knew was coming. This was their special game, and they played together whenever time permitted. Justin knew too well that his son would soon grow too old to play this silly game, so he was determined to enjoy the lad's innocence while it lasted.

"You two, stop it!" Virginia said, pretending to be upset by their loudness.

"Just building memories, Mommy," Justin replied, satisfied that the boy had had enough tickling.

Deciding to change the subject, she asked, "When will Wilbert and Rachel return from vacation?"

"I expect him back near the end of the week. Luckily, things are pretty quiet in town, but it does seem strange at times to be working alone." Justin glanced at his pocket watch. "Well, I better get back to work. See ya around the normal time." After kissing his wife goodbye, Justin left for the marshal's office. *Time is passing by so quickly now that the kids are back in school,* he thought. *I sure dread the thought of winter snow coming.*

Entering his office, Justin saw a well-dressed man sitting with his back to him. "Hello, I'm Marshal Blake. How may I help you?" The visitor stood and faced him. Justin's eyes widened, and his right hand instantly moved slightly toward his holstered weapon. "Henderson!"

The visitor slowly raised his hands in a non-threatening way and smiled. "Easy, Marshal. I'm not here to cause you any trouble but to fully explain what occurred while I worked for you. I feel I owe you that much."

Justin remained suspicious and seated himself behind his desk. "All right, go ahead. I'm listening."

"First of all, my real last name isn't Henderson, but Hayward. Russell Hayward. I'm a sheriff's deputy assigned to the Huntington County Sheriff's Department. I do have the proper identification to present to you." He pointed toward the inside of his coat pocket and slowly removed a small leather packet. It was then handed across the desk.

"Well, I'll be!" Justin exclaimed in total surprise. "Care for a glass of water?" he asked. Hayward only shook his head.

"There's so much to explain, and I wanted to speak with you before going to the Grant County Sheriff's Jail to provide my official testimony. The newspapers won't take long to catch wind of it, so you should hear it first. I'm sure you know how common it is for two county sheriff departments to work together to benefit both parties. About six months ago, our department received a tip from one of our paid informants that a stash of stolen jewelry was being smuggled through Huntington and Grant County and that a shipment awaited pickup inside an old abandoned shed south of Huntington. All he could tell us was that each county had one main boss who collected, organized various transportation methods, and then dispatched the stolen items out of their county to the next boss.

"Two of us responded and found bags of jewelry stashed underneath bails of chicken wire. We did catch a break when we discovered some rings wrapped inside a flyer advertising for a grocery store in Van Buren. Based on this clue, they decided to station an officer undercover in that Van Buren for a few months. I, being single and unknown to anyone in Grant County, volunteered, using the name of Henderson, but with no authority to arrest anyone in Grant County.

"I bet you had your hands full, from what I've heard," Justin said.

The deputy smiled and nodded. "In Van Burren, I found a job at a small freight company, which I assumed would be a logical starting point. Weekly, I sent a letter to my 'Uncle Charles,' by general delivery which kept both sheriffs informed, and I received additional information and instructions from them. So many stories were circulating about Marshal Montgomery and his two thug deputies being as crooked as a dog's hind leg. I passed everything on, assuming they were behind the smuggling operation. I habitually made rounds at drinking establishments, hoping to hear anything that might help us. Luckily, I made a friend who eventually helped me months later. Unfortunately, I wasn't getting anywhere though.

"One letter from 'Uncle Charles' advised that we should regroup and that I should apply for the nighttime deputy position the marshal in Gas City was advertising I must tell you, Marshal, it was a real pleasure working for you here. Then, weeks later, a letter from 'Uncle Charles' arrived instructing me to devise a plan to get fired, which was bound to be remembered, and that the terrible information would be supplied to all Grant County newspapers. I hoped my criminal involvement and return to Van Buren might attract the right people. I do have a favor to ask of you, though. Please inform that kind preacher that it had to occur this way. Even though I knew my criminal dealings to be untrue, I felt quite guilty about it. Spending that month inside the county jail was no picnic, but at least the presiding judge was aware of my involvement and played along.

"That was quite a scheme," Justin replied.

"Returning to Van Buren, I accidentally met up with that friend I mentioned earlier, met his employer who owned a larger freight company, and wormed my way into a job hauling everything under the sun. He also helped me find lodging at an old woman's boarding house, where he and another employee stayed. Things were looking up, and with all the negative publicity about your deputy going bad, I hoped to be contacted by the marshal or his men, as they were still my number one suspects. Unfortunately, they paid me no mind, but I followed their nightly activities at every opportunity. I eventually came to the opinion that two sets of criminal activities were underway, neither connected to the other. The marshal, Leo Montgomery, and the brothers Ben and Scott Emery were too careless and unprofessional to be the party I was sent to find. I did begin to wonder if Grant County had placed another agent in town as I saw someone else in old clothing sitting on a bench and trailing behind the nighttime deputies. But I soon realized he wasn't very good at it and recognized him as the son of the hardware store owner. I never figured out his involvement. However, after following the Emery Brothers, I witnessed them, and three of their agents set fire to the lumber and coal yard. You know, Marshal, maybe I'll take that glass of water after all."

Justin walked over and poured two glasses. "Thanks," the visitor said as he downed half the glass. "I didn't realize how thirsty I was."

"It must have been very rewarding for you to get the goods on those men," Justin said.

"Yes, but because I felt I had failed to uncover my main objective, I feared I'd be removed soon from my case. At least I knew I helped the Grant County Boys obtain enough evidence to jail the 'Montgomery Men,' so some good would come out of it. Then, one evening, on a hunch, I followed our company stableman to the freight company's warehouse. I wondered why he made so many off-duty trips to the building on the pretense of checking on the horses. I watched through a window as he entered and began stuffing small, wrapped containers of unknown items into a dray wagon load full of drill pipes I was to haul to a customer in Warren the following day. I suspected I had an important player and maybe even the boss I was searching for. Luckily, I made it to the Western Union office just before the nine o'clock closing and sent a hurried telegram requesting 'Uncle Charlie' and his friends to meet me in Warren the next day. When I arrived in town, they came out of hiding and searched a marked pipe. It was packed full of stolen jewelry. Thrilled at our discovery, Warren sent a telegram telling the Grant County Sheriff their main suspect was Johnny Day, an employee of the 'We Haul Everything Freight Company' in Van Buren. What I didn't know until this morning was that extra deputies accompanied them and arrested their marshal and nighttime deputies, all in one sweep. That only made sense to do so."

"Good work, Russell. I'm sure you'll go far in the sheriff's department, but if not, I can always use an extra hand here in Gas City." Russell stood, and both men shook hands.

"I better be going now. Please let your people know I wasn't the stinker they thought I was, will ya?"

* * * * * * * * * * * * * * *

The biggest surprise came later that evening. The deputies remained on alert, watching for unexpected departures by anyone associated with those in custody. The last evening train going west was due out of Van Buren at eight o'clock. A lone figure emerged from the darkness toward the railroad terminal carrying two large suitcases. The person approached the ticket agent and asked for a single ticket to Denver. But no trip would be taken tonight as two sheriff's deputies approached. "Leaving town rather unexpectantly, Aunt Millie?"

Startled by their sudden appearance, she attempted to come up with a story about having a sister sick and needing her help. Neither deputy bought into her story. "Come with us, Ma'am. We have a few questions we need to ask of you."

The old woman started cussing out each deputy to high heaven. She was instructed to open each suitcase for inspection. Inside, beneath the bundle of clothing, was a large stash of cash and wrapped bags of jewelry. She was placed under arrest on suspicion of transporting stolen jewelry. When later informed of her attempted escape, Johnny Day admitted to being her half-brother and that she, not he, was the Grant County boss behind everything.

Johnny told the officers, "She ain't gonna take off and leave me holdin' the bag! But I gotta hand it to her. She played the part of the religious, old lady down to a tee, even foolin' me a few times. Not bad for a prior actress, dancehall girl, prostitute, and madam of her own house of ill repute in Denver! Whoever would have suspected a kind, old religious woman anyway? We made a bundle while it lasted. I ain't got no remorse."

* * * * * * * * * * * * * * *

The next few days proved quite interesting to the readers of the local county newspapers. The ex-marshal of Van Buren shared the details about the graft he and his men received from various robberies and even provided the names of the men they hired to rob homes and businesses for cash and who torched the lumber and coal yard. This, and the beatings the Emery Brothers had conducted on their victims, would most likely put them behind bars for many years to come.

No charges were ever brought against freight company owner Jim Moore, who had no idea his business was frequently used for illicit purposes. The men housed in Aunt Millie's Boarding House were forced to find other sleeping arrangements.

* * * * * * * * * * * * * * *

The next night, the Van Buren town council met for an emergency meeting to appoint a new Marshal. Able Doby was offered the new position at the strong suggestion of Russell Hayward and with the unanimous support of the three councilmen. He humbly accepted and stated that interviews for the nighttime deputies would commence starting tomorrow, with his recommendations to be received with the full approval of the council. The tarnish that had plagued Van Buren for so long was finally removed. Councilman Roger Paxton was asked why he voted to keep the old marshal in place. He refused to answer, knowing that the old marshal had obtained dirt on his wife and promised to let it be known. When it comes to his loving wife, Paxton felt any early-in-life transgressions she might have committed should be buried and forgotten. Nobody's perfect, anyway.

THE KIDNAPPERS

MAIN CAST OF NEW CHARACTERS:

James Howell — Vice President First National Bank

Jane Howell — Wife/Mother
Steven Howell — Bank Teller/Son
Brad Lockridge — Part-Time Deputy
Horace Baxter (Retired) — Owner of Haynes-Apperson
Marsha Evens — Owner of Evans Haberdashery

Eugene Maxwell — Medical Doctor of Gas City

CHAPTER 34
BROOKS' BARBERSHOP

On Tuesday morning, the barbershop was full of waiting customers. The owner, Matthew Brooks, and his brother Jordan were busy cutting hair as they listened customer from Jonesboro tell a strange story. "I just couldn't believe it myself, but people who saw the tin box full of money swear it's true. According to Grandma Lucas, a woman claiming to be a clairvoyant came to her and said that through her powers, the mystic saw a tin box full of money that was buried in Grandma's flower garden and asked permission to dig for it. Grandma is a kindly old soul and was amused and intrigued by the possibility, so she gave her permission. She provided a shovel, and together, they walked around her property until the clairvoyant stopped and pointed down. She dug a deep hole and, sure enough, found a tin box. They took it into Grandma's house and opened the box, revealing a large sum of money. The two women agreed that Grandma Lucas would take half of the one hundred and fifty dollars as her share of the money.

"Then the strange woman announced that the property belonging to Fred Schrader, just south of Grandma's property, also contained a large sum of money. After displaying her money and the now-empty tin box to many residents, word spread, and people began trespassing on Schrader's land, digging holes here and there. Fred was so angry that he called the Jonesboro Marshal to run the treasure hunters off and threatened to prosecute anyone found digging there. The town is all excited about it, I can tell you that."

"So, what happened to that clairvoyant? Looks to me she'd hang around to get her next cut of that other money!" an old man asked.

"I have no idea. Folks say she just disappeared as mysteriously as she appeared."

"Maybe a ghost, then?

"More likely some rich eccentric woman who gets her pleasure from pretending to be something she's not." The customer in Matthew's barber chair said as he stood, paid his quarter, and left. Another man entered carrying a folded newspaper, which was not an unusual practice for men waiting to be served.

After sitting down and not hearing anyone speak, the newcomer asked, "Did any of you read the story in the Marion Chronicle about the plan to drown children who are judged to be idiots?" No one had, but they were interested in learning about it. "I brought along my paper, just in case anyone hadn't. The New York physician, Doctor Brown, from the Board of Health, recommended a system of classification recently adopted there by the school board for disposing of backward children. Allow me to read it to you.

"Quote: 'Every child with the slightest deficiency will receive a special examination, and if he is blind or deaf, will be sent to the institution where that deficiency will be given special treatment and possibly cured." So far, the man said, looking up from the paper, "this seems reasonable, but let me continue. In like manner, the imbecile often is made into a useful citizen. But for the idiot, there is no hope. When it is found that he is too far gone for the surgeon's knife to help, his life should be extinguished. Idiot children should be drowned. We would then have more time and energy to spend on children with possibilities of success. For imbeciles who have less mental depravity and weak-minded pupils, we have training classes. In these, many will be trained to become expert carpenters, while girls learn to cook and sew. Un-quote."

The room fell quiet until Jordan said, "Drowning of children? Sounds to me like their doctor is the idiot!"

"Yep, an educated idiot. Must be something strange in the east coast water that makes um' think like that," Matthew replied.

The old man turned to the man next to him and said, "Say, Charlie, ain't you one of dem carpenter fellers that doc feller was talkin' bout?" There was laughter at the insinuation. The joke and smear of being considered a trained imbecile made Charlie so mad that he abruptly walked out of the barbershop. "I was just funnin' and didn't mean nuttin' by it," the embarrassed old man replied.

"You better not kid around anymore; you're costing me business," Matthew said with a smile.

CHAPTER 35
A BUSY NIGHTS WORK

Brad Lockridge

Brad Lockridge had a busy night as Gas City's fill-in deputy. Just before dark, he received a phone call from J.H. Stein complaining that three teenage boys kept throwing rocks at his front door. The deputy recognized their names and caught the pranksters red-handed, arresting them on a charge of malicious trespass. They were scheduled to appear before Mayor Huffman at nine o'clock the following morning. Huffman took the lesser cases to prevent 'Squire Williamson's court schedule from becoming bogged down. Many small towns followed the same procedures, and Huffman enjoyed handling them. If the mayor followed his usual standard of punishment, he would only require a sound thrashing by the boys' mothers.

Ed Norton was also arrested that night for public intoxication and sentenced to fifteen days of jail time. At the same time, Mrs. Matilda Mittenger filed a report against her husband, Martin, claiming he came home drunk and beat their son over a small matter. He was charged with assault and battery and faced jail time and a stiff fine. Whether his family would welcome him back home or not, only time would tell.

Despite the busyness of the night, Brad enjoyed occasional police work after being a full-time deputy before enlisting in the army. Now home for good, he and his business partner, a retired doctor named Horace Baxter, opened the first auto repair and gas station in Grant County. At times, business was slow, and to help make ends meet, Brad made general repairs to all types of equipment. He planned on getting a few hours of sleep once relieved and then approaching his partner with two ideas that hopefully would improve their business.

* * * * * * * * * * * * * * *

The morning didn't slow down even after Justin Blake and Wilbert Vance started their shift. Between the telephone calls from townspeople complaining of window peepers the night before and Mayor Huffman complaining again that saloons were illegally selling alcohol out their back door on Sundays, Justin finally felt he'd had enough and went for a walk. Unfortunately, even that didn't work out as planned. He'd been forced to arrest Alvin Wright for obstructing the public highway. Wright was hauling a load of gravel and stopped his team in the middle of the street. When informed he was obstructing traffic and asked to move, Wright refused. Within the hour, he pleaded not guilty before Mayor Huffman. His trial was set for Friday morning. After posting bond, he was allowed to go on his way. *Why was Wright so stubborn in refusing to move his stupid wagon?* Justin thought. *He must have woken up on the wrong side of the bed or something.*

Back in his office, Justin sat to tackle a large stack of paperwork when a young boy entered carrying an envelope. It was young Billy, a messenger from the Western Union Telegraph Company. "Telegram, Marshal Blake," the lad stated as he handed the envelope over. Justin reached into his pocket and presented the boy with a nickel, which pleased the boy immensely, as he ran out the door. *I bet Billy is on his way to the candy shop right now.*

Justin smiled as he read the message. "Good. It's from the marshal over on Sweetser. They've captured Frank Detten." The man in question had boarded for some time in the home of the widow, Mrs. Williams, here in town and disappeared overnight, still owing her boarding money. Officers in surrounding towns were notified to be on the lookout for Detten, and it paid off. "Wilbert, get over to Sweetser and bring back our non-paying cheapskate. I wish I could go, but I'm buried in paperwork." Wilbert was soon on his way. *By tomorrow, Detten can explain to Mayor Huffman how he simply 'forgot' to pay his large boarding bill.*

Then, the phone rang again. It was the mayor. "I just contacted the Journal to run a warning advertisement to all saloons, gambling joints, and immoral resorts that they must close at precisely eleven Saturday evening or face arrest. I want your weekend deputies to enforce this order," he said. Justin said they would be briefed and hung up.

Pushing his work to the side, Justin began to look over yesterday's edition of the Journal to see the latest news. There was a strike at the Tin-Plate Factory over wages; someone had developed a way to use the telephone from a moving streetcar, and the county carpenters demanded their hourly pay be raised from thirty to thirty-five cents an hour. There was also a job posting for the post office due to George Harris's resignation. *Now that's the job I should try for … no more worries or early-morning telephone calls. Just pass out the mail and go home at a normal time!* As good as it sounded, Justin knew he and his men were in a thankless occupation, but one that was greatly needed to provide law and order within a free society. Unfortunately, things were about to become much tougher in the following weeks.

CHAPTER 36
THE GREAT RACE

Dr. Horace Baxter (Retired)

Horace Baxter loved to drive his Haynes-Apperson Runabout automobile up and down the brick streets, zipping along, scaring horses and people alike. *I may be old and retired, but I'm not dead yet!* Helping the young man Brad Lockridge develop his dream of a gas station and repair shop gave Baxter a new purpose in life. Though not mechanical, he could still sell gasoline and accept new business as it arrived while Brad was sleeping from working deputy marshal duties the night before.

Shortly before noon, Brad arrived at the gas station carrying a rolled-up poster and entered the small office. "Thanks again, Doc, for filling in for me," he said. "I wonder if you have a few moments before you go home?"

"No problem. Oh, here's a short list of items brought in for repair, listed with the owner's name. What's on your mind?"

Brad reached into his pocket, extracted a folded paper, and handed it over. Doctor Baxter unfolded the flyer and read:

First Run of The New Marion Automobile Club

"It's a distance race starting this coming Saturday from Marion to Peru and back, all on the same day. I checked on this, and so far, only seven automobiles have been entered. I think you should join the club and run the race in your Haynes-Apperson. Any promotion of automobiles, their safety, and durability is bound to help our business. There's no purse involved, though."

"I think it's a grand idea, but not for me. You should be the one to join the club and drive my automobile."

"Well, what if I rode along and served as your relief driver and mechanic?"

Baxter shook his head. "I'd only be dead weight. Pack it with replacement tires and tools. The lighter the automobile, the less strain upon the engine."

Brad saw his point and agreed. "There's one other thing," as he unrolled the poster.

"What if we become an authorized dealership for the Haynes-Apperson Motor Company? We'd be the first in Grant County. Also, dealers who sell one of their autos receive two hundred and fifty dollars in commission. Then, we would maintain those automobiles we sold. A win-win for us."

"Is there a cost in obtaining the dealership license?"

"Yes, twenty-five dollars, which I have in my savings."

"Leave it there, Brad. I'll cover the cost and you can repay me your half after we sell our first Haynes-Apperson!" He reached into his wallet and extracted the money. The men shook on it, and Brad hung the poster on the wall for all visitors and prospective buyers to see. Tomorrow, Brad would catch the train to Kokomo, meet with the automobile manufacturer, purchase the license, receive whatever training was needed, and the required order paperwork. Then, on the way home, he'd stop in Marion to join the auto club and sign up to drive Saturday in their big endurance race.

CHAPTER 37
FIRST NATIONAL BANK

Steven Howell

"You look very distinguished today, Steven," the seventy-year-old woman said.

"Thank you, Mrs. Walker. Here's your savings passbook back, all recorded properly," the young man replied. Steven

Howell, a teller at First Nation Bank, politely smiled. *If only she* were *eighteen*, he thought. He was the son of James and Jane Howell, employed for the summer till college started in the fall. He was set to attend Marion College and earn a degree in business. His father also happened to be the vice president of the bank, which caused a bit of teasing from his coworkers.

"Young Steven is a chip off the old block," people said. "One day, he'll be the president of this bank." The only problem was, that nobody ever asked him if this was his life's goal. Oh, he tried to tell his parents numerous times, but his parents never listened. Ever since he was a small lad, Steven has had one deep desire in life: to be a railroad conductor.

The very mention of it brought scorn from his father. "I want you to have a better life than that," he would say over and over again. "Someday, you'll thank me for pushing you into a professional career." So, it was at his father's insistence that he take work during the summer as a teller at the bank to get a taste of the business world before starting college.

"Next customer," Steven uttered without any emotion in his voice.

* * * * * * * * * * * * * *

One of the boldest small robberies ever to occur in Gas City in recent years happened early this morning. The house of A.J. Danta, a prominent groceryman living on South Main and Grant Street, was broken into. Sixteen dollars in cash and a gold watch were taken. At two o'clock in the morning, the thief used a ladder to reach the second story where Danta lived above his store. He silently removed the screen, and with a long hook, snagged the owner's trousers and vest off the bedpost. So clever was the work that Danta was not disturbed and knew nothing of it until morning. The trousers, the homemade hook, and the ladder were later discovered in an alleyway by a man on his way to work.

* * * * * * * * * * * * * * *

Friday morning, Brad Lockridge's business partner wished him good luck as he drove off towards Marion, where he would stay overnight to be ready for Saturday's start of the endurance race. The back seat contained four rubber tires that the Firestone Tire and Rubber Company had produced. Brad felt these to be superior tires made with a combination of rubber and layers of fabric, which was said to enhance durability and traction. He also brought what he hoped was an adequate supply of hand tools for repairs along the route. The weather appeared good for tomorrow's run and Brad felt excitement building within. He and the doctor successfully obtained the license to become the first authorized dealer of Haynes-Apperson automobiles in Grant County.

* * * * * * * * * * * * * * *

The weekdays moved slowly for James Howell, as issues at the bank had taken up much of his time. Finally, it was Friday evening, and he and his wife sat down for supper. "Where's Steven? he enquired of their son, who still lived at home.

"He came home just before you, changed clothes, and said he was going out with friends and might be late."

"Oh, to be young again," he joked. "Don't forget, Mother, this is lodge night. I'll be home around ten or so." James was an active member of the Ben Hur Lodge #115 in Jonesboro.

"Don't let anyone talk you into running for an office," she suggested. James only smiled.

"What are you going to do while I'm gone?"

"I thought I'd go next door to Mabel Doris's and visit her for a while. She's very sharp for an eighty-eight-year-old." The meal soon ended, and each went their separate ways.

* * * * * * * * * * * * * *

Just before dark, Jane returned home from a delightful visit and noticed a large sheet of paper shoved between the front door knocker and the wooden surface. She removed it and entered. After setting down her purse, she proceeded into the library and unfolded the paper. Jane had to read it over and over to fully understand the gravity of its terrible message. Each letter was printed in dark ink. This is what it said:

Rich Banker,

We are holding your son as hostage. If you want to see him alive again, follow these instructions. Do not involve the cops, or he will die. You are to walk to your bank late tonight at two o'clock, alone. Go to the rear door. There, you will find a suitcase. You are to fill it with $10,000 consisting of tens, twenties, and fifties. Then, you are to return the suitcase to where you found it and go straight home. We will be watching everything you do from a distance, so don't try anything foolish, or you'll find his severed head on your front porch. If we are satisfied that you have not attempted deceit, you will receive word regarding where he may be found.

Father, please help me. Don't let them kill me!
Steven

Tears swelled in Jane's eyes, and her hands trembled as she recognized Steven's handwriting. She paced the floor, looking up at the mantle clock every few minutes, wishing James would hurry home. The hours seemed like days until she heard him opening the door. Jane instantly shoved the paper into his face as she loudly attempted to explain its terrible meaning. "Wait, wait, wait! Give me a chance to come inside, will ya?" James hung his overcoat and hat on the tree rack before turning to her. "Now, let me read it for myself."

She watched his facial expression intently as the danger to their son became a reality. Still gripping the letter, James walked past his wife into the library and sat on the couch. "What are we going to do?" she cried.

"What else can I do but comply fully with this demand and steal from my bank? Right now, the only thing of importance is getting Steven home safe and sound. Then, I'll turn myself over to the authorities and face whatever charges they impose upon me."

CHAPTER 38
ROBBING HIS OWN BANK

The First National Bank,
Corner of Main and First St.

It was a dark, cloudy night when a lone figure approached the back of the bank. James Howell had entered it a thousand times before, but never at this ungodly hour, or for this devilish purpose. As he approached the door, he saw the kidnapper's suitcase. Reaching into his pocket, he fumbled in the dark to locate the entry key. Once found, he picked up the suitcase and entered. Though a very familiar place, it seemed odd and different at night, casting unfamiliar shadows on the wall. After striking a match, James located one of the candles put aside for emergencies. Though fully equipped with natural gas lighting, he was afraid its illumination might bring on curiosity from one of the night deputies. Being questioned would most certainly put Steven's life at risk, so every precaution had to be taken to follow the kidnapper's instructions to the letter.

His eyes quickly adjusted as he sat the suitcase down on a table and opened it. Then, holding the candle in his left hand, he approached the combination on the safe and spun the dial to the correct numbers. It opened without difficulty. Now, he had to obtain the currencies required to make up the ten thousand dollars, which he stacked in separate piles on the table. He took multiple trips into the bank vault, counting the amount silently until the funds were stacked before him. James hadn't become the vice president of the bank by being naive. Realizing that the stacks of ten-dollar bills would be the easiest for the crooks to cash locally, he began frantically jotting down as many serial numbers as he could. Once finished, that paper was safely inserted into his vest pocket. It would be given to the lawmen once Steven was safely released. Sensing he better hurry up, he stacked all the money into the suitcase, shut and locked the safe, blew out the candle, and was preparing to leave when, all at once, loud bells sounded. *I've been caught*, he assumed. But that assumption proved incorrect when he looked out the large glass window and saw the fire engine pulled by a team of horses heading south. Flames were visible off in the distance. James stepped outside, sat the suitcase back down, locked the door, and briskly walked home. *I am now an official bank robber.* Once back home, Jane peppered him with questions about how it all went. He decided not to mention the serial numbers, fearing his actions would make her an accessory to the crime. Now, all they could do was wait, hope, and pray for their son's safe release.

CHAPTER 39
THE RACE BEGINS

The first run of the Marion Automobile Club, with only eight entries, would be a success in every way. All would remember good, solid running, breakdowns, wrong roads, and scared horses. Here is what occurred. The group left Marion at nine o'clock toward Peru by way of Converse. Everything was going well until the group reached Converse when one of the entries blew a tire and had to stop for repairs. Soon after, another blew their tire out. Unfortunately, the driver hadn't brought adequate tools and could not continue to Peru until dark. The remaining seven entries, including Brad Lockridge, arrived in Peru and enjoyed a hearty meal before the return trip by way of Wabash. One entry was found to have three flat tires, and sabotage was alleged but was unproven.

After a hurried meal, one automobile tried to get a jump on their compatriots and left early, stopping along the way to ask a woman which road would take them to Wabash. "This one," she said, pointing to the north road. The auto continued onward for some distance before reaching North Manchester. Realizing they had been steered the wrong road, they backtracked and soon came back upon the same woman. "Wabash is a nice town, ain't it!" she laughed. Gripping the wheel in rage, they turned their car toward the right road. The only other incident that took place was an accident between one of the entries and a farmer's pony, buckboard, and children, all of whom landed in the ditch next to a barbwire fence. After ten minutes spent assisting the occupants back onto the road, the automobile resumed its journey. In the end, seven of the original eight entries arrived back in Marion before darkness set it. Driving a Haynes-Apperson, Brad Lockridge was third to arrive safely without a blowout, thanks in part to the vehicle's Firestone tires and luck in not hitting any deep ruts. Soon, there would be talk of an actual race in which entry fees would be collected and prizes would be awarded to the winner

* * * * * * * * * * * * * * *

Great despair and fear hung over the Howell household as the couple continued to await either word from the kidnappers or their son's release. Every few minutes, his mother checked the door knocker, looking for further communication. There had been none. Neither was able to get any sleep and felt quite exhausted. James strongly suggested that after breakfast the next morning, she should attempt to lie down and rest. A mother's instinct to protect her child remained strong inside of Jane Howell and offered many excuses to stay awake. It took a bit of coaxing, but she finally agreed. "Promise me you'll wake me the minute you know something," she insisted.

"You know I will, Mother." She left the table and went upstairs to bed. James returned to their library and tried to read a book but couldn't concentrate. *The minute Steven returns home, I'll take the kidnapper's letter and go straight over to the marshal's office and surrender myself. Then, they can contact the bank president and inform him of what I've done and why. I hate to think what the board of directors will think of me. But what if Steven isn't released? What then? The bank will* quickly *learn of the shortage first thing Monday morning, so they must be informed as soon as possible. Oh, Son, where are you? Are you all right? I would gladly exchange places with you if I could.*

By late evening, they decided to go to bed and hope for better news on Sunday morning.

* * * * * * * * * * * * * * *

George Woodruff, who managed the saloon at the corner of South H and First Street, evidently thought that Mayor Huffman was only joking about saloons, gambling houses, and immoral resorts closing on Sundays. As a result, Woodruff found himself arrested for staying open Saturday night past the required eleven o'clock closing time. He was scheduled to be taken before the mayor on Monday morning and faced stiff fines for disobeying lawful orders.

* * * * * * * * * * * * * * *

Sunday morning arrived and after breakfast, the Howells decided to go to morning services as usual and pray for their son's safe release. When they returned home, there was no note. By afternoon, James approached his wife. "I've made a decision, Mother. If Steven hasn't returned home by seven o'clock tonight, I will go to Marshal Blake's home and turn myself in. I simply cannot wait any longer to report the missing money." Jane realized there wasn't any further advantage in waiting any longer. With the marshal's help, perhaps volunteers could be assembled for a search party. Seven o'clock finally struck on the mantle clock as the disgraced banker put on his coat and hat, then kissed his wife goodbye, perhaps for the last time in a while.

CHAPTER 40
COMING CLEAN

An exciting new board game sweeping the country called 'The Landlord's Game,' which years later would change its name to 'Monopoly.' Wilbert Vance recently purchased the game, and he and his wife Rachel were teaching it to their friends, Justin and Virginia, at the marshal's home. In a bedroom, the couple's small children played with toys. Wilbert landed on the Chance position and drew a card. "Oh, no," he muttered. "It says advance to Boardwalk." That position, owned by his wife, had two hotels positioned on it.

Rachael giggled. "You owe me six hundred dollars in rent, buddy boy!" Just as he reached to count out his remaining stack of play money, there was a knock on the front door. Each person secretly hoped it wasn't anything important that would halt their fun evening together. Virginia stood and went to answer.

A male's voice could be heard asking, "Is the marshal in?" *Looks like duty calls*, Justin thought as the visitor entered.

Justin stood and approached. "Mr. Howell. Come in, sir. How can I help you?"

Realizing he was interfering with their fun evening, he thought about leaving and approaching the marshal in the morning but decided he'd better not delay any longer. After removing his hat, he said, "Marshal, I'm very sorry to barge in on you and your company, but you need to know I was forced to steal ten thousand dollars from our bank vault." The vice president handed over the kidnapper's letter for him to read. "We've made copies for ourselves," James said. Justin then passed it over to Wilbert. "My wife and I are frantic. I did exactly what they demanded, but they haven't released Steven."

The lawmen began asking questions. The banker produced the paper containing serial numbers for the stack of ten-dollar bills. "I wish there had been time to write down more," he said. Justin motioned for Wilbert to follow him into the kitchen to speak privately.

"Our bad luck continues," Wilbert said. "Where do we begin?"

"First, I need to contact Captain Benjamin Stewart of the Grant County Sheriff's Department. He'll know who needs to be contacted on the Marion police force and at First National Bank. When we're through here, I need you to obtain a complete description of Steven that I can pass on to Stewart. I think we'll handle this as a kidnapping and organize people in the morning willing to search all points of the town and along the river. Jonesboro will also be asked to help with the search. If they've killed him, his body may already be in the Mississinewa River, but let's keep that speculation away from the family and remain positive.

"Now, put yourself in the kidnapper's shoes. If Steven is tied up in a basement or attic somewhere, we probably won't find him, but outbuildings, barns, and sheds must be searched. My gut tells me the ones orchestrating this won't take him with them if, and I do mean if, they choose to leave town with their loot. If only we had learned of this two days ago, the railroad depot and trolley cars could have been watched. Unfortunately, they've had ample time to make their escape, but maybe the ticket agent might remember something. The one ace we have is the serial numbers for the ten-dollar bills. I'll let it be known that, unfortunately, no serial numbers on the bank's money have been recorded. If the group is still in Grant County, they'll read this and feel it safe to start spending. Let's ask the ladies to help us make many duplicate lists of the bill's serial numbers tonight. Tomorrow, we'll quietly pass them around to hotels, restaurants, and grocery stores. They may not receive ten-dollar bills very often. Maybe we'll hit paydirt."

Wilbert asked, "What about Mr. Howell?" Justin motioned to follow him back into the living room. "Mr. Howell, you're free to return home tonight under house arrest. Tomorrow morning, meet us at my office at seven o'clock, and we'll start recruiting volunteers to search for your son. Pray with your wife and have faith that Steven will be returned to you unharmed. Goodnight."

James Howell seemed surprised he wasn't being taken to jail. He nodded and started to leave—but stopped. "Oh, somebody needs to inform the president of our bank about this. I know him quite well, and I could call ..." Justin stopped him and said it would be best if he had no contact until this gets resolved. Realizing the marshal was right, he said he would also refuse any phone calls from them for the time being.

* * * * * * * * * * * * * *

The following morning, word of the kidnapping spread through the town, and men and women volunteers began assembling outside the marshal's office to await instructions. Matthew Brooks felt obliged to James Howell and decided to close the barbershop and join the search. His brother Jordan accompanied him. Even Gas City's mayor, Davis Huffman, and many city workers joined. Justin arrived at work thirty minutes early and was pleased by the turnout, with more still trickling in. James Howell was already waiting and speaking with night deputy Philip Curtis. Wilbert Vance entered as well. "Justin, I want to lead one of the groups this morning," Curtis said. "I'll eat and sleep after we find him safe and sound." James thanked the deputy.

"All right, here's the plan. We'll divide the volunteers into four groups and each of us will lead them. I'll take my group north. Wilbert, you go west, Philip, south, and Mr. Howell, east. Each group should have one man on horseback to inform the other groups if Steven is found. Remember, you are representing this office in your search. We cannot enter anyone's home unless it is offered, but sheds, barns, and any outbuilding need to be checked. If a problem develops, have the owner contact me later to resolve it. Now, let's go outside so Mr. Howell can thank the volunteers, and I'll explain what we'll be doing." Soon, the groups were split apart, with a few remaining unassigned. Justin pulled the mayor off to the side. "Sir, I need you to take those remaining, go straight down to the river bank, and check a mile or so downstream on both sides. I contacted the marshal of Jonesboro last night, and he's organizing people there to do the same. I just don't want Mr. Howell to know we suspect his son's body might be floating in the river."

The volunteers departed, and the search for the missing Steven Howell began.

CHAPTER 41
BOARD OF DIRECTORS MEETING

The group of businessmen assembled in their smoke-filled Marion boardroom to discuss the recent loss at their Gas City branch. "Gentlemen … gentlemen … your attention, please." The room fell quiet as the appointed speaker continued. "I'm sure by now, all of you are aware of what has happened. I just spoke with the chief of police, and he gave me a copy of the kidnapper's letter." He then began to read aloud.

Once finished, a member known for his foul temperament asked, "So, what's happened to our so-called bank vice president?"

"I was told large search parties are scouring the town, as well as Jonesboro. I would assume he's with them."

"The man ought to be in jail, where he belongs! He didn't have to violate the trust of our depositors. Forget the kid; they should be searching for our missing money!"

The comment didn't go over well with the other men. One replied, "That's easy for you to say, Alfred, you don't have children. But what if it was your wife who'd been kidnapped?"

"Then they could keep her, and good riddance too!"

The speaker had heard enough. "Gentlemen, we're not here for personal attacks but to keep everyone informed of the current developments. I was also told all railroad and trolly cars are being watched. If we hear anything new, I'll phone each of you. This meeting is adjourned."

* * * * * * * * * * * * * * *

Hours passed before a man in a carriage reached James to inform him that a discovery had been made by the northern search party led by Marshal Blake. The driver soon had the banker underway. "What is it? Did they discover Steven?" he begged to know.

"I have no idea, sir. I was just flagged down and asked to find you and take you there. That's all they told me." This worried James even more. *If Steven were alive, they would have said so*, he feared. Seeing Justin outside an old, dilapidated shed, the driver came to a halt. James jumped from the carriage, forgetting to thank the man for bringing him. The driver now felt compelled to wait and see what they'd found. "Did you find Steven? Is he all right?" he shouted.

"No, he's not here, but it appears to be where they held him captive. Come."

The men entered, and James's eyes fixed on an old wooden kitchen chair. Several men were standing nearby, one holding a piece of cut rope and a thick rag. "They had him tied up and gagged before cutting the rope. Maybe they freed him, and he's back at home," the man said, sounding as optimistic and hopeful as he could. Justin reached into his pocket and handed over a pocket watch to the banker.

James instantly recognized the watch as belonging to his son and placed it in his pocket. "It's Steven's, all right. We bought it for him for his sixteenth birthday. If he's been freed, I need to get home.

Please thank everyone for their assistance today, Marshal." Exiting, James saw that the carriage driver had stayed, and it soon had him on his way home. "They found where he was held. I pray he's alive and well, back in his mother's arms!" James told the driver.

Justin remained behind to continue his search for clues. Besides the footprints that could have been there for a long time, he found nothing else. "Have all the men gather around," Justin said. "I'll dispatch Frank to ride to the Howell home to see if the boy is there and report back. While he's gone, we'll take a break and wait. But I can only suspect the worst has happened if he's not been freed. Our search will then change from a rescue to a probable retrieval. By that, I mean there'd be no reason to take the hostage with them, so he's probably buried in a shallow grave or hidden under a thick brush pile. We'll then spread out and check everything within a quarter mile of this shed. If we don't find the body, we'll continue searching more north along the riverbanks," Justin said to the men. "Tom, since you're also on horseback, tell the other groups to stand down, but let the mayor's group keep searching. If you see Wilbert, tell him what's happened here and instruct him to ask Jonesboro to concentrate on searching their side of the river."

* * * * * * * * * * * * * *

The carriage halted at the Howell resident, and James remembered to thank the driver this time. Walking quickly into the house, he unfortunately learned that his son had not returned. "We found where he'd been held captive, Mother, and I assumed he'd be here now," he said as he removed the pocket watch and handed it over to her. She held the watch up against her heart.

So, where is he?" she whispered as a stream of tears flowed down her cheeks. For that, James had no answer. "I cooked a large meal, hoping and praying for Steven's return today. We might as well eat it." Both tried but realized they had little appetite as terrible thoughts flowed through their minds, but they were afraid to voice them out loud.

James finally pushed his plate to the side. "Mother, I can't just sit around here doing nothing. I think I'll go into the office and try to stay busy. Call me if anything develops." He changed his clothes and walked the short distance to the bank. *I don't know if I'm still employed there or not*, he wondered. Entering through the rear door, James paid no attention to the stares he was receiving as he entered his office and closed the door. After about an hour, James emerged and was greeted with kindness *by* the employees, all asking about his son. Returning home at his normal time, James felt better after being around people again. *I'll return in the morning and work all day unless the board terminates me.*

"I think I need to get out of this house tomorrow and visit with Reverend Stokes," Jane told him. He thought it was a good idea, knowing the power of prayer can sometimes work miracles.

* * * * * * * * * * * * * *

As hard as they looked, the body of Steven Howell could not be found. The search was finally called off by Marshal Blake.

* * * * * * * * * * * * * *

Questioning the railroad depot and trolley agents hadn't produced any tangible suspects. "Deputy, you gotta understand," the railroad depot agent said. "I'm here to sell tickets to people wanting to travel, not to eyeball every person or examine what type of suitcases they carry."

It seemed the search had come to a dead end. None of the marked ten-dollar bills had shown up in any of the local businesses, and Justin was beginning to wonder if the young man's body had floated past the point of their search. *Maybe somebody downriver will find it and give the Howells some bitter closure.*

The days passed without any tangible results. James Howell continued to go to work every morning, expecting to find a termination letter waiting on his desk.

CHAPTER 42
BAD NEWS CONTINUES

An early-morning natural gas explosion at the new Thompson's Glass Factory resulted in three men seriously burned. A new piece of gasoline equipment meant to furnish power to the plant was in the process of being lit for the first time when a sheet of flame burned their faces and hands. Workers rushed into aid and transport the men to the office of Doctor Maxwell. John L. Thompson and Sons, who owned the plant, were proprietors of the Thompson Bottling Factory that has been in operation for several years.

Later that evening, Miss Margarete Terrell, employed as a domestic worker at the Shamrock Hotel on First Street, was shot and killed in a grove in Gas City. She was in the company of her ex-lover, Everett Athens, whose .38 caliber pistol was used. Athens claimed she committed suicide as the couple visited in the secluded spot. He claimed he arrived from Summitville on the eight o'clock train and went immediately to the hotel to speak with her in the hotel's parlor. Afterward, the couple walked down First Street and then to the grove northeast of town. Athens admitted to having the gun in his position which he claimed was lying on the ground between them. He claimed she laughed, and said she would shoot herself, picked it up, and fired it directly into her right eye. His story didn't sit well with Deputy Davidson, who placed him under arrest. The proprietor of the Shamrock Hotel who knew the young woman quite well, insisted she was not suicidal.

* * * * * * * * * * * * * *

James Howell went to the bank every morning to check the ten-dollar bills collected the previous day. Several days passed until he finally made a discovery. One of the marked bills had shown up. He removed a ten from his wallet, exchanged it for the marked one, and then proceeded directly to the marshal's office. "Marshal, I found one of the stolen tens! I've been looking every day and did as you asked. I didn't tell any of our employees for fear of tipping off the kidnapper. It was taken in sometime yesterday by one of our tellers."

Justin was thrilled with the news. The discovery proved that the kidnappers were still in or around the Gas City area. Wilbert matched the serial number to the list, placed the bill in an envelope labeled as evidence, and tucked it into the office safe as the banker returned to work.

"Wilbert, I want you to go to all the businesses north of Main Street to ensure they still have a copy of the serial numbers and emphasize the importance of their vigilance. I'll do the same on the south side. Here, take a couple of the extra serial number lists in case they're needed. Just don't mention what we learned this morning." Wilbert then left.

If they've spent one bill, they'll probably feel free enough to spend a few more. If only we could obtain a description or, better yet, the name of the individual passing the bill.

CHAPTER 43
A POSSIBLE LEAD?

"Wilbert, I'm going over for a haircut before things get too busy here. You can hold down the fort," Justin said to his friend as he left for Brooks' Barbershop. Justin hadn't been gone for five minutes when James Howell entered the marshal's office.

"Deputy, another ten-dollar bill was taken in by a teller yesterday." He inquired if there was any new information on Steven. He was told there wasn't. Hearing this, he handed the bill over and returned to work at the bank. Wilbert checked it against their list; sure enough, it was one of the stolen bills. *Someone is feeling pretty free to spend the stolen money. If only we could get a lead on who it is.*

* * * * * * * * * * * * * *

After entering the barbershop, located on the ground floor gift shop section of the Mississinewa Hotel, Justin saw two customers sitting in the barber chairs while two others waited for service. He sat and picked up a days-old copy of the Journal to help kill time. One of the waiting customers, an old man nearing his eighties named Joe, said, "I saw a couple of sheriff's deputies coming out of the bank yesterday. Maybe they came to arrest that banker fellow." Justin knew the answer to why they were in town but declined to comment about it publicly. They were there to collect the stolen ten-dollar bill, see how the case was progressing, and pick up the man who shot his girlfriend recently.

The other waiting customer felt like picking on the old man. "From what I heard, Joe, they're here to investigate you. Something about you exciting young teenage girls into a frenzy."

The old man chuckled and answered, "It's quite true that young women find me irresistible. Unfortunately, I can't run away from them as fast as I used to, and besides, now I'd rather just take a nap anyway." Jordan could only shake his head.

"I bet their visit was about that fella who shot his girlfriend and then claimed she shot herself. Good luck convincing a jury to believe a wild story like that," the waiting customer said. "Gas City is turning into the murder capital of Grant County. Maybe we'll have to post warning signs for visitors outside of town that say, 'Enter at Your Own Risk.'"

Realizing this statement was intended as a dig against his friend Justin, Matthew Brooks replied, "That's simply not true. We have the finest lawmen in Grant County, and eventually, they get around to solving most of our crimes. No law enforcement agency is perfect, you know."

Somebody should write down all the wild stories told by men in barbershops, Justin thought. *On second thought, nobody reading them would believe them anyway.*

* * * * * * * * * * * * * *

Justin returned to his office to find a seated visitor waiting for his return. Wilbert smiled as he said, "I asked Miss Evans here to remain and repeat her story for you. I think you'll find it most interesting."

"Good morning, Miss, I'm at your disposal." Marsha Evans was the proprietor of Evans Haberdashery on downtown Main Street, dealing in all types of gentlemen's accessories.

"Well, Marshal, it's like I told your deputy. I felt I should drop by this morning and tell you of a strange occurrence that happened this week. My first customer on Monday morning was a young man I didn't know. He said he needed two tailored suits, six shirts, and a mixture of ties, hats, and gloves. Naturally, I quite skeptical as this would add up to a great deal of money, but I suspect he felt my suspicion because he casually withdrew a large bundle of cash from his pants pocket. I was thrilled with my good fortune and commenced to measure him. He didn't say much at first, so I did most of the talking. I promised to have everything ready for pickup after lunch on Wednesday.

"He then mentioned that his injured brother would also like a complete custom-fitted wardrobe. 'Tom was one of the men severely burned in the explosion at the Thompson Glass Factory recently,' he told me. 'If I brought in his measurements, could you use them to make his clothing fit properly?' I told him I wouldn't recommend doing so as there were bound to be small alterations my trained eye would catch, and for the costs involved, I recommended fitting him in person. He got quiet as if considering what to do. Then he told me he needed the clothes because he was taking his brother to Chicago on Sunday and that perhaps he could bring in his brother before then. Once I had completed his measurements, I asked for his name and address for my records. Here it is," she said, handing over a piece of paper.

"Lester Strong, 413 South D Street," Justin read out loud.

Miss Evans continued. "He paid with twenty-dollar bills. I assured him again that I'd have everything ready, and if his brother were physically up to it, I'd assist him, too. He then left my shop. So far, so good, Marshal, but there's more to come.

"On Wednesday, right after lunch, Mr. Strong came back, supporting the arm of a heavily bandaged man I assumed to be his brother. The poor man's head, face, and both hands were wrapped in bandages, with only his eyes and nose visible. The men looked over my display stocks, and the bandaged man pointed. Then he nodded yes or no to each item he was interested in purchasing. After measuring him as quickly but as accurately as I could, he sat in a chair, looking exhausted, while his brother paid. I promised to have the suits all ready for pickup today after lunch. The reason behind all of this is that I later remembered to check the serial numbers from the copy your deputy provided to me, and sure enough, two of the tens he used that day were on the list. Those were the only tens I took in on Wednesday." She handed them over. "Marshal, am I expected to absorb the loss of twenty dollars to my business?"

Justin ignored her question and checked the numbers for himself. Sure enough, there they were. "Can you give us a general description and age of this man?"

"I would guess twenty-one or twenty-two. He was tall, thin, and had no facial hair. I noticed his hands were very rough as if he's used to manual labor."

"Thank you for bringing this to our attention, Miss Evans. I must caution you not to speak about this to anyone, and when you see Mr. Strong again, try not to act any different that might give him cause for concern." She left to open her shop for the day.

"Want me to check up on this guy?" Wilbert asked.

Justin nodded, then wrote down the name and address on a note and handed it over. "Go see what the city records have on him. I'll call the personnel office at Thompson's and see if either of them has ever worked there." Wilbert left as Justin reached for the candlestick telephone on his desk. "Operator, this is Marshal Blake. Please connect me with the personnel office at Thompson's Glass Factory." Soon, he had his answer. Nobody by the name of Strong had ever been employed there. Justin poured himself a cup of coffee and sat to think things out. *I'm guessing that the address is a phony also. I think we'll be keeping an eye on this Lester Strong fellow.*

Wilbert soon returned. "The rent house at that address is owned by an old widow by the name of Bertha Lake. Of course, there's always the possibility the brothers are renters or family members, but my gut tells me we may finally be on to something."

"Mine too, and nobody by the name of Strong has ever been employed at Thompson's. Are you thinking about the possible identity of the bandaged man?"

"You mean that he's Steven Howell? Yes. I began to suspect it as soon as she told me the story. Without bandages, he would easily be recognized by someone in town. This way, he could move about under the pretense of being one of the explosion victims. How convenient." Wilbert went over to the corner and started thumbing through old copies of the Journal until he found one detailing the explosion. "Here it is. The names of the three men injured in the explosion were William Schultz, Thomas Jones, and William Freeman. Thomas Jones, Thomas Strong; A coincidence? It also says that the injured men were treated and released."

"Doctor Maxwell?"

"Probably," Justin said as he picked up the telephone again and asked the operator to connect him with the well-known town physician. Maxwell answered on the third ring. "Doctor Maxwell, this is Justin Blake. I have an official question to ask you. Did you treat the men who were recently burned in that explosion at Thompson's?"

"Yes, Marshal. There were three injured, one with serious burns to his face, ears, neck, and hands. Why do you ask?"

"Did you recognize him as someone you've seen around town?"

"No, I can't say I've ever seen him before. I wanted to keep him for additional treatment and observation, but the man's brother was determined to take him home. I tried to warn him of the risks of the wounds becoming infected, but he assured me he was capable of caring for his brother without additional help and left."

Justin thanked him for the information and hung up the receiver. "Well, that puts the Steven Howell theory to rest. Maxwell certainly would have recognized him as he's a family friend of the Howells. I think we still need to check up on Mr. Strong, so let's position ourselves across the street from the Haberdashery around noon this afternoon and monitor his arrival and departure to his real residence. So go get yourself an early lunch. Also, check over your weapon, just in case. I'm going over and speak with 'Squire Williamson now about the possibility of getting a search warrant."

CHAPTER 44
THE SUSPECT

Wilbert Vance positioned himself directly across the street in the shadows of the entry door to the bakery. At the same time, Justin Blake hid in an adjacent alleyway with a clear view of the Haberdashery. Finally, just before one o'clock, a lone figure approached from the west and entered the shop. He matched the description given by Marsha Evans. A few minutes later, the man departed, carrying two large cardboard suit boxes. Both lawmen casually stayed apart and kept some distance from their suspect as they followed. The man continued walking back westward, then turned north onto Grant Street, and after two blocks, entered a small house. *So much for the fake address*, Justin thought. *The shed where it appeared Steven was held is just up the street on the edge of a wheat field. How convenient.* Justin had been unable to obtain a search warrant since the suspect's property address was unknown, but entry could be made if there was probable cause.

"Wilbert, we're dealing with at least two men and maybe more. I wonder if a little backup might be helpful," Justin said. "Since we're so close to Brad's gas station, see if he's available to help us. I'll stand watch until you return." Wilbert thought it was a wise idea and left. Justin saw that the front blinds of the house were all drawn shut. *The more I think about this, the more I'm convinced these are our kidnappers.*

Wilbert entered the office of the service station only to find it empty. He walked out into the service bay and saw a pair of legs sticking out from under an automobile. Wilbert lightly nudged one of the exposed boots and said, "Is that you, Brad? It's Wilbert."

The night deputy slid out from under the auto and began wiping grease off his hands with a shop rag. "Hey, what's up?"

"Justin sent me to see if you could help us." He then briefly explained everything up to the point of the house on Grant Street. The mechanic smiled. "You bet I'll help!" Realizing that his weapon was back inside his bedroom, Brad grabbed a crowbar from the workbench and placed his 'Sorry, We're Closed' sign on the window. "I'm ready, let's go."

After a brisk walk, the pair saw Justin standing across the street behind a tree. "Thanks for your assistance, Brad," Justin said. "Here's the plan. Brad and I will approach the front door, and I'll identify myself while Wilbert covers the rear door. Have your weapon ready, as anything might happen. Hopefully, he'll open up, and there won't be any trouble. Questions?" There were none. "All right, let's get in place. I'll yell loud enough for you to hear me when we move in," he said to Wilbert, who then circled behind the house.

Justin stood before the door and was about to knock when Brad motioned for him to move over to the side. *Yea, better safe than sorry.* Brad took his crowbar and pounded hard three times. Justin shouted, "Gas City Police! Open up!" They waited for about thirty seconds before Brand pounded the crowbar again. This time, pieces of the thin door exploded as three bullets passed through. The close call startled Justin. Brad jammed the edge of his crowbar between the frame and lock and popped the door open. Two more shots rang out from inside. Justin couldn't make out where the shooter was, so he dived through the doorway onto his stomach as he fired his pistol twice. Both shots went high, and he could make out the figure of the shooter aiming for his prone figure. Justin knew he was about to die.

Suddenly, the shooter screamed and grabbed his face in pain. Brad had managed to throw the crowbar, striking the shooter squarely on the nose. Blood gushed between the shooter's fingers as he stumbled back and fell to the floor. Justin was quickly on him, taking the gun, cuffing his wrists, and searching for any hidden weapons. They heard pounding at the back door, so Brad went into the kitchen just as Wilbert was shattering the door's small glass window, trying to enter, and opened it for him.

"I heard shots. Is Justin all right?" Wilbert asked, his eyes wide.

Brad said Justin had the situation under control. Spying a dish towel, he grabbed it, reentered the room, and began applying it against the broken nose of the shooter.

"My brother's very sick and needs to see a doctor," the injured man managed to say.

Wilbert searched the house. "There's a bandaged man lying on the bed in there. I checked and he's not armed."

"Wilbert, find a telephone and call for Doctor Maxwell. Ask the neighbors if they have a telephone you can use."

"All right, you," Justin demanded. "What's your real name? None of that Strong nonsense either."

"You broke my nose!" the injured man complained.

"And you tried to kill me. Now, I'll ask you one more time, what's your real name!"

"I'm Lester Floyd, and he's my brother Thomas. He needs a doctor, please. Tom hasn't spoken all day, and I'm worried about him."

"I sent a man to call the doctor for your brother." *Now, the big question.* "What did you do with Steven Howell?"

Lester Floyd hesitated, and Justin's frustration only grew.

"If you want your brother treated, you better answer the marshal, pronto," Brad said with authority in his voice.

"Outback. His body is in the fruit cellar. We had no choice. He was trying to back out of our deal," the dejected man stated. Brad left to investigate and returned a few minutes later coughing, looking pale, and waving fresh air into his face. He nodded to the marshal, confirming Lester's story was true. The case had gone from a kidnapping to a murder.

"Where's the bank's money?" Justin asked.

"Under Tom's bed. It's still inside the suitcase we used. We didn't spend all that much of it, and if it hadn't been for his terrible injuries at the factory, we'd be long gone, Marshal." Brad went into the bedroom, got on his knees, and located the suitcase. It was still packed with paper wrappers identifying The First National Bank.

Wilbert returned. "Doctor's been called and is on his way." He then joined Brad in looking over the money. It was more than either of them had ever seen before.

A carriage pulled up outside, and Brad waved the doctor in, pointing to the bedroom where Tom Floyd lay. After a brief examination, Doctor Maxwell returned to the living area.

"He's dead. And from the looks and the smell, I would guess he died from an infection. His wounds have not been kept clean or his bandages changed, like I instructed your prisoner here to do. I'll know for sure after I examine the body later. I'll send a couple of men to pick it up."

The prisoner burst into tears. "You better look at his nose too, Doc," Justin said.

After a brief examination, he said, "It's broken. Just keep clean compresses on it until the bleeding stops. It'll look worse than it is. Expect bruising and maybe a black eye or two."

"Also, there's a body out back in a fruit cellar. We were told it was Steven Howell." Doctor Maxwell and Wilbert then went outside.

Justin reached over to shake Brad's hand. "You and your trusty crowbar were a big help to me today. Thanks! By the way, how's the Haynes-Apperson car business these days?"

"It's just the Apperson Car Company now, and so far, we've sold three automobiles!"

Soon, both bodies were removed, and Justin and Wilbert, with a suitcase full of bank money, escorted their prisoner to the jail. Once Doctor Maxwell called and confirmed it was indeed Steven Howell, Justin grabbed his hat and made his way to the bank to inform James Howell of the bad news about his son and that most of the stolen money had been found.

CHAPTER 45
LIVING WITH THE TRUTH

One of the hardest things Justin has ever had to do was inform James Howell that not only his son Steven was dead but that the young man was named, by the prisoner, as an accessory in the phony kidnapping and bank extortion. When he heard the news, he seemed as if the life force had been drained from him, and Justin was concerned that he might collapse or have a heart attack.

Finally, he looked up from his desk and said, "I don't know how Jane will take this. It will break her heart. If that's all, Marshal, I need to go home now."

After returning to his office, Justin couldn't help but stare at the accused murderer before reaching for his telephone and asking the operator to connect him with the Grant County Sheriff. After identifying himself, he explained everything that happened and that a prisoner was safely behind bars. Justin was congratulated on solving the murder and bank extortion plot and that two deputies would be dispatched tomorrow afternoon to escort the prisoner to the Marion jail. Wilbert entered the office, and Justin told him to go home, that he'd handle everything until Deputy Davis came in at seven o'clock. Wilbert thanked him and left. For the rest of his remaining shift,

Justin didn't feel like doing anything and just sat drinking coffee. Thirty minutes until his relief would arrive, a visitor entered the marshal's office. It was James Howell. "I just wanted to see the face of the man who murdered my son," he said to Justin.

The prisoner stood up and said, "So, you're the rich banker. Ha! You ain't much to look at!"

Suddenly, the banker pulled a pistol from underneath his coat and pointed it at his son's killer. Justin reacted quickly and got between Howell and the prisoner.

"Put that gun away, Mr. Howell!"

"Sorry, Marshal. I feel I must do this, as he's destroyed our happy home."

Lester Floyd started laughing. "Happy home, you say! That's a riot, old man. Happiness for you is your twenty-four-hour businessman mode you couldn't leave at the office, making Steven miserable. Oh yes, I've heard about you. You and you alone brought all that pain and misery into Steven's life. From an early age, it was you who demanded your son follow your path in life. You had his entire life planned out for him: work in a bank to gain a taste of business for counting nickels and dimes, enroll in a business course at a college Steven didn't even want to attend, then follow in your footsteps at your stupid bank. Yes, you pushed and pushed but failed to listen to your son's pleas, his desire to make his own way in life. Many times, he told us that he begged you to allow him to attend a locomotive engineer conductor training program; that was his life's dream. But no, you ran his dream down as his dream wasn't good enough for the son of an important vice president of a bank! You were molding him to one day fill your shoes. That's all that mattered to a father who refused to even listen to, love, and support his only son. I may be the one who ended his life, but you began that very slow process years ago. So, go ahead and shoot me, Mr. Important Banker. Then it will be you that hangs from the gallows and not me!"

Howell stood motionless, finally letting the words he had refused to listen to for years be uttered by a stranger. He slowly lowered the gun, then laid it on the marshal's desk.

Relieved, Justin said, "Go home, Mr. Howell, and comfort your wife. She needs you now more than ever." The banker nodded and left as he contemplated what he now realized about himself was the truth. This day, and those to follow, would be a painful memory involving deep regret. Justin never mentioned the incident to anyone.

* * * * * * * * * * * * * * *

The funeral of Steven Howell was well attended by the townspeople. Due to the condition of the body, there was no open viewing. This was especially hard for his parents, forced now to say goodbye to a sealed brown casket. The bank's board of directors attended in a show of support and solidarity for their vice president. In time, the bank's blanket bond insurance covered the two hundred dollars the Floyd brothers had spent.

* * * * * * * * * * * * * * *

One day, an envelope addressed to Marsha Evans arrived in the mail. There was no return address. Upon opening it, she found two ten-dollar bills wrapped in a blank sheet of paper.

CHAPTER 46
-EPILOGUE-

Lester and Thomas Floyd
During Happier Days

After a few days in confinement at the Grant County Jail in Marion, prisoner Lester Floyd asked to make a statement. The sheriff's office was more than happy to provide a stenographer. The prisoner was brought to the interrogation room and offered his full confession. This is what he said:

"My name is Lester Floyd. My younger brother Thomas and I were born at our parent's small farm north of Pendleton, Indiana. We grew up doing hard labor, as farmer's sons are expected to do. But we each hated it and dreamed of a time when we could leave it all behind and make our way in life. Our father inherited the property from his father, and Pa naturally assumed we would one day pass it on to our future children. He just couldn't come to grips with what we told him; we didn't want any part of farming. Pa was a great believer in using the leather strap to get his way, as was his own Pa. I'm a man of twenty-two years, and Tom was twenty. We were long past being beaten by a strap for small infractions, or we should have been. But not in Pa's eyes. Then, one evening, he came at me with his strap while Tom and I were out in the barn. It was over some silly indiscretion I had made, but this time, I refused his punishment, and we fought. After Pa went back to the house, I told Tom I had enough and was leaving that night. My brother said he'd go also, but we didn't have any cash. I suggested we take the money Ma stashed in her cookie jar on the pantry shelf. After they were asleep, I pocked the sixty-two dollars while Tom saddled our old workhorse, and together, we rode away for good. I'm telling you all this to give you a better understanding of what drove us into a life of crime.

"We finally arrived in the big city of Muncie. We sold the broken-down horse for ten dollars and rented a small rundown apartment there. From that point on, I became Lester Smith, and he was Thomas Jones; we were not brothers but only friends. Soon, we needed more cash, and I hit upon an idea. Just down the street was a family-owned grocery store. The owner had a lovely young daughter named Mary, probably about sixteen years of age. The local boys were infatuated with her. She appeared to have a new beau every evening. Together, Tom and I sent a letter to the owner, saying that

I saw his daughter with a young man in the back seat of an automobile parked in a secluded forest and that she was in a compromising position if you follow my drift. Earlier that day we saw her blue flowered dress hanging on their clothesline, so I described it in detail and that she had removed it completely from her young body. The letter then went on to say that I would forget what I had witnessed for a hundred dollars. Otherwise, all his customers, friends, and neighbors would hear the story. He was instructed to hide the cash in a secluded location, and he had only twenty-four hours to decide. A father's deep desire to protect the reputation of his young daughter came into play, and sure enough, we found the cash. I have often wondered if her unchaperoned evening dating had come to a screeching halt. We tried the same routine with a few other businessmen but achieved mixed results.

"We grew restless and one day decided to purchase two train tickets to Gas City. That little town is the talk of the state right now with all the gas and oil business, so I figured we might score big there. Once we arrived, we rented a little house on Grant Street, but after a few days of just walking the town, I suggested we get jobs to fit in. That way, we would meet people and find some bigger prey, no more hundred-dollar con jobs. Tom got a job at the new Thompson plant while I worked as a teamster. It was about then that we met Steven Howell. Tom recognized him as a bank teller, and came up with the idea to rob the bank. The young man seemed lonely, so we did our best to become his trusted friends during the evening hours at our house. He soon opened up about being forced down a career path he hated and told us of his love for locomotives and a training school he wanted to attend. In this respect, Tom and I could relate to his pain as our Pa's seemed cut from the same hard mold.

"One evening, we outlined a new plan that would involve him being kidnapped and held for a ten-thousand-dollar ransom. I told him, 'It's the banks' money, not your parents, so no real harm would come of it.' Split three ways, he could go where he pleased, take whatever training course he wanted, and have ample money to live on, and nobody would be the wiser. Steven liked the idea and agreed to the plan. I began scouring the area, looking for any abandoned outdoor location to stage the supposed kidnapping, and found the perfect little shed on the edge of a field. One night, I snatched an old chair off a person's back porch and placed it in the shed. Then, the following night, the three of us went inside and stomped all around, leaving heavy tracks, pieces of cut rope, his pocket watch, and a gag cloth. We then returned to our house, and I wrote the kidnapping letter, which Steven signedand delivered after dark to his parent's door. From that point on, he lived with us, and the suitcase full of money. What he didn't know was that Tom and I decided a two-way split was far better than a three-way one. He was also showing signs of backing out of our deal. And like many of the local homes, we also had a small unused fruit cellar out back. After dark, we got him drunk, and we took him out to the cellar after he passed out, tied him up tightly, and gagged his mouth. This was where he would eventually die. We suspected that the train stations and trolley cars were being monitored closely, so we decided to just sit tight and wait a few more days until we could depart for Fort Wayne. I had it all worked out, and it would have worked, too, but the next morning, there was an explosion at the factory, and Tom got seriously injured. We obtained clothing for the journey, but Tom's burns got worse. I just couldn't go off and leave him and I was afraid to call a doctor, so I just waited. Somehow, the town's police suspected me, and the rest is history. We both liked Steven, but he was young and might return home to his mommy one day and give up our names to the authorities. No, we just couldn't take that chance. In retrospect, I wish now that I'd taken that beating, and then Tom would be alive, and I wouldn't be facing the hangman's rope."

The End

Dear Readers:

The following short story came to me one day recently and has nothing to do with my normal historical fiction, murder mystery series. It's a bit of science fiction set in what was Indiana in the not-too-distant future. I hope you will give it a chance and read it to completion. p.s. If you do enjoy my books, I would greatly appreciate positive reviews on Amazon. Thank you!

Alan E Losure

Alan E. Losure

THEN CAME THE MIGHTY HUNTERS

CAST OF CHARACTERS

Chieftain Samuel	Leader of the River Rats Tribe
Vice-Chieftain Paula	Tribal Advisor, River Rats
Survivor Lee	Honored Guest Speaker
Chieftain Elder	Founding Father of all Tribes
Chieftain Jor-EL	Leader of the Giants Tribe
Advisor Tiger	Friend of Jor-EL
Fieldhand Audrey	Ex-Advisor for the Giants Tribe
Ex-Fieldhand Trent	New Member of the Security Detail
Ex-Minister Noah	Firewood Provider
Chieftain Del	Jones Tribe Leader
Chieftain Ken	New Leader of the Swayzee Tribe

CHAPTER 1
THE MEETING

The vast number of twinkling stars shone down from the heavenly, dark sky like miniature campfires. One could easily spend a lifetime attempting to count their number, but they would fail. The vastness of God's creation could not even be imagined or explained. Still, every beam of starlight gave hope to those who continued to remain alive and pray for a better future for their children. Such was the case of the River Rats Tribe. That night, men and women sat side by side in a large circle, eager to hear the purpose of the hastily called tribal council meeting. As usual, a large bonfire burned brightly at the center of the group, providing light and warmth. Soon, the flap of a large ceremonial tent opened, and two people emerged. A man and a woman. The man was Samuel, Chieftain of the River Rats Tribe. The woman was Paula, Vice-Chieftain and Samual's right-hand advisor for all tribal matters. Both remained standing in the vacant places left for them by tribal members. Silence gripped the assembled group as they waited patiently to hear the words spoken by their leaders.

"Peace and joy to all of you," a smiling Samuel said as he clutched his right fist and touched it over his heart before extending the arm outward in a salute of respect to his people. The members of the Tribe returned the salute. "Vice-Chieftain Paula has an important announcement to make, and I encourage you all to listen carefully."

Paula enjoyed her position of authority, a rare one for a woman. It was not handed to her because of her good looks or sex but earned through countless hours of hard work and dedication to the tribe. After sensing everyone's attention, she began to speak. "We received wonderful news today from a scout from The Tribe of the Many Lakes who informed us that an original survivor and his party will arrive here sometime tomorrow morning. His name is Survivor Lee, and he wishes to speak before our council tomorrow night.

"As you know, there are fewer and fewer original survivors left, as many died within the moon's first full cycle or changed into the wild beasts of the night. We have been reassured that Survivor Lee has a clear memory of *The Great Before* and that he has made this his life's work now to travel and speak among the different tribes and share his important message with our youth." She turned and addressed two council members directly by name. "Teachers Rachel and Philip, please direct all your students from ages six to eighteen seasons that they must be present. We also encourage everyone else to participate in this extremely rare opportunity. We were told there would be a question-and-answer session afterward, a rare chance to learn the truth from someone who witnessed and survived that period known as *The Annihilation* firsthand." Both teachers nodded their compliance. The Vice-Chieftain then sat.

All eyes fell upon the middle-aged Chieftain. "We recently experienced an unprovoked raid on Stockman Harris's farm, which, sits near our established boundary with the Giants Tribe. Stockman Harris said he heard a loud commotion in his barn late one evening and, upon investigating, discovered two unknown young men later identified as members of the Giants Tribe, who were attempting to steal his donkey. Stockman Harris captured them, and Arbitrator Donna was contacted to help resolve this issue with their tribe's arbitrator. Since the donkey was not harmed, the Giants Tribe agreed to hand over two hens as compensation for the attempted theft and pledged to punish the young men. I wish to thank her for her efforts in preventing this situation from getting out of hand. The last thing any of us needs is a return to the terrible days of raids upon each other's tribal assets." Many heads, male and female, nodded. "Does anyone else have anything they wish to bring up?"

Doctor Neal stood. "Yes, Chieftain Samual. I recently treated two small sisters who drank contaminated water directly from the river. Everyone here must understand that river water must be boiled before consumption, or a serious illness such as Cholera or Typhoid Fever may develop. Luckily, I was called in time, and am pleased to report that the children are on the road to full recovery. Parents, warn your children of this danger. That is all I have to say." He then sat back down. Seeing that there was no other subject to discuss, the tribal council meeting was concluded.

A few people remained to speak about unimportant subjects until finally returning to their lodgings. "I'll see to it that ample food is provided for our honored visitors and bedding placed in the ceremonial tent, as I'm sure our aged guest will be quite tired upon his arrival," Paula said before leaving for her family's farm. Samuel was tired but excited about the upcoming visit. He walked the short distance across the old, dilapidated street toward his family's place of lodging. It was also occupied by their son, his wife, and their three small children. Life was normal for large families to live together these days, but he knew this had not always been the case. Samuel had seen old photographs of beautifully cared-for homes, strangely cut grassy yards, and people wearing clean, well-fitting clothing made by others. There were only two other places of lodging nearby. An old high school with a strange-sounding name had once stood on this now-vacant land. It had been torn down long ago and its bricks scavenged. Samual should know, as he had been known as Bricklayer

Samuel before being chosen as the tribe's chieftain and had done much of the recovery work himself. Why he was chosen as chieftain had always confused him. *Others are more worthy of this honor than myself,* he thought.

CHAPTER 2
THE ARRIVAL

The sun had reached full height when a small caravan of people came from the north and approached the assembled group there to welcome them. All were walking, with one older man being lead on a horse. Chieftain Samuel gave a salute to the new arrivals. It was returned. "Peace and joy to you, Survivor Lee, and welcome to the River Rats Tribe. My name is Chieftain Samuel. Please, sit yourself here in this comfortable chair. We have ample food and drink for all your party. This tent has also been equipped with bedding should you desire to rest before tonight's meeting."

"Peace and joy to you also, Chieftain Samuel," the old man replied as two members of his group assisted him off the horse and walked with him to the waiting seat. "Ah, much better! Your chair is a lot more comfortable than the back of my horse," he joked. Survivor Lee was handed a plate of smoked pork, potatoes, bread, and a drink before the others were served. All the newcomers seemed impressed. "You're too kind," the old man said. "This truly is a feast to behold. You should have seen the skimpy food the Giants Tribe offered us to eat days ago." He began to devour his meal as if he hadn't eaten in a long time. "Aren't you eating Chieftain Samuel?"

Samuel smiled. "I ate early to ensure all was ready for your group's needs. We are very excited to hear your talk tonight."

"Do you have any survivors in your tribe?"

"We had an elderly woman who passed away a few seasons ago, but her mind just wasn't there, if you understand my meaning."

"Yes, I most certainly do. Many who did survive simply could not cope with the massive changes that occurred during and after *The Annihilation*. I was one of the lucky ones who managed to live and bend to the new ways. Oh, while I'm thinking about it, I suggest your tribe form a close ring around me tonight so that all can hear my words and for me to hear their questions. I'm just not the young man I used to be," he grinned.

"That will be done, Survivor Lee. In the meantime, feel free to relax and take a nap. Blankets and a pillow are inside the ceremonial tent for your convenience. So, unless you have any questions, I'll leave you now to rest up." The survivor thanked him and was soon sound asleep.

By early evening, the crowd began to assemble. The comfortable chair had been brought inside the tent for Survivor Lee's comfort as he visited with his family group and began making plans for their upcoming journey and talk at the Deaner Tribe. Food was again provided for everyone as he waited to be introduced. *I wonder why these people called themselves 'the River Rats Tribe?'* Survivor Lee pondered.

CHAPTER 3
THE GREAT BEFORE

The eager crowd assembled as directed and waited patiently for the appearance of their anticipated speaker. A few times, Chieftain Samuel and Vice-Chieftain Paula directed those sitting too far out to move closer inside the circle. Finally, satisfied that all appeared ready, Samuel whispered a few words inside the tent, then stood to the side, ready to make the appropriate introductions. The flap of the tent was pushed open, and two men carried the comfortable chair outside and placed it facing the audience. They then re-entered and assisted the aged man outside and safely into the chair. Samuel knew it was now time. "My friends, we are honored to have with us tonight a man, a survivor, who lived during The Great Before who will tell us much about life during that time. I ask that you join me in welcoming to our tribe … Survivor Lee."

"Peace and joy to all of you," the old man said in a strong voice. "On behalf of my traveling family, we wish to thank you for your kind hospitality." The old man paused and looked deeply into the smiling faces of the assembled young people. He then continued. "I was born Leeland Edward Walker in the year 1972 in Huntington, Indiana." He paused again to view the expressions on most of the faces. "I realize that using a full name is outdated today, as well as identifying dates that are no longer important and seldom used. I always begin my presentation this way to demonstrate to my audience how so much has changed since *The Annihilation* nearly ended mankind's existence. If you bear with me, I will address a few of those differences I feel are worth discussing. It is my earnest hope that all of you have learned to read and write and, just as important, read every old book you can lay your hands on. I realize many of the reading subjects are strange since our places of lodging are no longer powered by the wonders of electricity. But please, read and learn anyway, and perhaps one day, some of those conveniences you read about may become a reality once again.

"One big difference between back then and now is … time. During *The Great Before*, time controlled everything. Seconds, minutes, hours, days, weeks, months. Time controlled how people lived. You would wake up at a certain time, eat at a certain time, go to work at a certain time, leave work at a certain time, well into the evening when you spend your time playing with your smartphone or watching television until bedtime. Then, the next day repeated itself. Today, we awake in our lodging at sunrise, work until the sun goes down, and then go to sleep after dark. Ask yourselves this: which system seems less stressful? And speaking of smartphones, if a person back then misplaced their phone or lost their connection to the internet, the owner often went near crazy until the system was up and running again. Worldwide communication may sound like a fairy tale to you, but I assure you, it did exist, and people at that time were obsessed with it.

"Another subject I should mention is food. A large portion of our population back then was overweight. Food was abundant everywhere. Just lay down money or a plastic card, and you could have all you wanted to eat, everything imaginable under the sun. Grocery store shelves were packed full of items to choose from. Not just one selection but many different versions of the same item. These foods were generally not produced locally but trucked in from faraway locations. This system worked great as long as food could be transported safely and securely. When that system failed, people starved.

"I don't wish to give you the wrong impression about life back then. It was the best of times in many ways. I could purchase an airline ticket in the morning, fly across the ocean to Europe, and arrive that afternoon. A total of twelve men walked on the surface of the moon. I have watched the films many times, so don't let anyone tell you it didn't happen. One could order an item, let's say a heavy blanket off the internet, and it would be delivered to your door in a day or two. You could plan a family vacation in Florida and drive the entire way, knowing there would be ample food, gasoline, and lodging. Sports were an important part of people's lives. Movies, weddings, television, concerts, there was always something going on if you looked for it. Of course, we lived our lives in fear of nuclear war from our enemies: Russia, China, North Korea, and Iran. I swear, if there were only two men left on the Earth, they would eventually try to kill each other. I guess that about does it. Are there any questions now about life during *The Great Before?*"

There were many, some serious, while a few were rather silly. Still, Survivor Lee did his best to answer each one as thoroughly as possible.

"I now come to the difficult part of my presentation, where I'll try to describe the events leading up to *The Annihilation* as I experienced and heard firsthand from other survivors. I cannot vouch for the accuracy of everything, but I feel this to be a good representation of what little was known at the time." Survivor Lee paused and drank from the glass of water he'd been handed by one of his people. With a nod of thanks, he continued.

"My friends, we never stood a chance. The attack came completely out of nowhere; I heard from the few surviving military personnel later on that all of our air, sea, land, and space and military capabilities were eliminated in a matter of minutes. One must also assume the same occurrences happened throughout the rest of the world. On that day of infamy, I was living and working in a small northern Indiana town called Angola. I remember waking up to the sight of massive, flashing lights like bolts of energy outside my bedroom window. Pulling back the curtains, I saw the sky was full of beams of intense light, lightning if you will, emanating from the sky. These covered the entire skyline, and I thought I could hear faraway rumblings of heavy thunder in the distance. Just as quickly, the power went off. Suspecting a major storm was about to hit, I sought shelter in my apartment's bathroom but soon realized this was a storm unlike anything I had ever witnessed. Suspecting the worst, I jumped into my shower while I still had hot water and dressed, ready to stay put or leave. If I were to die, I would do so clean and dressed, not in my pajamas. The bolts of energy became even more numerous, and dark smoke filled the sky. I was truly terrified. After hearing loud voices in the hallway, I saw other renters and joined them, hoping to discover what exactly was going on. Most suspected this to be a bad storm or tornado tearing up our town, while one man kept saying, 'We are under attack!' His words terrified the assembled group but later, unfortunately, proved to be true.

"We were soon joined by other attendants who felt the hallway was our safest place to be. One man brought a small battery-powered radio, but nothing was being broadcast … only static. He ran the complete dial, and we still couldn't hear anything. At that point, I knew this was more dire than any weather storm. By mid-afternoon, it seemed that most of the light flashes had ended, but heavy smoke filled the air, making breathing very difficult. Occasionally, we could hear explosions, which seemed to be drawing even closer to us. While I tried not to show it, I was terrified. By early evening, the light flashes seemed to end, but a new, more deadly force was about to be unleashed: *The Silver Hunter Orbs.*

"Explosions and fires wracked the night as what seemed like millions of silver orbs floating through the air near the ground emitted their own small but just as deadly beams of light. We called them hunter orbs as they seemed intent on vaporizing large groups of people fleeing from their presence. These were the hunters who destroyed the population of small towns and villages. I watched one instance through the broken hallway window, where an orb went out of its way to vaporize three people attempting to run from a building on fire. Killing men, women, and children appeared to be a hunting sport to '*The Demons from Above*,' as we came to call them. To the best of my knowledge, nobody I later spoke with ever claimed to have seen one of their kind in person, as they remained safely tucked away inside their protected orbs. The battles continued to rage into the next day, but by evening, an eerie silence gripped the land. The orbs had disappeared. Fires continued to rage unchecked, and our group decided it was time to make our escape before our building was inflamed. If we thought the worst had passed, we would soon learn otherwise.

"Obtaining food became a priority for everyone who survived. Gangs of armed militant men and women soon broke into buildings still containing food and began killing other gangs to obtain their resources. Stocked supplies quickly disappeared, so the gangs invaded individual homes, killing the occupants if their hidden resources were not produced. Perhaps the reason *The Demons from Above* did not finish exterminating all of mankind was that they knew enough about us that we'd eventually do it to ourselves. Men and women who, weeks before, were normal, hard-working citizens had reverted into wild animals, willing to kill anyone for a mouthful of grain. Farms were attacked, and livestock was slaughtered. It was feared that all wildlife would soon become extinct and doom mankind to follow shortly after. Even house pets disappeared.

"You should understand that most survivors knew nothing about raising corn, wheat, or caring for livestock. Just as all seemed hopeless, one great man stepped forward. His name, as you already know, was Chieftain Elder. He brought together a small band of survivors and convinced them that to live, each must learn to rely upon the works of the other. In this, The Tribe of Hope was formed, and he, its elected chieftain. Elder brought farmers, stockmen, seamstresses, carpenters, and other skills together to teach their knowledge to the untrained ex-townspeople. Work assignments were issued so that the occupation assigned would appear before the person's first name. For example, John Smith became Stockman Smith. Schools were instituted, and anyone with medical skills became a doctor. Before long, his tribe became self-sustaining, and confidence among members grew. Now possessing the needed agricultural skills, volunteers stepped forward to pass on tools and skills on to other gangs so they could form a successful tribe as well. Many were killed, but eventually, these efforts produced rich results, and raids between warring groups diminished and eventually ended. Today, peaceful tribes co-exist next to each other and work together in harmony for the betterment of all. We must continue to build upon the great works of Chieftain Elder, and perhaps one day, a better world will result. Thank you. Are there any other questions?"

There were several, but one stood out in particular. "How did you become a wandering historian?" a middle-aged man asked.

"It's funny you should ask that. You see, one night last fall, I had a vivid dream. In it, I saw myself and a group of friends going between the tribes and telling stories about life during *The Great Before*. Then, for the next several nights, I had the same reoccurring dream. Finally, I spoke with a few trusted members of my tribe, and I told them God was calling me for this mission in life. They tried to talk me out of it since I was approaching eighty seasons in age, but I was determined to give it my best try. So far, I have spoken with nearly all the tribes in the northern sector and am now working southward. Just a few days ago, I spoke to your neighbors, the Giants Tribe. My next goal, Lord willing, will be the Deaner's Tribe, then continue onward wherever I am welcome. As a survivor, I feel it's important to tell my story so that our history will not be lost."

Sensing it was time to bring the meeting to a close, Chieftain Samuel thanked their speaker and dismissed their assembled tribal members to return to their lodging. "Peace and joy to all of you," the visibly tired old man uttered as people began leaving when a small child stepped forward to asked a question.

"But will *The Demons from Above* return?" The child's serious question had to go unanswered.

"I bet there'll be a few nightmares tonight," Vice-Chieftain Paula whispered to Samuel. He nodded in full agreement. Samuel pulled one of the aids to the side. "Please enjoy our hospitality tonight. There are plenty of logs to keep the fire going, and we'll provide something for you to all eat before you leave tomorrow."

"Thank you, Chieftain," the man said. "You have no idea how much we appreciate everything you have done to meet our needs. Your hospitality is sure different here than we experienced in the Giants Tribe. Talk about a cold reception! And what little food was offered seemed to even upset a few. You could see it in their faces. My gut feeling is they are having serious difficulty. Even their clothing appeared more ragged and dirtier than most of the tribes we have visited. Well, goodnight, and thanks again."

That night, Chieftain Samuel was unable to sleep as the statement made about the Giants Tribe kept resonating over and over within his mind. *I just can't shake the feeling that there's gonna be trouble.*

Alan E. Losure

CHAPTER 4
TROUBLE BREWING

It had all been so easy. Last fall, when the old chieftain of the Giants Tribe lay dying, Fieldhand Jor-EL and his band of thugs began plotting a takeover. Three of Jor-EL's associates paid the Vice-Chieftain a friendly visit at the man's lodging to encourage him to step aside. After receiving a severe beating, the vice-chieftain promptly resigned from his tribal position. In reality, Jor-El hadn't even waited until the chieftain passed away before announcing he would become the new tribal leader. His first official act was to abolish the position of Vice-Chieftain and appoint his friend Fieldhand Tiger as Advisor Tiger. The remaining roughens then became members of Jor-EL's personal security detail. The first thing Advisor Tiger suggested was to host a celebration party to win over the tribe with a brief increase in their food allotment. The announcement of added food to their daily ration had indeed proven very popular, but a few warned the tribe might be facing a hard winter of reduced rations if this grand party was carried out. The security detail quickly silenced those voices. Seeing certain advantages, more and more young men and a few women began siding with Jor-EL's bunch, with a few new members added daily. Realizing that bad times had indeed returned, the remaining members of the tribe could only continue to work hard and hope that, somehow, things would eventually work out.

The attempted theft of the donkey from the nearby farm had also been a ploy to test the resolve of the River Rats Tribe, and Jor-EL had been very pleased to see their first impulse was to negotiate a settlement rather than the urge to fight for their property. Of course, there would be no delivery of the promised two hens, and the young men, members of his security detail, were rewarded, not punished.

"It's only right that we, as the largest tribe in the area, have the greatest resources," Jor-EL told his advisor. "Continue to have our men collect every rifle, shotgun, pistol, bullet, and even bows and arrows from our population and store everything here in the basement of the old city jail building. I've decided to move into the old sheriff's office. You are welcome to sleep in one of the empty rooms if you like. Also, start moving our people into those old jail cells for living quarters. Force out any riffraff that might already be there out on the street. Also, obtain as many local women as you need to prepare meals for all of us daily. We're lucky this place was built with masonry blocks, unlike those metal ones that didn't last. Once we're fully armed, we won't need to worry about any future resistance from the tribe, or any other tribe for that matter."

"Yes, I fully agree. I'll instruct the men we want everything collected quickly, but there may be some scattered resistance," Tiger replied.

"Break a few heads if need be. That should put an end to any challenge to my authority. Then, fully armed, we'll display a show of power to that little Swayzee Tribe and demand they fork over half of their corn, grain, poultry, horses, and livestock, or we'll come in and take all we want and let um' eat grass," Jor-EL said.

"What about the River Rats Tribe?"

Jor-EL smiled. "We'll move on them soon enough. The main thing now is to train our men to shoot at what they aim for. Bullets speak louder than words, my friend. But, in the meantime, I need you to send two of our female recruits into the Swayzee Tribe's area to obtain information on who their leaders are, where they lodge, food storage areas, poultry and livestock locations. I need their information returned within four sunsets. This will give the women a chance to prove their worth as spies. Once this knowledge is obtained, you and I can sit down and work out a plan to hit their tribal leadership fast and hard before anyone there has a chance to fight back."

Tiger liked what he was hearing. "It will be done as you say. Anything else?"

"No, not for the time being. Just get our people collecting the weapons. I want to see all our men walking around fully armed. That should stop any further complaints or trouble among our people." Tiger left. *Once Swayzee falls, word will spread quickly not to resist my efforts to merge other tribes into mine and eventually form a super tribe with thousands of armed men, women, and children, all under my authority!*

CHAPTER 5
A PLAN TAKES SHAPE

Oh, how the mighty have fallen. Fieldworker Audrey stood up, stretched, and rubbed the lower part of her aching back. At thirty-two seasons old, she felt as if her lower back would explode. *How do people do this day in and day out and not be crippled up for life?* she wondered. Her career in the Giants Tribe had gone from Seamstress Audrey to Advisor Audrey and now to this. Still, Audrey knew she didn't have a choice in the matter. This working title had been personally chosen for her by Chieftain Jor-EL, a man she considered a crazed, power-hungry man. If she had one last advisory word to give him, it would be, "Resign!"

"Hey you!" a voice sounded. "Get back to work." It was one of Jor-EL's thugs who was assigned to ensure the wheat crop was properly cut, turned, thoroughly dried, hand-pressed into box balers, and finally, hauled by wagon and placed within the overhead barn loft. Reluctantly, Audrey began using her rake to separate the wheat from the weeds and the man walked away. *Strange,* she thought. *I know him and his family. The power he and the others now hold over us has gone to his head.*

Several within the tribe had recently sought her council, but she had to remind them that she was only a fieldworker now and couldn't help anyone, even herself. Seeing the disappointment appear on their faces haunted her sleep. Great anger swept through her, knowing that Jor-EL and his thugs were eating all the food they wanted, with no thought as to the severity of the impact it would have on the people this winter. Hunger and starvation were soon to come unless something drastically changed. A rumor spread that morning that lodgings were being searched for weapons. This was not good. As she raked, a familiar voice near her broke her concentration. "Are we having fun yet?" It was her twenty-two seasons old step-brother, Carpenter Trent. She was happy to see him until she noticed he was carrying a scythe.

"You were demoted too?" she asked with sadness in her voice. Hardly anyone within the tribe knew they were related through marriage.

"It would seem so, or at least until our new dictator decides he needs a few leaking roof lodgings repaired." As he spoke, he pretended to be cutting with the scythe. "I saw you from a distance and worked my way over to see how you are doing."

"As well as anyone could expect, I guess. What are you hearing about lodges being searched for weapons?" she asked.

"It's true. They came to my humble dwelling this morning and searched. I didn't own any guns, but one fellow stole our father's smoking pipe. I can still picture him today, pretending to smoke that pipe even though we couldn't afford to trade for tobacco. The men were armed, so I couldn't say or do anything about it. Sis, what are we to do about this nightmare?"

"If only we had someone on the inside who could keep us informed about what Jor-EL is up to," she said.

Suddenly, a smile appeared on Trent's face. "That gives me an idea. Why don't I volunteer to join his happy band of wayward brothers, learn all I can, and then keep you informed? Does that sound workable to you?"

She paused before responding, and Trent knew she was concerned about his safety. "If they discover you are a secret mole, I fear what they may do to you. Also, once you are publicly accepted into their security detail, your friends and neighbors you've known all your life will despise and spit at you."

Trent's mind was set. "I need to try anyway. They may not take me, but I must attempt this. Well, I better move along before someone suspects I'm talking to you. Goodbye and be safe. If this works, I'll have to put on an evil act, you realize." He then worked himself away and was soon only a distant figure in the field.

By the end of the day, Trent approached one of the security team members. "How do I join your merry band anyway? I'm ready to change teams." Trent's name was written down on a clipboard.

"Just show up here tomorrow and work until you're called." Trent could only wait and hope from now on. He was told to report to Advisor Tiger for an interview three days later. Excitement and fear began to trouble him. He knew he needed to sound legitimate, or Tiger would see through his act. Trent waited for nearly an hour before being called inside. Advisor Tiger sat behind a desk with a harsh look on his face. Before him was a list of names of possible selectees.

"Past-Carpenter Trent, huh? Why do you want to join our team?"

"It's better to be a wolf than one of the sheep, sir." Tiger could easily relate to that statement.

"Ya think you could build us a shooting range? We're about to start training our people on firearms."

"That would be no problem at all, sir. I know where the materials are located. It may not be pretty, but I'll build it solid to last for many seasons of use. How soon do you need it?"

"Yesterday," the advisor said in an aggressive tone.

"Then I'll work all night and have it ready for you tomorrow," Trent said.

It was then that Tiger seemed to relax. "Good. I like your style. Welcome to our team, Security Detail Trent." After obtaining a horse and wagon, Trent brought the needed supplies to the designated location, and by daylight, it was completed. By the time the sun was directly overhead, teams of shooters were at work toning their skills and building the confidence they would need if called upon to do so. Jor-EL was well pleased with their progress. But perhaps even more important was the message continuous firing of weapons sent to the tribe: We are in control and don't forget it.

CHAPTER 6
PREPARATIONS BEGIN

The following morning, Jor-EL and Tiger were sitting in the planning room of the old jail building when the two female spies returned. The ladies had accomplished their task with precision, even drawing a clear and accurate sketch of the area with the locations of the tribe's food resources, livestock, and the chieftain's lodging. Jor-EL was impressed. "Were there any problems? Were you stopped and questioned as to why you were there?"

"No, sir. We told them we were traveling north to visit family. They were very friendly and even fed us." Jor-EL thought he detected a bit of remorse in the woman's voice, which he chose to ignore. "You have done well. Report to the old jail section, and quarters will be assigned to you, as well as food. You are dismissed." The women then left.

The two men studied the map intensely and soon developed a plan for the raid, including the direction of travel, estimated travel time to arrive, and the number of horseback riders and wagons needed to bring as much food and livestock back to the Giants Tribe as possible.

"When are you thinking the raid should commence?" Advisor Tiger asked.

"We'll move to strike now, late tonight, so we arrive around sunrise and catch them totally off guard. Compile a list of names of men we can trust for my approval. Have all our most stout wagons made ready and our horses properly fed, watered, and saddled to save time. I plan on triumphantly returning around mid-morning tomorrow to the cheers of our people," Jor-EL replied. "Tiger, tonight's adventure will only be the start of what's to come to eliminate once and for all those stupid, binding agreements not to raid each other's resources. Soon, after our success has been achieved, other tribes beg to join us!" Both men smiled broadly at the thought.

* * * * * * * * * * * * * * *

Security Detail Trent was at his wit's end. The large occupant sleeping in the adjoining cot was snoring loud enough to wake the dead. Nothing Trent tried could muffle the terrible noise, neither a pillow over the head nor fingers in the ears. So far, not one minute of sleep had been achieved, and he was tempted to strike the large man with his pillow, but he knew that 'Sleeping Beauty' was over twice his size and probably would smash him into a puddle of goo. *I better not. I have no desire to die today, anyway.*

Someone entered the hallway and began beating together metal pan lids, yelling, "Wake up! Wake up! We have an important mission to undertake tonight. If your name is called, get dressed, go to the basement armory for a weapon and adequate ammo, and meet outside. Hurry!" Two other men holding lanterns passed by the open cells, also yelling. The unhappy security detail men reluctantly complied with a couple complaining about being awakened during the middle of the night.

Once the dressed men stepped out of their open cells, the yelling man shouted, "Silence!" He turned out to be Advisor Tiger. The complaining abruptly ended. Name after name was called, including

Sleeping Beauty, but not Trent's. "The rest of you can go back to sleep." Trent flopped down upon his cot, still fully dressed, and was asleep almost instantly without a care in the world. If he only knew what terror was about to be unleashed on the Swayzee Tribe.

Outside, the large group of men were all talking at once, trying to make heads or tails out of everything. Finally, a shout of, "I said silence!" was heard. It was Advisor Tiger again. "That's better. Now listen up. All of you have been chosen for a very special mission tonight, a raid upon the Swayzee Tribe to obtain the needed resources we require and are entitled to. That means more food for you and your families. This raid will be the first of many to come. You are now trained and well-armed to complete this vital mission. Tonight, history will be made. All hail Chieftain Jor-EL!" He gave the salute, which was duplicated back by all the members of the security detail.

Jor-EL looked upon his men with pride. "Thank you, men, for your support and loyalty. Tonight, we shall become the hunters descending upon the hunted. We have a long ride ahead of us and we must arrive by daylight for the element of surprise to occur. So, mount up now, and good luck to all of us. Onward to victory!"

* * * * * * * * * * * * *

Word spread quickly at breakfast among the non-participating security detail about the raid assumed to be in progress against the Swayzee Tribe. Many boasted of their disappointment at not being chosen and left behind. Trent, on the other hand, felt sick to his stomach and guilty for returning to bed. *But there wasn't anything I could have done to stop this terrible raid*; he kept telling himself. Even if he had he known and left the building to wake Audrey up, there was nothing she could have done either. Perhaps if they had learned a day in advance, some sort of uprising or revolt by the Giants Tribe might have stopped it from happening. Sadly, he knew this would have only been wishful thinking now that the tribe had been disarmed and the time for challenging the legitimacy of Jor-EL and his thugs had passed.

Work assignments were issued and the newest detail members were assigned to supervise the fieldworkers. This pleased Trent as he suspected he could work his way over into his sister's field or trade out supervisory positions with another security detail member. *Maybe Sis will have an idea of what we should do now.*

* * * * * * * * * * * * * * *

It didn't take long for news of the raid to spread. Public discussions had to be handled discretely as Chieftain Jor-EL had outlawed any gathering of over three people, enforced by his security detail. The older members of the tribe remembered the awful raids and the feeling of fear that prevailed during their childhood. Death and destruction would have continued had it not been for Founding Father Elder, who influenced weary tribes to adopt a policy of peace, charitableness, and support among the people. And now, because of power-mad Dictator Jor-EL, all that had been achieved was in great peril.

One man dared to speak among his fellows and criticize what was occurring. He used to be Pastor Noah, but now he was titled Firewood Maintenance Noah, after Jor-EL outlawed all forms of public religious services. Nearing sixty seasons of age, Noah found the cutting, splitting, hauling, and stacking of firewood a back-breaking task. Call him as you will, but Noah will always be a pastor in the service of the Lord. He prayed daily that God would somehow intervene, but so far, things had only gotten worse for the tribe. Though his work party only consisted of six woodmen, Noah asked for their attention. "My friends, you have heard the grave news that members of our tribe, under the direction of Jor-EL and Tiger, are at this very moment on their way to raid and loot the properties of the good people of the Swayzee Tribe. I ask you to join me in prayer that no one will be harmed and that our leaders may realize the utter stupidity of their violent actions."

After seeing this group illegally assemble and offer prayer, a security detail member ran over and extracted a wooden club from his belt. "You know the rules, old man," he shouted as he commenced to beat Noah over and over until the injured man fell to the ground. With a sick look of satisfaction, the security detail man kicked Noah in his side. "The rest of you, get back to work, or the same will happen to you," he warned.

* * * * * * * * * * * * * * *

Security Detail Trent had no difficulty working through the field to speak with his sister, Audrey. "So far, Sis, I haven't been much help to you," he said with sincere sadness.

"You will be, Trent. Just hang in there. I have a plan to welcome our illustrious Ceasar's return to Rome all worked out, and my team is spreading the word about how I need them to meet up and stand when the sun is nearly overhead."

"Great, but please be careful and let me know if I can help."

"If it's possible for you, meet me before dark tonight along the river bank just north of your jail, and maybe by then, we'll know the details of the raid, and I'll have another plan worked out," she told him. He agreed and, with a slight wave of his hand, returned to patrolling the fieldworkers.

CHAPTER 7
A TRIUMPHANT RETURN

It had all been so easy, and Advisor Tiger couldn't be any happier with the results. There had been almost no interference from anyone in the Swayzee Tribe. Oh sure, a couple of people strongly objected to the raider's thefts, but a few warning shots in the air seemed to quiet things down. Horses and livestock were driven away while other security detail men searched for, discovered, and began loading as many food supplies as each wagon could hold. One brave man stepped forward and shouted, "What gives you the right to steal from us?"

Tiger responded, "By order of our illustrious leader, Jor-EL, Chieftain of the Giants Tribe." Tiger then ordered him beaten for daring to question his authority. Those who witnessed this were terrified.

A short distance away, Jor-EL had no difficulty locating their chieftain's lodge. As a show of force, Jor-EL kicked open the door and entered. The tribe's chieftain was sitting at a small table eating his breakfast. Looking at the intruder, he demanded to know the meaning of this intrusion.

"Shut your mouth, old man! I'm Chieftain Jor-EL, leader of the Giants Tribe, here to help ourselves to as much of your food, horses, and livestock as we desire. Dress quickly, as you are now my hostage and will ride out of town with me to ensure there won't be any trouble or interference from your people." Seeing he had no other option but to comply, the chieftain dressed. Out front, an extra horse was waiting for the prisoner along with eight mounted members of Jor-EL's security detail. "Mount up," the old chieftain was told. The group proceeded to leave as the men briefed their leader on the success of their mission. Jor-EL couldn't have been more pleased. About a mile out, he ordered the group to stop. "I guess we need you any longer," he said to his hostage.

"Good," replied the old chieftain. "I must return and begin assessing the severe damages you and your men have caused my tribe that violated our hard-fought peaceful agreement. Trust me, you haven't heard the end of this!" Just as the man prepared to pull away, the horse's reins were grabbed.

Joe-EL laughed at the foolish threat. "You don't understand. You're no longer needed, period!" He pulled out his pistol and shot the old man twice. Their chieftain was dead before hitting the ground. If any of the men hadn't taken Jor-EL seriously before, they certainly would from now on. "Time to head for home and a grand reception welcoming from our people," he bragged.

* * * * * * * * * * * * * *

"Looks like they're lined up to welcome your triumphant homecoming, sir," Tiger said to his boss. Up ahead, twenty-five to thirty men and women were lined up on both sides of the road awaiting the group's arrival. Jor-EL smiled broadly at the thought of this impromptu welcoming. As the mounted riders began to ride between them, a voice in the distance yelled, "Now!" Everyone on both sides abruptly spun around, showing their backsides to the group. The shock and rudeness of their meaning were apparent to Jor-EL. A terrible insult had been inflicted upon him and his men.

Anger boiled deep within him. "How dare they show contempt for me! Find out who orchestrated this great insult and have them publicly shot! As for these people, hold them captive on half-rations until I say otherwise."

"At once," Tiger said, but before his men could act upon the order, the men and women scattered in different directions, trying to escape, making it difficult to capture them. Eventually, only eleven were taken prisoner, though none claimed to know the identity of the mysterious voice who had organized this terrible insult and who, somehow, managed to escape during the confusion.

* * * * * * * * * * * * * * *

Audrey and Trent compared notes on what each had heard of the raid on the Swayzee Tribe. The full extent of the theft, and especially the murder of their chieftain by the tyrant Jor-EL, made Audrey sick to her stomach. But the immediate concern fell upon those poor eleven people who were being held captive. "You know, Sis, it won't take long on half rations before some hungry person identifies you," he warned. "They're being kept in that small block building near the corral. Tiger assigned all of us newcomers two-hour shifts of guard duty. I'm to be there in the middle of the night."

"My main concern is not about myself being identified. We need to figure out their successful escape, then get a warning out to the other local tribes to start preparing for Jor-EL's upcoming invasion of them. I feel I know how this can be done, but I hate to ask for your involvement as it would point a figure directly at you."

"Tell me, Sis."

"Can you get hold of a flat head screwdriver?"

"Sure, no problem. Why?"

"Tonight, as soon as you begin guard duty, you need to slip it under the door so they can pry it open from the inside. Then, tell them everything we know and that I need them to break up into groups of three, steal horses from the corral, and escape toward our local tribes to warn them to be prepared for a probable raid. But the worst part of all this is they will have to beat you up, good and proper, to make it look convincing to Jor-EL's men."

Trent smiled. "I can handle it! Don't you remember when I was thirteen when that Morgan kid beat the 'ever-lovin' crap out of me! Don't worry, I'll see that I'm properly bruised, bloodied, and torn to pieces to make it convincing enough."

"Just be careful, they're not fools," she replied. They split up and went their separate ways. Unbeknownst to either, they had been observed in the distance by another security detail member who felt it his duty to report the meeting to Advisor Trent.

CHAPTER 8
QUESTIONING BY TIGER

One of Jor-EL's thugs approached Trent. "Tiger wants to talk with you."

Trent suspected this was not good and wondered if his connection with his sister had become known. *Oh well, I'll face any trouble as it happens.* Entering, Trent could see the advisor sitting at his desk. *I'll try to make a good impression.* "Security Detail Trent reporting as ordered, sir!" he said louder than needed, offering the proper salute. Tiger looked him over with suspicion before returning the salute.

"It's been reported to me that you are meeting with a woman, once observed in a wheat field, and then this evening on the river bank. What do you have to say for yourself?"

Trent knew what to do now. He broke out with a big smile.

"What's so funny?" Tiger demanded to know.

"Well, sir, yes, I meet on the sly with a woman who's … ah, married. I hope you can … ah, understand my awkward predicament."

Tiger's face instantly softened. He even chuckled briefly and shook his head. "Yes, I fully understand your predicament. But I suggest you become more discreet, or her jealous husband may pay you a not-so-friendly visit with a club in his hands." Tiger looked down at the guard duty schedule list. "You did well with the shooting range, so I'm going to take you off tonight's guard duty schedule and give you an evening off to … peruse more important personal matters. Be safe and try to be more careful. You are dismissed."

Trent agreed that he'd have to be more careful and left. *Everyone, it seems, is watching everyone else. The Giants Tribe is on its way to becoming a total police state, as the old books describe.* Trent ate, then sat around talking with other detail members before leaving the old jail. Instead of walking straight to his sister's lodging, he purposely tried to lose anyone who might be following. Finally feeling confident he was alone, he approached her modest dwelling and knocked. He was ushered inside.

"Change in plans," he then told her everything and handed over the screwdriver. "I was thinking about it. Once, I made repairs to that door, and I don't think there's enough room to slide the screwdriver underneath, but there's a tiny window for light you could break out, but doing so requires taking out the guard first."

"Yes, that's why I'm switching to Plan B. I'll be right back." Audrey was only gone for a short time before returning, this time wearing a long blonde wig with a scarf tied under her chin and carrying a metal flask. "This contains homemade moonshine I was given a while back by a secret admirer. Late tonight, I'll put its strength to the test. Go now and stay safe." Trent returned to the jail and remained inside its walls all night, wondering just what his sister was planning.

CHAPTER 9
THAT NIGHT

Dressed as seductively as she dared, Audrey, wearing the blond wig and scarf and carrying a handbag, poured a bit of the moonshine in her mouth for effect. She planned to be staggering as she approached the security guard. Thanks to the full moon, he couldn't help but smile as a seemingly intoxicated woman came into view. Stopping about ten feet in front of the guard, she pretended to take another swig from her flask and spoke in a slurred voice. "Aw … now that's some great shine!" She then pretended to notice him. "Hey there, soldier boy! Care for a little nip? It's might-good stuff!" She couldn't make out much detail on his face until he responded.

"I guess a little swig won't hurt. Much obliged, pretty lady." It was much more than a little swig, then another, and another. "You're right, pretty lady. This is great shine!"

"Keep it. I guess I've had too much anyway. My head is swirling and I need to sit down a bit." Before he could ask her to move on, she sat near where he was standing. Sensing a possible opportunity, the guard sat beside her and took another long swig.

"What's your name, pretty lady?" he asked.

"Lola. Seamstress Lola."

"A real pleasure to get ta know ya, Lola." As he took another swig, she struck the back of his head with her handbag containing part of an old brick. He slumped over, out cold. Realizing that time was limited, she removed the brick and smashed it onto the small glass windowpane. Though too small for an adult to pass through, it was perfect to hand a screwdriver into the waiting hand of a captive. On her second smashing attempt, the glass shattered. Everyone inside was now on their feet wondering what was going on.

"Here, take this and pry open the door so I can come inside and brief everyone. Don't worry, the guard's out cold," she told them. Within a short time, the lock popped open, and she hurried inside. "Listen carefully and don't interrupt. We haven't much time before the relief guard arrives." She told everyone what had happened during the raid. "Break up into groups of three, decide upon a local tribe, then quietly go over to the stable barn and steal horses. Ride fast and don't look back. Warn the tribes of the coming danger from Jor-EL. Now, go!" Audrey then made her escape, located an unattended campfire, and tossed the wig and handbag into the flames. Seamstress Lola was now gone forever.

* * * * * * * * * * * * * * *

Chieftain Jor-EL was in the middle of a seductive dream when a loud pounding on his door awakened him. Angry at being awakened in the middle of the night, he flung open his door. "Sir," one of his men stated, "We found our guard passed out dead drunk, and the prisoners somehow pried open the door, escaped, and stole eleven horses!" Jor-EL was furious.

"Work him over and discover what happened! Once we find out who helped them escape, take that fool down to the river and make him disappear permanently," the chieftain ordered. "I'll dress and join you shortly."

The guard eventually remembered that a blond woman named Seamstress Lola had given him moonshine before knocking him unconscious. A quick check of tribal records revealed that no such person matching that name or description existed as a seamstress. The ex-security guard soon mysteriously disappeared and was never seen again.

Later, the two leaders met in the planning room to discuss the escaped tribal members. "I suspect they had two choices to make," Jor-EL told Tiger. "Either they simply fled in panic to unknown locations and will not bother us again, or they split up and went to warn the other local tribes. That's exactly what I would have done in their place. We may have lost the element of surprise, but the River Rats Tribe will soon feel the wrath of our power anyway. Right after our noon meal, you and I will start planning for their complete capitulation. Now, I'm heading back to bed for a few hours of sleep. I suggest you do the same."

After getting some extra sleep and an enjoyable full lunch, Jor-EL and Tiger met again to discuss the next raid. Viewing an old torn and faded paper map, the leader asked, "Tiger, if you were to make plans for the next raid, from which direction would you advance?"

"That's easy, right here at our closest point between them," pointing with his index finger.

Jor-EL slowly shook his head. "Put yourself in their place. If they've been warned about us, that's exactly the direction they'd expect us to come from by posting sentries on their side of the border to watch for our advance. We must do what they least expect: take the long way by going south and then cut over eastward and attack. Afterward, we'll take the shorter route home over our bridge. We have a golden opportunity to strip the small Jones Tribe, on the other side of the river, of its meager resources simultaneously. We'll take all of our men with us, then before the river, split off around fifteen to twenty to easily overcome them, while the remainder of us continue across the old bridge to overcome the River Rats. But we must first verify that their bridge is still standing and will hold our wagons. Ask around and see if any of our men know of its current condition. Once we know, then I'll choose the day of our next attack."

Tiger left and soon returned. "We're in luck. Two of our men crossed over it last fall to visit friends. It naturally has a few large holes, but they say a wagon can pass over it." "Splendid!" Jor-EL said. "In the meantime, qualify any new men on the shooting range. We'll need at least fifty to hit both tribes at the same time." Tiger left to begin a rigorous enlistment and training program. What Jor-EL hadn't suspected was that his 'friend' hoped he would be killed during the attack, paving the way for Tiger to be installed as the new chieftain.

Alan E. Losure

CHAPTER 10
THE BAD NEWS SPREADS

Chieftain Samuel of the River Rats Tribe's recent gut feeling was proving to be true. He and Vice-Chieftain Paula sat in stunned silence as the three Giant Tribe escapees explained what had happened and the dangers local tribes now faced. "Jor-EL is a madman bent upon power, and his advisor, Tiger, seems committed to accomplishing the man's every whim," Fieldhand Nathan said. "We pray that you and your people won't blame our tribe for this outrageous attack. They've collected all our weapons, outlawed all public gatherings, and placed most of us out working in the fields. We are powerless to act, and our people fear what may lie in store. Our one true leader, Ex-Advisor Audrey, now Fieldhand Audrey, risked her life to set us free to warn you, and we now fear for her life as well. Jor-EL has no qualms about killing anyone. His thugs even had Ex-Minister Noah severely beaten for daring to speak out and pray to the Lord for help."

Samuel turned to an aide. "See to it that our friends here have adequate food, drink, and a place to rest. Tonight, we'll call an emergency meeting to provide each of you an opportunity to tell our people what they may be facing and the chance to ask questions. But before you leave, there is one thing I must ask. Don't suggest any course of action or advocate violence. That will be up to Paula and myself to decide. Thank you for all you have done and we'll see you this evening." The three hungry and tired escapees left. "Paula," Samuel continued. "I want you to ride over to the Jones Tribe and brief Chieftain Del on what we've learned. Tell him about our emergency meeting tonight and invite him and his people to attend. This dire threat concerns all of us."

Later that evening, a large crowd gathered and were split into groups of threes so each of the escapees could speak separately and be heard. Many had only heard bits and pieces of the raid, prompting fear and anxiety. Many questions followed the briefings, some that the escapee' simply could not answer. Once the briefings had ended, the groups were instructed to form a tight circle around their leaders. "Gather around us, my friends," Chieftain Samuel shouted as loud as he could. "Please, we require silence from everyone." The voices diminished. "If you cannot hear me, ask others later to relay what was said. As you have heard, a crisis has developed, affecting all of us. For so long, we have lived in peace with our fellow tribes, helping when we can and, of course, being helped. Our children have not experienced tribal war, and I never thought I would see the day that I must warn all of you that the probability of being raided by the Giants Tribe is very real. I ask that in your hearts you harbor no ill will against their tribe, but only in their self-appointed chieftain and his power-mad thugs. As you have just heard, their people have lost their freedom to speak their minds, assemble in groups, or worship as they wish. These are the basic liberties all men and women in all tribes are entitled to enjoy. I will now turn this over to Vice-Chieftain Paula, who will discuss our plan of action. Afterward, my friend Chieftain Del from the Jones Tribe can address us if he chooses." He then nodded to Paula for her to continue.

"Thank you, sir. First, we ask that everyone remain calm as we suspect we have time to prepare for a raid. When you return home this evening, we suggest hiding any excess food supplies in a safer location. Unfortunately, there is little you can do if you own livestock or horses. Tomorrow, two temporary outposts, to be constructed miles apart, will be placed on our northern and northeastern boundary. Their purpose is to create a viewing lodge for any approaching intruders. Three watchers will man these from morning to morning when another relief team arrives. Men aged eighteen to seventy seasons old will be utilized as watchers. They will be named Outposts A and B. We will leave it up to each team to work out their work schedule, as long as one pair of eyes watch around the clock, come rain or shine. We have established a list of names to bring the wagons of food and materials to build the temporary viewing lodges. They are already packed and waiting to depart at dawn tomorrow. The other two watchers will arrive and depart on horseback." She then read the names aloud. "An identical list of names and dates will be posted inside this lodge and the stable for viewing. It is the responsibility of every man in our tribe to check the list daily, and when you see your name, arrive at daybreak at the stable as a relief, fully armed and with plenty of ammo, and ride to each outpost together. We cannot tolerate any lateness or 'I forgot' excuses. I strongly suggest you all bone up on firing your weapon as your life and those you love may soon depend upon it.

"Now, should one of them catch sight of an impending raid, send one of the men to ride back and report directly to the fire lodge to start ringing the fire bell loud and long. I have arranged for the fire bell not to ring should we suffer a fire in the immediate future. Therefore, should you hear it ringing, grab your weapons and report to your assigned locations to guard livestock, horses, food storage, and, of course, if necessary, fight off the incoming raiders. Mothers, please consider where you and your children can hide during the attack. Hopefully, God willing, that day will not come. I now turn this over to Chieftain Del of the Jones Tribe for his comments."

"It sounds like your leaders have developed a workable plan," he said. "I will schedule our men to construct Outposts C and D to serve as watchers and place them west and south of our tribe, though I doubt the raiders would take the long way to reach us. That way, we have each direction well covered. In the morning, I'll send my vice-chieftain to warn the larger Deaner Tribe and ask for their support. The idea of the fire bell as an early warning makes sense, and I'll see that arrangements are made for us to do the same. So, if you hear our bell, you'll know an attack is underway. Thank you for including us here tonight. Peace and joy to all of you." Chieftain Samuel then asked the Reverend Jason to lead the group in prayer. Then the meeting ended.

CHAPTER 11
ANOTHER PLAN IN THE MAKING

The following morning, Trent worked his way over to the field where his step-sister Audrey was working. "Sis, the scuttlebutt going around says something big is probably in the works for tomorrow. Horses are being attended to, and every workable wagon is parked outside the corral. This appears to be in preparation for another raid."

The concerned fieldhand nodded. "Yes, I've caught wind of it. I heard two security thugs discussing the condition of the old bridge leading to the River Rats Tribe. If only we had a way of warning them ahead of time."

Trent paused a second before responding. "Maybe I could try to steal a horse. It might prove difficult as the area is buzzing with armed security workers, but if you want, I can try."

"No, don't even consider it. But let me ask you a couple of questions. Do Jor-EL's thugs keep their weapons and ammo in their possession while eating and sleeping?"

He shook his head. "All weapons are collected and kept inside a wire cage in the basement armory room once anyone enters the building."

"Is this cage you mentioned locked?"

"I don't think any of the old locks work anymore, even in the cell block. They post an armed guard around the clock to protect anyone from getting their hands on them."

"Have you ever been tasked with guarding the cage?"

"No, not yet, only as the main entry guard to the jail. It's also guarded the same way. I've had to do that twice now at night, and it's hard to just stand there without curling up on the steps and going to sleep."

A plan began to form in Audrey's mind. "It would be suicidal for an unarmed man or woman to attempt to storm the front door, then fight your way into the armory, but someone already positioned inside …" She then laid out a workable plan to steal the weapons. "No available weapons," she joked, "No raid."

* * * * * * * * * * * * * * *

It was in the early morning hours as Trent struggled to stay awake. He had read some, then walked the empty hallway, waiting for the proper time. Finally, the cage relief guard came into view. "I just can't sleep," Trent told the man. "I'm just keyed up thinking we may see action tomorrow, as people say. How about letting me take your shift for you? Maybe working can help calm my jitters."

The relief guard smiled. "Sure thing! Thanks a lot, pal. I'll do the same for you sometime." He then returned to his waiting bunk. It had worked. Trent then entered the basement. The guard happily handed over the rifle to his relief without saying a word and left.

"Sleep tight," Trent offered. Now, the first part of Audrey's plan had been accomplished by eliminating one of the two guards.

Trent leaned the rifle against the cage door and left the basement for the first floor. The outside guard heard the entry door opening and turned to see who was up at this time of night.

"I just can't sleep, knowing we'll be in action tomorrow," Trent told him. "Want me to relieve you early? I don't mind it." The guard's smile could not be seen in the darkness as he silently passed his rifle to this volunteer. As the man began to walk past him, Trent whispered, "Have a nice sleep," then brought the rifle butt down hard against the back of his skull. The man dropped to the ground. Trent drug the unconscious man over towards the tall bushes, then returned to the steps and began motioning frantically. *What if they can't see me, or even worse, Audrey wasn't able to assemble a small group of men?* His doubts quickly ended as six men and his stepsister, who had been hiding and watching, appeared out of the darkness.

"Everyone listen up; no talking from here on out," Audrey whispered. "Trent, show us the way." The group entered the building and proceeded down the stairs and into the basement. Each person was carrying an old cotton feed sack. Trent moved the rifle he had left over to the side and opened the cage door. There, before them, were pistols, rifles, shotguns, ammunition, and even a few bows and arrows. The group silently began to load each bag full of weapons.

Great confidence swept over Audrey until she heard a loud voice. "We fully expected some sort of assault tonight," Advisor Tiger said mockingly. Standing beside him was Chieftain Jor-EL. Each man was holding a pistol aimed straight at them. Three other security detail members then appeared as well. Tiger continued to gloat. "I can't believe you seriously thought I had fallen for your phony girlfriend story, and I see you brought her here to help you. Welcome, Ex-Advisor Audrey, and now properly titled Fieldhand Audrey."

Jor-EL spoke. "We've had you both watched and now, seven traitors have been captured. As soon as we return from our glorious raids upon two nearby tribes, all of you will be lined up against a wall, in public view of the tribe members, and shot by a firing squad."

Audrey finally said, "You are a delusional madman, Jor-EL, and the same goes for your lapdog here!" In retaliation, Tiger slapped her hard across the face.

"Put them all together in that large vacant cell," Jor-EL ordered. "We'll deal with them soon enough." The security detail carried out the order. Since none of the cell door locks worked anymore, the bars were tied shut securely with rope. The guard gave the cell door a pull and was satisfied the prisoners would be unable to escape.

"We hope you enjoy your stay with us," he said sarcastically as the detail left to join Jor-EL and Tiger, who were waking up the sleeping men at that moment,

"Wake up, men! Everyone goes," Tiger shouted. "Report to the dining room for a quick meal, then meet outside for final instructions and duty assignments. Today, history will be made, and we'll take what is rightfully ours from the Jones and River Rats Tribes! The security detail men gave a cheer and the proper salute, which Jor-EL was pleased to return. Soon, mounted men and wagons left the stable area. The plan was to take the longer trek southward before finally cutting east where teams would split up and attack both tribes simultaneously. This out-of-the-way movement was bound to trick anyone watching for the expected closer raid coming from the north and catch them with their pants down.

* * * * * * * * * * * * *

A great sadness of failure overcame the confined group. Finally, Audrey said, "I'm sorry I got all of you involved in this." No one answered. What would be the point of doing so, anyway?

Trent pulled her to the side and whispered loud enough for her to hear, "They didn't search us very well. I have a pocketknife stashed inside my boot. I can cut our way through those ropes with no problem. Just give the word." Upon learning this, the group's morale suddenly improved a great deal.

"That was good thinking on your part, Trent. I'm very proud of you. I suggest we wait a bit and let Jor-EL's men leave before we try to make our escape. He's bound to have a few men stay behind, so we must be careful. Once we're out, I want you other five men to storm the armory guard and grab any weapons left behind. Jor-EL's boasted of a raid upon two tribes. They must be the Jones and the River Rats. We must assemble every armed man who can ride a horse and follow behind to fight these thugs who have shamed the name of the Giants Tribe. Beg and plead if you have to for volunteers, but ride hard and catch up to us. Tell them this may be our last opportunity to fight back. In the meantime, Trent and I will steal two horses and ride hard to warn the tribes. We should be able to detour around Jor-EL as they won't be traveling all that fast. Trent, start cutting on our side of the knot so it won't show from their side if anyone comes to check on us." Luckily, no one entered, and soon, the knot was cut, and the cell door opened. "Everyone knows what to do. Let's not fail, no matter what the cost." The group separated and wished each other good luck. The five men made their way carefully toward the basement stairway. So far, they had been lucky not to be seen. "Now, here's the plan. We rush the guard all at once, and hopefully, he will hesitate before raising his rifle," the new leader said. "The cage is right through that doorway. We move to the count of three. One … two … three!" The men barged into the room but stopped dead in their tracks. There was no posted guard, and the cage was loosely tied shut by a small rope.

"We are in luck," one man muttered.

The empty cloth bags had been pitched earlier in the corner when the detail men removed the weapons and returned them to storage. Around thirty pistols and a couple of rifles, along with boxes of ammo, were left behind. "Load up everything we see," the leader ordered. "Now, if Audrey and Trent can't overcome the front step guard, we may have to shoot our way out."Once the men and their bags of weapons arrived inside the front door, they couldn't see any guard standing outside either. "I hope Jor-EL took everyone with him," the leader said. "Now, let's line up as many volunteers as possible. Have them bring their horses and meet at the corral and barn. Lord willing, we'll have enough animals to help get us there in time to prevent a bloodbath."

* * * * * * * * * * * * * *

It was already sunrise when Audrey and Trent made their way out of the jail without any difficulty. "Jor-EL's taken every man he could round up," she said. "Let's go steal a couple of horses, shall we?" They arrived at the corral near the old, rusted railroad tracks. Due to the prior raid on the Swayzee Tribe, ample horses remained behind. there were enough horses. Entering the horse barn, Audrey saw an old man and a small boy working.

Before she said anything, the old man assumed the new arrivals were part of Jor-EL's raiding party. "They're gone," he said. "And to blazes with the lot of um. Go ahead and report me fer speakin' my mind. We used ta have freedom around here until your stinkin' boss grabbed power and closed da schools and …" He stopped speaking and looked closely into the woman's face. "I know ya, you're Advisor Audrey or … were. So, ya went and joined up with dat devil of a man, did ya!"

"No, no! Please listen to me! We need two horses to ride fast and hard and warn the two tribes of Jor-EL's raid. If not, many, many people will be killed, and it'll be even worse than the Swayzee raid. Did you hear anything they said or which direction they rode off to?"

The old man's face softened. "Praise be to God," he said with relief. "Yes, I heard them bragging. They said they'd go south, then cut over to surprise everyone. Then, just before the bridge, some were ta break away from da group and hit the Jones Tribe while da rest hit the River Rats. Yes! Take these two horses. They're da fastest we have. Warn dem good people; we ain't behind this great evil, only dem crazy men and women. Oh yes, I saw two or three women riding away, too."

"Listen carefully, friend. There should be a large group of armed men coming here for horses soon. They are not part of Jor-EL's bunch but patriots standing with us. Please saddle as many horses ahead of time as you can and tell them everything that you told me. They must take the shorter route to arrive early. That's the way we're heading, too. About how many people would you estimate were in his raiding party?"

"Shucks, Advisor Audrey, I didn't count riders ... I count horses. Fifty-four total."

"Please tell our men to hurry. Many lives are at stake today."

CHAPTER 12
BOREDOM AT OUTPOST D

I can't believe I begged for this duty assignment; fifteen-year-old Fieldhand Bert of the Jones Tribe told himself as he lay upon the grassy meadow. Overhead, a large hawk was circling its potential prey. From the edge of a nearby wood, he heard the chattering of a squirrel. *We are very lucky that all our wild animals and birds were not killed off immediately after The Annihilation occurred.* Chieftain Del had scheduled each three-man watch crew to perform their duties for two days instead of one before being relieved, and this morning was the start of the last one. Not at all used to sleeping in a lodge with two other grown men, Bert desperately needed a good night's rest. *When I get home tomorrow, I'm going straight to bed.*

The recent visit and lecture by Survivor Lee had made quite a sobering impression on him, as well as others within his tribe. Viewing photographs in old books couldn't compare to hearing a first-hand account of what life was like before mankind's near extinction. As a result, he had been unable to sleep that night, fearing the possible return of The *Demons from Above*. And now, his tribe was facing a new potential enemy bent on destroying everything multiple generations had strived so hard to build upon and accomplish.

Looking skyward, Bert found it easy to imagine clouds taking the shape of people or animals. It would also be quite easy to close one's eyes for a brief bit of rest, but Bert knew he hadn't been posted there to sleep on duty. Bert glanced southward at what appeared to be a dust cloud or storm in the far distance. Assuming impending bad weather was moving his way, he made mental preparations to become soaking wet. *Great, just what I needed.* But there was something odd about this storm cloud, something that continued to hold his attention, glimpses of individual movement. *If only there were enough of those old binoculars left to go around, I could make this out.* Soon, Bert could see that it wasn't an approaching weather storm but a storm of a different sort: a large group of riders. *Oh, my God! It's the Giants Tribe raiders!*

Bert jumped on his horse and rode back to the outpost at a fever's pitch. After hearing an approaching rider, the other two watchers exited the temporary lodge. "They're coming up from the south!" Bert shouted.

Both men squinted hard to see anything, but could only make out what could be dismissed as a dust cloud.

"Are you sure you saw riders?" one man asked. "We don't need to set off any false alarm."

"I'm positive. From my watcher position, I could make out individual movements."

"Then ride hard and warn the others to start ringing that old bell. I never expected them to attack from that far south," the other man said. "Tell Chieftain Del we'll stay here and try to delay their approach as long as we can hold out." That statement sounded like a self-imposed death sentence to Bert, who nodded and rode off to warn his tribe. *There would be no sleeping today unless it were to be eternal sleep* the youth thought.

Bert rode straight toward the large group of members assembled on the outskirts of their village. "I've seen them!" he shouted. "The

Giants Tribe raiders are coming in from the south. The other two watchers told me to start ringing that bell at once!"

The news shocked the group. Their leader instantly thought it made no sense for the raiders to have traveled such a long distance to attack them, but doing so might catch anyone watching off guard. Bert was told to ride into the village and tell the assembled men to start ringing the fire bell. Secretly, as a kid, he often wanted to sneak in and ring it himself, but today its sound only foretold of death and destruction. Hearing their neighbor's bell warning sounding, the River Rats Tribe's bell soon joined in the warning. Armed men and women assembled at their pre-assigned locations, the size of the horseback riders more than tripling.

Chieftain Dell, now with Audrey and Trent, responded quickly to the bell's location, where an excited Bert remained. "Are you the watcher?" Del asked. The young man answered he was. "Tell us what you saw."

"Well, sir, at first, I thought it was some sort of dust cloud or rain storm approaching from the south, but then I made out individual movement of horseback riders. There are so many, maybe a hundred. I'm assigned to Outpost D. My fellows remained behind to try to delay the raider's arrival."

All knew that the men had little chance of doing that. "Let's get into position," Del suggested as the three walked the short distance to his horse and the mounted men. Audrey and Trent remained standing and looked southward. "I've got around sixty or more armed riders ready to ride southward to meet the enemy head-on." He told them. "If they want a fight today, we'll give um one!"

* * * * * * * * * * * * * *

Back at Outpost D, the two remaining outpost watchers gazed intently at the advancing group of riders. Both men, with rifles trained, knew their chances of survival were slim. From behind, they heard the fire bell warning, soon followed by another bell over at the River Rats compound. "They will alert everyone now. Maybe help will arrive soon," the optimistic watcher said. The other man estimated the raiding party consisted of around fifty riders, certainly better than the one hundred plus that young Bert had given them.

"They'll be on us soon. Get ready to fire." Then, a strange thing happened. The raiders halted, and a lone horseman approached, slowly waving a white cloth.

"Want me to pick him off?" the optimistic watcher asked.

"No! He's asking for a truce. Probably asking us to surrender."

"Maybe they want to surrender," the other watcher joked.

"Let's ride out and see what he wants." The men met up in the open field.

"Hello! We're from the Deaner Tribe and are here to help. Your vice-chieftain told us of the Giants Tribe's impending attack on the Jones and River Rats. Where do you want us?"

The two watchers were overjoyed. "That's wonderful news! Please, bring your men forward, and I'll send my friend here into camp to let our chieftain know of your arrival. We thought you were them. His name is Chieftain Del. He'll suggest positioning your men where they're most needed."

"Are you sure they're on their way today?"

"Yes. We were told so by two friendly members of their tribe who rode all night to warn us."

The rider motioned for his men to come forward, then stepped off his horse. "By the way, I'm Carpenter Nolan," he said as both men shook hands.

"Teacher Carl. Happy to know you, Nolan. Our chieftain will be overjoyed with your arrival. To be honest with you, I thought I'd be dead by now. Feel free to go ahead, as they've been advised of your arrival by now. I'll remain here and continue standing watch."

The Deaner volunteers were welcomed by the Jones Tribe with open arms, food, and refreshments.

Chieftain Del welcomed each man. The group's leader explained that they left an equal number behind to guard their supplies.

"Just in case we failed to stop them here." It was an idea that nobody wanted to consider. Del explained that with the Jones and Deaner men, and the River Rats, he hoped to discourage anyone from making any foolish attack.

"Nolan, I want to join your men up with ours. The River Rats have an equal number. Combined, we are a force to be reckoned with," Del explained. Now, all anyone could do was wait.

CHAPTER 13
THE ARRIVAL

A lone horseman arrived at the camp of the Jones Tribe volunteers. Chieftain Samuel of the River Rats was there to confer with his friend, Chieftain Del. "I'm pleased to report that about thirty-five armed mounted friendly riders from the Giants Tribe have just arrived and are being inducted into our force under the direction of my vice-chieftain." Audrey and Trent were happy to hear the news. "So, we need to come up with a battle plan soon, or it'll be too late."

Del smiled. "I think we may have one. Let's assume that my advanced watchers report Jor-EL's raiders are coming at us through the open field before us, moving straight east toward the village. I'll line up twenty of our men to provide a false indication as to our weakened strength. Now, look a quarter mile toward the left and right of the field. Those thick forests may very well be the key to our success today. Once we're positive of the raider's travel route, the Deaner men and the rest of the Jones riders will hide inside the woods to the left, while the Giant's volunteers and the River Rats will hide on the right. Once Jor-EL takes the bait and advances closer, both groups will move in, with about a third of each group splitting off and riding in behind the raiders, effectively boxing them in. Comments?"

"But what do we do if we're wrong and they come in more northward and attack my tribe first?" Samuel asked.

"Then, all the men hiding in the woods will quickly ride northward, come in from behind, and circle them. I'll have two riders standing by to inform each group of men about any change in orders." Audrey liked the plans and said so. Chieftain Samual said he must return home now and brief his people on the two-plan options. About thirty minutes later, a watcher rode in to report that the raiders had been spotted about two miles away. Samuel sent a rider to report this information to the vice-chieftain of the River Rats. "I think it's time to position both groups as planned. Let's assume they'll come straight in, for now."

* * * * * * * * * * * * * * *

Although the Giants Tribe raiders were nearly two miles away, the faint sound of two fire bells ringing in the distance could only mean one thing: despite their precautions, they had been seen. Realizing he needed to offer a bit of encouragement to his men, Jor-EL turned in his saddle to speak. "Have no concerns about those bells, men. By now, the Jones and River Rats Tribes are running around like a bunch of scared rabbits, or maybe I should say, scared rats!" Whether his words calmed any nerves could not be known. "Let's speed up, boys. We have an appointment today with Destiny!"

CHAPTER 14
SURRENDER OR DEATH

Jor-EL and his men were close enough to make out the defensive line of the mounted troops from the Jones Tribe. He was not impressed, and he laughed at their small numbers. Turning to Tiger, he said, "A slight change in our attack plan. We'll stop short of them, and then I'll ride up and demand their immediate surrender. If they agree, which I fully expect they will, we'll return to our original plan and leave a third behind to loot while the rest of us attack the River Rats." Tiger offered to ride beside him as added safety, but Jor-EL said no. "This way, I can display my bravery to our men." Once the group arrived, the leader held up his arm to halt, then slowly rode toward the Jones camp. Seeing the rider's approach, Chieftain Del rode alone to meet him.

"I am Jor-EL, Chieftain of the Giants Tribe. You only have two options today, old man. Either you order your men to drop their weapons, surrender, and stand aside, or all their deaths and those that follow will be on your conscience. What say you?"

The chieftain smiled. "Actually, Jor-EL, we're expecting your tribe's surrender today. What say you?"

Anger flashed over the thug's face as he abruptly turned and rode back to his waiting men. Del waved his arms before returning.

Joe-EL hadn't seen the chieftains signaling, so upon his arrival, he instructed his men that prisoners would not be taken today.

"Wipe everyone out!" he shouted.

Seemingly, out of nowhere, large bodies of armed men mounted on horses began emerging from the forests on both sides of the raiders. A signal was given, and about a third of each group broke away and formed behind the raiders.

Jor-El's men realized that three times their strength had boxed them in. The hunters, it seems, were now the hunted. No longer confident of a fast victory and the inevitable spoils of war, each man scanned his neighbor's troubled faces and saw fear. Silence followed as each man felt unsure of what was to happen next.

Then, a loud voice shouted orders. It was not Jor-EL, but Tiger. "This ain't gonna work, men. Let's get out of here!" Just as his horse turned to make a break for it, a shot rang out, and Tiger sagged in his saddle and fell to the ground, shot in the back by Jor-EL's pistol.

"No stinkin' coward gives orders to run away to my men!" He turned to face them. "We've never backed down before, and we ain't gonna do so now to a bunch of untrained farmers. Follow me, boys, to fame and glory!" His horse dashed toward the smaller line of Jones men but, after a glance backward, saw that none of his riders had followed him. His unquestionable authority over them had just ended.

"All of you men out there, drop your weapons and raise your hands. Do it now!" Chieftain Del yelled at the top of his voice. One by one, the men of the Giants Tribe realized their situation was hopeless and dropped their weapons to the ground ... that is all but one; the man who had gotten everyone into this terrible mess to start with.

"Don't ever forget the name of your great leader and warrior, Jor-EL!" he shouted as he spurred his horse forward. With rapid, but poorly aimed shots at the Jones men, the lone tyrant was cut down with a hail of bullets from the new arrivals while in the act of taking prisoners.

"Thank God, our nightmare is finally over, Audrey, "Del said with great relief in his voice.

"Yes, sir. Jor-EL chose to die by the bullet, rather than by the rope."

* * * * * * * * * * * * * * *

After the raiders were arrested, their hands were tied, and they were placed under guard. While the victorious men celebrated, Chieftains Samuel, Del, and Ex-Advisor Audrey met to decide their next course of action. At her strong recommendation, Carpenter Nolan of the Deaner Tribe was included. "Some sort of trial will be required for the prisoners at some point," Samuel said.

"Yes, and the Giants Tribe has a large serviceable jail to hold them until we do," Audrey suggested. Soon, a plan emerged. The trial would take place within the Giants Tribe area, conducted by a five-person panel of judges, all of whom would be the chieftains from each of the tribes involved. The prisoners would be confined to their cells for thirty days to allow ample time to organize everything, transport witnesses, research any documentation, and provide adequate time for the appointed defense team to present their cases.

"Audrey," Del said, "Samuel and I've discussed this, and we feel you should be appointed as Chief Judge on our panel. If it weren't for everything you and Trent did to undercut Jor-EL and his thugs, we all might have eventually been overrun."

"But sir, I'm not the chieftain of my tribe."

Del laughed. "I'm guessing that may soon change."

Carpenter Nolan and his men departed to return to the Deaner Tribe with news to pass on to his chieftain. After saying their goodbyes, the volunteers of the Giants Tribe loaded their prisoners into the supply wagons brought with them. Instead of returning to the tribe as concurring heroes as they'd assumed that morning, instead, they are now a defeated lot, with bound hands and the promise of securely tied cell doors waiting to greet them.

CHAPTER 15
PICKING UP THE PIECES

Del's prediction soon came true, as the greatly relieved citizens of the Giants Tribe asked Audrey to assume the position of their new chieftain. After a bit of soul searching, she humbly accepted but worried about not being up to the difficult tasks that lay ahead. For the time being, she decided not to appoint an advisor until after the trials had ended. Trent could only smile. "Does that mean I have to address you as Chieftain Audry like everyone else?"

"Sis will do nicely, thank you."

She had assumed Jor-EL's old office and was pleased to discover that Tiger had kept documented records on the number of horses, livestock, and food supplies stolen from the Swayzee Tribe. That would make their return much simpler, though his men had wasted a great deal of the pilfered food. Somehow, atonement must be provided by the Giants Tribe to the Swayzee people for allowing this to happen in the place. "Trent, I have a job for you. Take this letter to the Swayzee's new chieftain. It explains everything that has happened up to this point and the upcoming trial for them to attend, along with any witnesses wanting to testify." He took hold of the envelope, but she held fast. "That's not everything. Here is a list of horses, livestock, and food supplies stolen from them. Pick seven good men with strong horses and wagons and return everything to them."

Trent had a strange look on his face. "Sis, I'm not a drover, I'm a carpenter."

"Today, you're a drover. Have a nice journey, little brother."

Audrey's first decision as the tribal chieftain had been to restore the God-given freedoms that had been taken away from her tribe. People could return to their prior work assignments unless they chose not to. Schools opened to educate the future leaders of their tribe. Happiness and joy soon appeared on the faces of her people.

Now that life seemed to be returning to normal, it was time to begin planning the location of the upcoming trials. Unfortunately, the old courthouse had long ago collapsed and wasn't safe to use. *I think the only solution is a location that is close to the jail where tribal members can watch the return of law and order. That large pole barn east of the old railroad tracks can be emptied and would work just fine. But who can we get to represent the rights of those men during the trial in an unbiased way? It is apparent that nobody wants the job, and frankly, I can't blame anyone.* That was a question she had asked repeatedly that no one had answers to.

When it came to enforcing law and order, every tribe had its way of doing so. Normally, it was left up to the tribe's chieftain, who, after hearing the charges against one of their members, and hearing their side of the story, decided guilt or innocence and any appropriate punishment required. But in this case, forty-nine men and three women, each to be tried separately for their uncontested involvement, would require something far more structured. The complicated laws and procedures of the past could no longer apply. Each person charged would be allowed to speak in their defense, but a tribal-appointed person to assist them and, at times, speak for them must be required to avoid the wrong impression of unfairness. There are no lawyers or judges to introduce or object to complicated courtroom tactics and strange laws. Audrey had once read an old book based on a character named Perry Mason and wondered why the old laws had been so strange and unnecessarily complicated back then.

* * * * * * * * * * * * * * *

Two weeks passed. The appointed prosecutor, Teamster Ian, had little difficulty finding witnesses willing to testify about what they observed. It soon became apparent that only a handful of individuals would be charged with brutality, while the majority were guilty of believing in Jor-EL's lies and going along with the group. Each man or woman was captured, armed, and ready for battle. That fact could not be denied. Each would stand alone and be tried.

Since Audrey would serve as Chief Judge, she avoided any mention of the trial, the prisoners, or anyone wishing to discuss the subject altogether. The few who tried were stopped and told to save it for the trial. Her biggest concern remained not finding anyone suitable to defend the prisoners with fairness and without bitterness. The trial date was fast approaching and the thought of telling the arriving chieftains of her failure to secure someone sent chills down her spine.

The next morning, Audrey sat at her desk reviewing the projected fall and winter rationing when she heard a knock on her door. This was an all-too-familiar sound these days. Without looking up, she asked, "What is it?"

"I wonder if I might have a word with you, Chieftain Audrey?" Looking up, she saw it to be Minister Noah. "Yes, Noah, please come in and have a seat. How are you feeling these days?"

"I'm just fine, ma'am. I was wondering if you've appointed anyone to represent the prisoners yet?"

"No, not yet, but we're beating the bushes looking for someone willing to be impartial."

"Then, I'd like to volunteer to defend those men and women."

His request caught her a bit off guard. "You? Don't you recall being beaten by one of the defendants, the one called Mechanic Mike?"

"Of course I do. How could I ever forget? The real question you should be asking is, why me? The simple answer is that I feel God has directed me to do so. Please let me try to help those people. I promise to do everything within my power to ease their burden of guilt. Perhaps I shouldn't even be speaking to you, but I don't know who else to turn to."

"What does your wife think of this? After all, defending them may very well tarnish your reputation with some tribal members."

"We have prayed about this, and she fully supports me. As for the latter part of your statement, I'll just have to wait and see, as their defense is more important. In time, our people will come to understand my motives."

Audrey smiled. "All right, the job is yours. Go down the hall to the office that used what used to be Tiger's office and speak with the prosecutor, Teamster Ian. Tell him I said to arrange an office for you to work out of."

"I'd prefer to work and study from home if that's all right, but I will require something from you saying I have permission to speak with my clients as often as I desire." She agreed and wrote out a pass. He thanked her and left. Down the hall, he introduced himself to the prosecutor.

"Teamster Ian? I'm Minister Noah. I've just volunteered to represent the prisoners." The men shook hands. "I'll require a copy of the charges you intend to bring against them."

"I don't envy you, sir, but our lists are incomplete as we're still waiting on the arrival of the Swayze Tribe's statements. Once we get the complete lists, I'll make you a copy and let you know," Ian said.

"I'll take a copy of what you already have for now."

"Give me a little time, and I'll get to work on it."

"Fine. I'll go over to the cell block now and speak with them, then drop by on my way home later. Will that work for you?"

Ian replied he'd have it waiting for him. "Good luck, Minister Noah, you'll need it." With a smile and a wave, Noah left.

After showing the guards his pass to see the prisoners, Minister Noah entered the cell block and slowly walked the hallway, looking into each cell containing two prisoners. "My name is Minister Noah, and I have volunteered to help represent you at next week's trial. I will return tomorrow morning with a partial list of the charges brought against you and meet with you individually to discuss everything. It's a partial list because the witnesses from the Swayzee Tribe have not arrived to make their statements. Once they do, I'll get with you again. Have faith and trust in the Lord, and I'll see you tomorrow morning."

Inside the cell holding Mechanic Mike, his cellmate said, "Say, ain't that the guy you beat to a pulp?"

"Yeah, it is, and there ain't no doubt now that I'm gonna hang by my neck for sure!"

CHAPTER 16
THE TRIALS BEGIN

The day before the trials started, several members of the Swayzee Tribe and their new chieftain arrived. "Peace and joy to all of you," Audrey said as she greeted everyone. "We have comfortable lodging you to rest from your tiresome journey. Food and drink await. Two of our men will tend to your horses."

One man stepped forward. "Chieftain Audrey, I'm Chieftain Ken." They shook hands. "I gotta tell you, ma'am, I'm not used to my new fancy title yet, and I still feel like Mortician Ken inside."

She smiled and nodded. "I know that feeling very well, so just call me Audrey, and I'll call you Ken. Follow me, and I'll introduce you to Samuel of the River Rats and Del of the Jones Tribe. We're still awaiting the arrival of Chieftain Parker of the Deaner Tribe." Within the hour, Parker arrived, and the five judges worked well into the evening outlying tomorrow's court procedures.

Work crews brought in three tables with comfortable chairs for the presiding judges, as well as whatever chairs they could locate for the prisoners, guards, witnesses, Prosecutor Ian, and Defense Council Noah. Chief Judge Audrey would sit in the middle of the other chieftain judges. All other visitors would be required to stand at the rear, allowing them to come and go as they pleased.

Rumors had a way of spreading quickly among the tribal members concerning the punishments those found guilty were to receive. One such rumor stated that each man and woman would receive a severe flogging. Another swore that the local blacksmith was forging a branding iron with the letter "T" for traitor. It would be heated in a fire, then branded upon the cheek of each guilty party. The person would then be banished so that, wherever they may go, others would recognize their crime. That rumor sent chills down one's back. But it was the hard-nosed members who were begging for a group hanging to take place involving the worst of the lot and long prison sentences imposed for the others. Soon enough, everyone would hear the court's final conviction judgments anyway.

The trial began mid-morning the following day. The first group of five prisoners were brought in under heavy guard and seated. Before the audience sat the five chieftains, reviewing papers containing the list of prisoners to be called and in what order. Prosecutor Ian appeared confident, while Defense Councilor Noah was observed lowering his head to pray silently. Excitement filled the air with loud chattering from the large crowd of assembled visitors. It was time for the proceedings to begin. Looking side to side to make eye contact with her fellow judges to ensure they were ready to start, Audrey struck a wooden gavel. "Silence! We must have silence!"

The make-shift courtroom fell quiet.

"We are about to begin, so I will cover the rules agreed to by my colleagues on the bench. First of all, we will not tolerate any interruptions or loud talking from anyone in the audience. If it happens, you will be escorted out by our security volunteers. Is that understood? Fine. Let me begin by explaining how this is to work. The bailiff will call out the first defendant on the list, who will stand as the prosecutor reads the charges pending against him or her out loud. At the conclusion, I, as the Chief Judge, will ask the defendant whether they plead guilty or not guilty to those charges. If the plea of not guilty is rendered, any witnesses wishing to testify will be brought forward, one at a time, to swear that the man or woman is the one standing before them. Then, the prosecutor and the defense counsel will question each witness. At the conclusion, the defendant is free to make a statement if they desire. At that point, each of my fellow judges will annotate a guilty or not guilty verdict on their list, next to the defendant's name, and if guilty, their ruling on the length of punishment. Then, the process will begin all over with the next defendant. Our volunteers escorting the prisoners are asked to keep one group standing by to not delay the court's proceedings. And finally, upon the completion of the trial, my colleagues will assemble and review each rendering. Mine will not count unless the decisions are split evenly at two against two. Once a full agreement has been reached, the defendants will be informed first, followed by the prosecution and defense counsel, and finally, all of you. So, if we're ready, Bailiff, call the first defendant."

Each trial proceeded relatively smoothly, with most pleading not guilty while a few admitted their part. Defense Council Noah occasionally attempted to convince the judges that those who had not taken part in the Swayzee raid were only recently recruited and hadn't realized the depth of their involvement. Most tribal members felt Noah's efforts were falling on deaf ears. Then, it was Mechanic Mike's turn, and he pleaded not guilty to the charge of severely beating a minister who was offering a public prayer. Two witnesses who'd been part of the wood-cutting group that morning testified they'd seen the beating occur and had no doubt who inflicted the pain. Most of those listening to their testimony realized who the minister was: Defense Council Noah, whose job was to defend his attacker.

Chief Judge Audrey cleared her throat loud enough to be heard. "Defense Council Noah, I realize this puts you in an awkward position today, having to defend the man accused of your beating. If you desire, I'm sure the court would be willing to overlook your position temporally and allow you to testify if you so desire."

"Yes, Your Honor, I would like that." He took the witness stand. "What the two previous witnesses have testified is true, but I ask the court to overlook the incident and treat it as a non-event. You see, I have completely forgiven Mechanic Mike. The people now on trial were our friends and family before getting caught up in Jor-EL's crazy, power-mad scheme. As anyone listening to today's testimonies can attest, the promises of more food and an improved social position were critical in their decision to follow him. Anyone who studies the old history books that were left to us has read of entire societies of good and kind people who were swayed and deceived into becoming hateful, killing people, seemingly overnight, by a ruthless, evil tyrant who promised a better life at the expense of others. Is this not the same thing happening again? Mechanic Mike has a skill we today, as well as our descendants, will need if we're ever to start becoming an industrial nation once again. That's all I have to say, thank you."

The trial continued that afternoon and picked up the following day, ending just before night set in. The judges were exhausted from two full days of testimonies and decided to sleep on it and meet the next morning before deciding the fate of the forty-nine men and three women.

CHAPTER 17
THE VERDICT

"The following is the official ruling of the court of chieftain judges, appointed to conduct the trial of forty-nine men and three women defendants, for unlawful activities and attack upon the Swayzee Tribe, and participating in the attempted attack on Jones Tribe; all under the supervision and direction of the late Fieldhand Jor-EL and Fieldhand Tiger. All were found guilty of those charges," Chief Judge Audrey read aloud from the bench.

The verdict:
"The court has weighed heavily as to what form of punishment must be inflicted and has come to the following conclusion. Each defendant will undergo complete and total public shunning within his or her tribe during each sentence. No member of the individual's tribe, family member, or friend may speak with the parties mentioned, commencing immediately upon their release from jail. Any attempt to speak with other ex-security detail members will result in an additional season of shunning added to their sentence or, if required, a more physical form of punishment to be inflicted. The public is required to watch for and report any violations of this decree

and to report such parties to the authorities for questioning. If found guilty, the party or parties will also become publicly shunned by their tribe for a period of one season. A second violation will result in their immediate expulsion from the tribe. These rulings will be vigorously enforced. All convicted persons are required to wear a large red cloth pinned to their outer garments to identify them as shunned persons while out in public."

"Sentences will consist of one or two season periods commencing upon this date. (See the second page of this ruling for the list of names and duration of sentences.)

Audrey, Chieftain of the Giants Tribe

Del, Chieftain of the Jones Tribe

Ren, Chieftain of the Swayzee Tribe

Parker, Chieftain of the Deaner Tribe

Samuel, Chieftain of the River Rats Tribe

* * * * * * * * * * * * * *

Upon hearing the verdict passed down by the five judges, the ex-security detail members rejoiced, thinking they had gotten off easy. Once released, it didn't take them long to realize that the constant silence and shunning by everyone around them was indeed a terrible sentence to endure. In the first week, three people trying to whisper to the ex-raiders were reported and brought before their chieftain, who imposed the red cloth and shunning fine upon them. It didn't take long for word to spread among the tribes that their chieftains were deadly serious. After about a month of teaching the three violators a lesson, each person's shunning penalty was quietly revoked upon swearing it would not happen again. Lessons were quickly learned.

Three of the forty-nine thought this shunning was a joke and continued to speak to one another. Each received an additional season added, then with hard labor, and finally reduced rations. The threat of a public whipping finally got their complete attention.

Mechanic Mike just couldn't understand why the man he had nearly killed appeared in court as a witness in his defense. As a result, he only drew one season of shunning rather than the two he fully expected. *Maybe there's more to that church stuff than I realize*, he kept thinking. That fall, a new man entered the church building on the day of worship. It was Mechanic Mike who returned again and again thereafter, always sitting alone in the back row.

CHAPTER 18
−EPILOGUE−

The cooperation between the tribes continued to flourish through the seasons, resulting in many improvements that were shared equally. It was decided that tribal leaders should meet every spring, summer, and fall, rotating between tribe locations, to discuss current events and recommendations.

Paper was being produced again by breaking old rags down into pulp, then soaking them in water, and beating them into a fibrous mixture, which was then pressed and dried. Another ingenious person cast a complete set of backward typesets, which allowed for the printing of documents. His design was passed on for others to follow. Based on old book illustrations, a working but crude printing press would follow. Soon, the return to using a seasonal day/week/month calendar was proposed and eventually approved by the tribes. The hangup was deciding the actual year that nobody could agree on. Finally, someone recommended just not worry about it for the time being. "Perhaps in time, many other tribes will work hand in hand with us, and together, we'll decide then," Chieftain Parker suggested.

Mechanic Mike, now happily married with a son, became obsessed with developing a machine that might once again travel on the old rail lines. After discovering a deteriorated railroad maintenance car, he began disassembling it piece by piece. In time, he constructed a two-man pump handle that propelled the car forward. Chieftain Audrey saw the benefit of having a way to travel more easily and faster between the tribes. Still not completely satisfied, Mike set about trying to build a larger car and a small steam engine to propel a similar car down the track. It would eventually fall upon his son Noah to complete the project.

Area tribes were soon routinely using and repairing railroad tracks to ensure safe travel and communications. Many hoped that one day, public travel by rail might return. A new industrial age was slowly beginning to take shape. Agricultural methods improved, and those with extra food could barter for useful hand tools. After all, a chicken only lasts a family for a brief period, but hand tools would last many generations.

As more and more contacts were made with other tribes, along with those who preferred using the term town rather than tribe, the Indy Tribe proposed to host a large gathering of chieftains. The meeting idea was printed and distributed far and wide early in the spring to allow for adequate planning and travel. The dates of July 4-6 were chosen, and the location of the grand meeting was the interior of their huge old racetrack. The promise of sharing all new improvements equally among the attendees was a good incentive to attend. In all, fourteen tribes and towns attended. Many topics were discussed during those meetings, giving every chieftain an equal time to comment or propose new ideas. All such were voted upon. The host tribe proposed forming a combined agreement among the tribes that pledged full cooperation and friendship and the pledge never to attack one another for resources or land. The idea was discussed at length, but the hangup was choosing a name. Finally, one was chosen: The United Confederation of Tribes and Towns, or United Confederation for short. The document was printed and each chieftain signed it for his or her people. Then, fourteen copies were produced for each chieftain to take back home.

Three other proposals were made: (1) The adoption of a standardized calendar already in use by most of the tribes. (2) To agree upon the year that all signers would use on their calendars. (3) The proposal to return to using the original name their ancestors once called Indiana. The adoption of the already in-use calendar was approved with much discussion. It seemed to depend upon old memories to agree upon the year. Some said it to be 2095, while others swear it is 2105. Finally, a suggestion was made to split the difference and use 2100 as the perfect starting date. A near-unanimous vote eventually approved this. As for the term 'Indiana,' that proposal was tabled for the next year to allow each chieftain time to reflect and obtain the opinions of their tribe or town. A suggestion was made to set aside a day every year to honor Chieftain Elder, who had brought peace and stability to the land. April 1st would forever be known as 'Founding Father's Day.'

The following year, the name of Indiana was adopted. Within a few years, more and more new groups joined The United Confederation organization. One speaker at their conference spoke about being on a sailing ship two years earlier and visiting far-away places with people speaking different languages. It was very reassuring to everyone that other had survived *The Annihilation* and were prospering without the need to make war upon one another. Seven more years passed by.

* * * * * * * * * * * * * * *

Audrey knew that the grave was calling her name. Cancer had a way of doing that. Not many men or women live to be eighty-eight years old. She had long ago passed on her responsibilities as chieftain to a much younger person. As she lay on her cot staring up at the ceiling, Audry hoped she had made all the right decisions in her life, one being not to marry. Movement in her room caught her attention. Her brother Trent pulled up a chair, sat down, and took hold of her hand. She couldn't help but wonder what had happened to the young man she remembered so well. Now, he was an old, balding man bent over with arthritis and pain from a bad knee. "How are you feeling, Sis?" he asked.

She attempted a slight smile. In reality, the pain in her stomach was severe, but there wasn't any use in dwelling upon it with others. "I'm fine. What's the latest news out in the real world?"

"Seamstress Barbara had her baby last night. A boy, seven and a half pounds, I hear. The passenger train from The Indy Tribe is due to arrive tomorrow. I thought I might go down to the station and see if any pretty girls step off," he joked.

"And what would your wife think about that, you dirty old coot?"

"What she doesn't know won't hurt her … unless you tell on me." Trent tried his best to cheer her up, but both knew it was hopeless. Her doctor told him she only had a couple of days left. Trent decided to cut the humor and be serious.

"Is there anything you want me to take care of, Sis?"

"No, not really. I'm glad you didn't bring the boys with you today. I wouldn't want them to see their Aunt Audrey like this." He sadly nodded in agreement. "Go now. I need to take a little beauty nap."

Trent understood and bent over to kiss her goodbye. "I'll drop by tomorrow," he told her. What neither of them knew was that Audrey would not awaken from her beauty nap, which, if you think about it, is perhaps God's way of saying, "I'm ready to bring you home now."

Early the following morning, explosions and flashes of light filled the sky as hundreds of small silver orbs returned and were seen targeting the terrified population with rays of death. Perhaps this was God's way of saying, "I'm ready to bring Mankind home now."

THE END

HISTORICAL TIDBITS

1. The story about the presidential assassin possibly being seen in Marion before the shooting was reported daily in the Marion Chronicle. The Secret Service later learned that Czolgosz was not in Indiana during the supposed time he was spotted in Marion. Wishful thinking, perhaps.
2. The burning of the covered bridge in Gas City on November 4th, 1901 was a true event.
3. The photo of the oil gusher credited to Gas City happened east of Van Buren on December 1, 1913. At one time, Van Buren led the state in oil production.
4. Unfortunately, as reported in the 1902 Marion Leader newspaper, the story about Van Buren's presumed corrupt marshal was true. Here is the published quote:

"Editor Diliion, of the Van Buren News-Eagle, who has been making a fight against vice in his town, and has forced the town council, through public sentiment, to take steps toward the removal of the town marshal, who is charged with being in cahoots with blind tigers and other disreputable places. (Blind Tigers: a place where liquor is sold illegally)

"As the marshal could not be removed by the town council, his salary was reduced from fifty to five dollars per month. One member of the board voted not to reduce the salary.

"The marshal says he will remain on the job if the pay is reduced to a nickel, which leads the News-Eagle to remark

that the officer is getting liberal compensation for his inactivity against them."

5. On July 9, 1902, it was also reported that a bear was killed in Van Buren. The animal escaped from the den of Matthew Doyle and terrorized citizens who turned out and killed it. The animal's body was skinned and a big bear roast was given to the public.
6. At two in the morning, thieves blew open the Van Buren post office safe and stole between $300 and $400 in cash, postage stamps, several registered letters, and packages. They had earlier set fire to a sawmill to attract the attention of the watchman and, during his absence, committed the robbery, stole a horse and buggy, and made their escape out of town going south. After reading this article, I had to wonder if the town's marshal received his cut of the take too.
7. Though newspapers at that time had acquired the ability to publish photographs, they often appeared dark. Here's an example and some ads that appeared as shown.

EASTER HEADGEAR FORECASTING SUMMER MODES.

House of Murder

Beer as a tonic?

303

8. The story about the clairvoyant finding a tin box full of money in Jonesboro did appear in the Marion Chronicle. Also true was the story about the New York Board of Health doctor advocating the drowning of mentally challenged children.
9. The events involving the new Marion Automotive Club endurance race were also true.
10. The Haynes Automobile Company, formally known as Haynes-Apperson, produced automobiles from 1905-1924 in their factory in Kokomo, Indiana.

Milton Keynes UK
Ingram Content Group UK Ltd.
UKHW031038020824
446373UK00004B/271